Thomas Fenner Curtis

The Human Element In The Inspiration Of The Sacred Scriptures

Thomas Fenner Curtis

The Human Element In The Inspiration Of The Sacred Scriptures

ISBN/EAN: 9783741180767

Manufactured in Europe, USA, Canada, Australia, Japa

Cover: Foto ©Andreas Hilbeck / pixelio.de

Manufactured and distributed by brebook publishing software (www.brebook.com)

Thomas Fenner Curtis

The Human Element In The Inspiration Of The Sacred Scriptures

THE
HUMAN ELEMENT

IN THE

INSPIRATION

OF THE

SACRED SCRIPTURES,

BY

T. F. CURTIS, D.D.,

LATE PROFESSOR OF THEOLOGY IN THE UNIVERSITY AT LEWISBURG, PA.

"The Bible presents to us in whatever way we regard it, two distinct elements, — the Divine, and the Human. This is a matter of fact." — LEE ON INSPIRATION, LEC. I. P. 32.

.... "There seems no need to fear the admission of a human element as well as a Divine, in Scripture." — AIDS TO FAITH, ESSAY VII.

"The Lord will build himself in Science, as well as in Life, a new tabernacle in which to dwell ; and neither a stubborn adherence to antiquity, nor a profane appetite for novelty, can hinder this work of the Lord which is now preparing." — NEANDER'S LIFE OF CHRIST, AUTHOR'S ADDRESS.

NEW YORK:

D. APPLETON & COMPANY,

443 & 445 BROADWAY.

1867.

PREFACE.

IN preparing lectures, year by year, for the Theological Department of the University, I found on each occasion increasing difficulty in expressing any set of views on the subject of Inspiration, at once clear, consistent and satisfactorily meeting all the difficulties that presented themselves to my own mind. Each successive year these lectures altered, or rather grew, slowly and steadily, but always in one direction. A greater degree of importance attached itself to the consideration of the *Human* Element in the interpretation of many difficult passages of Scripture. By degrees, following many, if not most, of the present age, whose studies have led them to this class of investigation, I had so far entered into Neander's views, and drifted from the former accustomed teachings of the denomination whose future ministers I was instructing, that I found it best to give the students fairly an historical digest of the various opinions that have grown up in the course of centuries, including those that are being advanced in our own times. Having done this, I then mentioned in what direction the truth seemed to me to lie, at the same time frankly declaring that in some of these respects my own mind leaned increasingly to views broader than the current opinions. I was well aware, however, that in all the Evangelical denominations a growing number of the most intelligent and influential ministers, including some conspicuously active and useful in every good word and work, were quietly drifting in the same direction. But they were not obliged annually to define their position as I was. It therefore seemed to me the most proper course to resign my professorship, examine the whole subject more thoroughly and independently, and publish such conclusions as might seem calculated to assist others tried by the same difficulties and struggles that have cost me at times so much perplexity and pain.

Having, however, taken the first of these steps, I at one time seemed to myself exempted thereby from the necessity of taking the second. While I was an appointed Theological Instructor, it was clearly my duty, humbly, honestly and prayerfully, to investigate for truth, and then, so far as I had found it, utter it faithfully and impartially. But having resigned this position, might I not now safely leave the theology of the age to take care of itself? If, as I believe, it is a mere question of time, how long mistaken and antiquated opinions can survive, why should I undertake to molest views quietly dying out among the most thoughtful, and wound the feelings of pious brethren whom it is impossible not to love, and who might even think it doing God service to assail with bitterness what has been written from a trembling but earnest desire to promote a living Christianity in place of a dead formality.

But it appeared to me that men in Evangelical religious circles were for the most part too cautious in speaking with candor, or in making any concessions not absolutely wrung from them by the force of circumstances, and that the tendency of much of the teaching in our Theological Seminaries is to stifle deep thorough and candid enquiry on all these points, and therefore to leave our rising Ministry quite unprepared for the work of the age before them. To adhere only to that which is old, seemed to me the final tendency of the exhortations of even such men as Dr. McCosh when at Andover last summer. This was the great lesson he appeared to bring over from his past experiences in Europe. It is with regret I see so little real and hearty fellowship with that which is living and therefore growing, and which must be more warmly welcomed by the religion that is to guide the coming age.

A most valued friend advised me not to publish until I felt "a woe upon me" if I uttered not what

I think to be true. And such is my dread of all want of candor and want of courage to utter freely well considered convictions of truth and duty, that perhaps I might say it is some what in this spirit that I write. It is, indeed, the fool who uttereth *all* his mind, and there is much truth in what Dr. Pusey has written as to that "economy" which should be the law resting on the lips of the religious teachers of mankind. But the duty of candid utterance of Christian truth and experience, at any cost of personal feeling, is also a part of that Cross which each follower of Christ may not refuse to bear. The Master declared: " In secret have I said · nothing." " Proclaim it on the house tops." In fact, it is this religious *reticence* that is now most to be dreaded. But it is hope of good, more than fear of woe, that impels me to publish the following pages. There are many whose minds are now filled with most painful anxieties lest in yielding respect to the reason God has placed within them, they should be refusing to walk by faith in his Revelation of himself in the Scriptures. This is often caused as I know through experience, by the want of a sufficiently broad consideration and honor of God's *other* Revelations of himself in *Nature*, those 'elder Scriptures;' in *Providence*, where God daily unfolds his will; in *History*, where his past dealings are made prognostics of his future plans; and in *Re-*

ligious Experience, where the Spirit of God reveals his will directly to the Christian consciousness. The true harmony of all the Divine methods of teaching us his will, best show the real position and divine intention of the Christian Records.

The Bible for the purposes for which it was given, cannot be prized too reverently; it can never lose its hold on the hearts of the good. Viewed from the true stand point, and interpreted not in opposition to, but in harmony with all God's other teachings and revelations of himself, it will unfold new wonders and beauties to each age yet to come, and exhibit the progressive development of the Religious Spirit in the history of man, among those who have followed the teachings of Him who spake as never man spake. I have sought earnestly to attain and express correct views on this subject, independently of their bearing on any party or creed; yet not for a merely speculative purpose, but to find a religion by which to live in all sincerity, simplicity and wisdom; by which to die also in peace, charity and hope, handing down to my children as the best of all riches, this inheritance, that cannot fade away, — a firm faith in Christianity, because it is true, and the essence of Universal Religion. Next, however, to the possession of its Spirit which giveth life should I desire them to grow up free from that bondage to the letter, which too often killeth both the light of reason and the growth of love in the soul.

For many years I conscientiously and earnestly struggled to maintain the current theories of the Infallibilty of Scripture Inspiration until all possibility of doing so reasonably and honestly was gone. Only very slowly, unwillingly, and against every earthly pre-possession and interest, have I felt obliged to relinquish long cherished and early opinions in respect to this point. And I wish here only further to express my conviction and testimony as to the little alteration it necessarily involves in the experimental parts of Christian Theology while yet giving them a progressive tendency and movement which is, in fact, a new life and vividness, of value incalculable to those who like myself have been ever prone to settle down into an excessive conservatism except as shaken from its sloth by Divine Providence and grace. It need and ought not to involve controversy among Christians. And humbly do I pray that the change which I see inevitable on this subject, may take place quietly in the Evangelical Churches of our land, without strife and bitterness, but marked with an increase of gentleness, charity, earnestness and zeal. Such surely was the spirit and intention of the Master.

T. F. C.

4 INMAN STREET,
CAMBRIDGEPORT, MASS.,
MAY, 1867.

CONTENTS.

CHAPTER II.

Two Leading Theories. I. Those which Magnify the Divine Element alone. 1. The Roman Catholic View, (p. 54.) 2. The Modern High Church View, (p. 56.) 3. View of Modern Orthodox Protestants, (p. 57.) 4. The Dynamical Theory, (p. 58.) New Hampshire Confession, (p. 59.) Dr. Dwight, Dr. Hill, Dr. Henderson, Dr. Lee, (p. 61.) II. Theories which Ignore the Divine Element, (p. 62.) 1. Strauss, (p. 62.) 2. Baur, (p. 68.) 3. •Renan, (p. 74.) 4. Theodore Parker, (p. 77.)

CHAPTER III.

Eclecticism in Philosophy and Religion, (p. 81.) 1. Schleiermacher, (p. 84.) 2. De Wette, (p. 89.) 3. Neander, (p. 91.) 4. Dr. Priestly, (p. 92.) 5. Dr. Pye Smith, (p. 93.) 6. Coleridge, (p. 94.) 7. Arnold, (p. 103.) 8. The Broad Church, (p. 109.) 9. Aids to Faith, (p. 110.) 10. Colenso, (p. 111.) 11. Dr. Davidson, (p. 111.) 12. Robertson, (p. 115.) 13. Westcott, (p. 118.) 14. Farrar, (p. 119.) 15. Summary of the whole, (p. 120.)

CHAPTER IV.

I. The Chronology, (p. 122.) II. Geology, (p. 131.) The Deluge, (p. 131.) Berosus, (p. 133.) Belgium Bone Caves, (p. 138.) Six Days or Periods, (p. 140.) Antiquity of Man, (p. 157.)

CHAPTER V.

1. The Allegorizing System, (p. 168.) 2. The Points, (p. 170.) 3. Documentary and Anonymous Character of Genesis, (p. 174.) 4. Formation of Old Testament Canon, (p. 182.) .

CHAPTER VI.

The Popular View begs the Question, (p. 193.) The Teachings of Jesus Recorded by others, (p. 193. Sermon on the Mount, (p. 194.) John 10 : 35, (p. 199.) St. Paul, (p. 202.) II Peter, (p. 203.)

CHAPTER VII.

No Promise Specially for these Writings, (p. 208.) Writers Claim no more for Words Written than Words Spoken, (p. 209.) John 14 : 25–26, (p. 209.) Matthew 10 : 19, (p. 210.) Paul Bases his Whole Claim on his Apostleship, (p. 212.) Luke 1 : 1–4, (p. 215.) Revelations, (p. 217.) The Genealogies Disprove it, (p. 222.) The Relations of the Three Synoptical Gospels, (p. 224.) The Gospel of John, (p. 229.)

CHAPTER VIII.

Sir William Hamilton on Authority and Reason, (p. 238.) Natural Religion a Science, (p. 240.) Dr. Mansel, (p. 240.) "Reason in Religion," (p. 241.) Paley's Defect, (p. 242.) Comte's Philosophy, (p. 242.) Renan's Error, (p. 245.) Christianity supposed by some to Exclude Reason, (p. 246.) Natural and Revealed Religion not Antagonistic, (p. 247.) Knowledge of all other and of Religious Truth Corresponds in the same Three Methods, (p. 250.)

CHAPTER IX.

The Paraclete, (p. 256.) Classical Sense, (p. 256.) How far the Comforter, (p. 260.) Its Comprehensiveness, (p. 261.)

CHAPTER X.

Clement's First Epistle, (p. 269.) Paul's Epistles, (p. 270.) The Acts, (p. 271.) The Gospels, (p. 275.) The Catholic Epistles, (p. 278.)

CHAPTER XI.

1. That we Give up Every Thing, (p. 283.) 2. That it Leads to Rationalism, (p. 287.) Mr. Lecky's Work, (p. 288.)

CHAPTER XII

INTRODUCTORY CHAPTER.

"The theory of a servile literality of Inspiration has put the most ostensibly powerful arms into the hands of the foes of God and man." —Dr. J. Pye Smith on the Person of the Messiah, Book I, ch. 2: Notes 5, Appendix

THERE will, perhaps, be much in the following pages, that some excellent Christians will esteem highly dangerous concessions, as tending to favor, and even to foster scepticism. Let such read before they decide. The object in view is certainly not to *unsettle* the faith of any in regard to the Inspiration of the Holy Scriptures, but rather to establish it on a true and solid basis. I do not desire to unsettle anything, and should not feel called upon to write this work merely to disabuse the minds of those who can and do continue devoutly to hold such views of plenary Inspiration as are advanced even by Gaussen, though they seem to me in a mistake, and to a certain degree as holding on to a superstition that is rapidly being exploded.

It is not less, but more reverence that should be cherished for these holy books as our guides, especially in regard to the Divinely authorized and "profitable" objects of "doctrine, reproof, correction, and instruction in righteousness." Here it is that we find the best proofs of their inspiration.* It is not narrower, but broader, loftier and more enlarged views of that subject that I desire to exhibit even if at the risk of momentary and perhaps painful trial of the faith of some to whom such views may be new. F. W. Robertson of Brighton well says, " It seems to me that this feeling of vagueness is inevitable, when we dare to launch out upon the sea of truth. I remember that half painful, half sublime sensation in the first voyage I took out of sight of land when I was a boy, when old landmarks and horizon were gone, and I felt as if I had no home. It was a pain to find the world so large. By degrees, the mind got familiarized to that feeling, and a joyful sense of freedom came. So I think it is with *spiritual* truth. It is a strangely desolate feeling to perceive that the " truth " and the " Gospel " that we have known, were but a small home farm in the great Universe, but at last I think we begin to see sun, moon, and stars as before, and to discover that we are not lost, but free with a latitude and longitude as certain and far grander than before." Enlarged

* 1 Tim. 3 : 16.

views of our subject, will produce just such effects as these.

Negative assertions of Inspiration, such as those of Gaussen, that there are *no* mistakes in our Bibles as to matters of science or fact will hardly be found profitable to the Church at the present time. It is, rather, the *positive* truth, much more easily made clear and certain, which is needed, that here vast bodies of living principles are revealed, and that these writings are channels through which God and the soul are brought near to each other, and Divine truth and life infused into the heart of the believer.

In asserting this view, it is better for the friends of Christianity, if they must err, to begin by claiming too little rather than too much, and to proceed with the utmost caution from that which is clear and easily proved by experience, to those points which must require at least more faith and deeper consideration.

But there are many even of the most devout Christians, and of those piously educated, whose minds are in danger of being hopelessly alienated from the Scriptures, or at least from all sense of their Inspiration, by the assertions put forth by well meaning friends of Christianity, which they are unable to reconcile either with the claims of science, or of the books themselves.

Geology has taught every educated youth, facts in

regard to the world's antiquity, that cannot be made to agree with any fair interpretation of the six days of Genesis. In England, the leading young men intending to go out either in the Civil or the Military service to India, study Sanscrit, the Zend and other Indian languages, and when they do so, they are startled at some things they find in the Avestas and the Vedas. Within a few years, full English translations of many of these works have been published in London as well as the fragments from Berosus, Sanconiatho and others. These all suggest difficulties. He who examines the antiquities of Egypt, finds dates most respectably given for it as a flourishing kingdom, which it will be impossible to reconcile with that of the flood, at least according to Usher, or even Hales B. C. 3254. Indeed, Bunsen does not hesitate to assert it as a well established fact, that Menes the first king must have lived B. C. 3643, while Lepsius places it 3893.

But what are dates like these, to the Geological periods which Sir Charles Lyell thinks indicated by the sixty feet of penetrated mud of the Nile, throughout which he finds burnt brick and other evidences of civilized man, without having yet reached the bottom. They appear to prove not less than twelve thousand years, and perhaps thirty thousand, while the Hebrew Bible allows us but six thousand, and the Septuagint less than eight thousand years since creation. And further, the deepest of these borings on the banks of the Nile show man surrounded by no species of animal now extinct, while it is clear that the human race has existed in company with many species now no more. The race of man must, therefore, be much older. It is in this way Lyell argues, that "geologically speaking, and in reference to the first age of stone, these records of the valley of the Nile may be called *extremely modern.*"

This subject was brought to my own attention first in 1845. Bent on finding arguments to substantiate the Hebrew Chronology, a summer's vacation from ministerial duty had been spent in looking into Egyptian Antiquities. I was invited to see, what Dr. Koch foolishly called, the fossil skeleton of a sea serpent, recently brought by him from near Clairbourne, Alabama, to New York. Seeing me interested in the account of his more important discovery of the Missourium, he took me into another apartment and showed me two Indian arrow heads of rose quartz and then explained that he had discovered them directly underneath the huge femur or thigh bone of this enormous animal. According to his account, this creature must have been bogged in the bed of a river, and attacked by Indians who had shot these and other arrows into him, thrown large quantities of stones and rocks at him, and finally built large fires around him, some of the charcoal and charred bones of the legs showing this. The legs broken, the feet remained in the bog upright, and the body had fallen over on its side, thus burying the arrows. Incredulous that any race of Indians could have been contemporary with an animal of this species, I cross-questioned the man very closely. At last he gave me a full printed account of the matter, assuring me that I might rely on the truth of every word. I left sick at heart, for I saw that if that should ever be proved true, there was an end to the usual opinions as to the date of the human race, since, according to his account, the stratum covering up this animal, was of the upper post pliocene, of about the same period as that in which the arrow heads and other relics of human existence have been since found in France, but older by many thousand years than the Alluvium or Recent formations in which alone human remains were supposed to be traceable.

To show how reluctantly and against all his prejudices, Sir Charles Lyell must have come to regard these as proofs of human existence at so early a date, I may mention that a few months later, when he visited Tuskaloosa, I took occasion to relate what Dr. Koch had so solemnly assured me. He became quite indignant against Dr. K., called him an imposter, and declared his utter disbelief of the whole story. So should I have done, but for the *circumstantiality* of his statement. I therefore carefully preserved the pamphlet, and when eighteen years later, Sir Charles Lyell's work on the Antiquity of Man was published, I at least knew it was not the work of a theorist trying to establish a preconceived notion, but of one convinced against all his earlier prepossessions. It is thus becoming every day more difficult for a candid mind to be a firm believer in Geology, and, indeed, in any of the modern sciences, and yet retain faith in the old and accustomed views of Inspiration commonly taught in our childhood.

And if from science and ordinary literature, we turn to Theology, everything betokens a very great revolution of opinion rapidly approaching. For the last thirty or forty years, scholars whose writings have been in most esteem for profound culture combined with deep piety have also been conspicuous for avowing their abandonment of the old views of Inspiration. Arnold, of Rugby, the Apostle of Christian culture of Young England in its best form, with his faith in earnest living Christianity, and his adoration of the person and teachings of Christ, openly exhibited a freedom from, and dislike to the current belief in the infallibility of the Inspiration of the Bible; while he foresaw in this, as he said, as great a shock to the feelings of Protestant Christendom as Roman Catholic Christianity had received three hundred years ago, from the downfall of the belief in the infallibility of the Church.

Coleridge may be said to have broken ground on this subject in England, and his Confessions of an Inquiring Spirit, published after his death, have produced a greater effect morally among thinking Christians, than all he had published during his life. When Neander wrote his Life of Christ, in answer really to Strauss' Life of Jesus, he felt it necessary to "distinguish what is divine from what is human in the Gospel record." "I am certain," he says, "that the fall of the old form of the doctrine of Inspiration and, indeed, of many other doctrinal prejudices, will not only not involve the fall of the essence of the Gospel, but will cause it no detriment whatever. Nay, I believe it will be more clearly and accurately understood, and men will be better prepared to fight with, and to conquer that inrushing infidelity, against which *the weapons of the old dogmatism must be powerless* in any land, and that from such a struggle, a new theology, purified and renovated in the spirit of the gospel must arise. Everywhere we see the signs of a new creation; the Lord will build himself in science as well as in life, a new tabernacle in which to dwell, and neither a stubborn adherence to antiquity, nor a profane appetite for novelty can hinder this work of the Lord which is now preparing. May we never forget the words of the great Apostle: where the spirit of the Lord is, there is liberty."

By the "stubborn adherence to antiquity," Neander probably referred chiefly to Puseyism and the High Church generally, which was one of the first reactive effects from the giving way of the old doctrine of verbal inspiration, carrying back men like Newman and Manning into the bosom of the Roman Catholic Church.

On the other hand, what Neander calls " an appetite for novelty," has carried others into extremes far more startling to many excellent Christians. The learned and candid Professor Maurice, and F. W. Newman led off in this direction.   A man being arrested for preaching infidelity in England, was able to plead in reply, that he was only in the habit of reading and expounding passages from the Essays and Reviews, written chiefly by clergymen of the Church of England. But Bishop Colenso goes so far beyond these Essayists as for a moment to produce a great scandal even in their eyes, by devoting much ink to prove a series of negatives, such as, that Moses was *not* the author of the Pentateuch, and that it is *not* contemporary history. From efforts like these, there arises a new school of clergymen whose lives and whose sermons would do honor to any age of the Church, embracing such men as F. W. Robertson, of Brighton, and Dean Stanley. Even the " *Aids to Faith*," written as a reply to the Essays and Reviews by the most conservative Churchmen, and for getting out which, the chief mover was made a Bishop, admits that in matters of science and history at least, it is not necessary to believe that infallibility is involved in Inspiration, but that on such points, good men may safely agree to differ.[*]

" The Inspiration of the Bible," says F. W. Robertson, " is a large subject. I hold it to be inspired, not dictated. It is the word of God, — the words of man ; — as the former, perfect, as the latter, imperfect. God the Spirit as a sanctifier, does not produce absolute perfection of human character. God the Spirit as an Inspirer, does not produce absolute perfection of human knowledge. Men of science smile at the futile attempts to reconcile Moses and geology. I give up the attempt at once, and say, the inspiration of the Bible remains intact for all that. I look upon Bibliolatry with quite as much dislike as Arnold did, as pernicious, dangerous to true views of God and his revelation to the human race, and the cause of much bitter Protestant Popery. I believe Bibliolatry to be as superstitious, as false, and almost as dangerous as Romanism."

Dean Stanley in his last published volume of the History of the Jewish Church, has contrived to say almost all that has made Bishop Colenso so conspicuous, but in so Christian and fair a spirit of building up the true views of Scripture, rather than merely attack-

* Essay 7, Sec. 22.

ing the erroneous, that few would feel their faith seriously ruffled by his mode of questioning the Mosaic authorship of the Pentateuch.

" One of the most striking differences between the existing differences of the Jewish people and those of Greece and Rome is their anonymous character. Whereas the Classical historians, almost without exception, claim their books for themselves, the Sacred historians, almost without exception, leave their names undisclosed. For a long time this was unperceived, owing to the groundless assumption that the subject of a book must necessarily be the author of it; and that therefore Moses, Joshua, Samuel and Job, must have written the books which bear their names, even though their own deaths are recorded therein. This mode of argument was confined to Sacred criticism. It was never imagined, in classical literature, that the Odyssey was written by Ulysses, or the Æneid by Æneas. It is now generally abandoned in regard to sacred literature also, and the singular self-abnegation of the Sacred historians has proportionally been brought into light. A more delicate question is opened by the discovery, not only that many of the Sacred books have no known author, but that in single books different elements from various sources are combined. This detection of the composite nature of the Hebrew writings, though sometimes pushed to excess by the German critics, is nevertheless one of the most interesting and certain results of their labors. The telescope of scholarship has resolved what before were dim nebulous clusters, into their separate distinct stars; and there are very few of the books of the Old Testament which have not received additional light from this restorative process. Almost all the historical writings partake of this complex character. The Pentateuch in the earlier period, the books of Samuel, Kings, Chronicles, and Ezra in the latter period, are now universally acknowledged, in their present state, to be the work of several hands."

It is not only in the Established Church of England that matters are taking this turn. In the Presbyterian Church of Scotland, Dr. Hanna, formerly the able editor of the North British Review and the son-in-law of Dr. Chalmers, the leader of the Evangelical movement of fifty years ago, had to resign his position because his writings were so variant from the former theories of Inspiration. Peter Bayne has also had to give up the Editorship of the London and Edinburg Weekly Review for a similar reason. Among the English Dissenters, Morell's Philosophy of Religion, the later writings of Dr. Pye Smith, and those of Dr. Davidson have distinctly avowed that the old views are untenable, and the last named of these gentlemen has resigned his Professorship an account of his teachings of this character. Henry Ward Beecher boldly avows very broad views on this subject in the Plymouth Church, and the most recent confession of faith has been wisely left of breadth convenient for the reception of those entertaining such opinions in the Congregational Church.

While on the one hand, faith in the verbal views of Inspiration seems to be dying out among all thoroughly educated men, even of the warmest piety, there appears to be no great or marked change in the tone and style of preaching in the great masses of the Churches, and congregations either in this country, or yet of England. Rev. Mr. Spurgeon, who adheres to the old Evangelical view, is as popular as ever in London, and the great bulk of the preachers of all denominations, *say* little, even when they think much on this subject.

When a mighty river has been frozen over, through the long, dark winter, and the thick, ribbed ice under the influence of the sun of returning spring is.honey combed, and beginning to wear through the old beaten tracks, it may appear strong enough to the solitary and superficial foot passenger and much the same as ever. And yet the experienced traveller sees that the whole mass is loosening from the shores, and just ready to break up, drift to sea, and leave a living, navigable stream, over which commerce shall spread its wings,

2

and navies float and streamers fly. So is there at this moment in the Theological world, notwithstanding all the smoothness with which old forms are preserved, every precursive sign to an experienced eye, of a breaking up of ancient creeds and party ties. This change will prove destructive to such as can only superficially glide over the icy surfaces of form, though one which will open up treasures from the deep, oceans of divine truth and love for those prepared to navigate through waves, where others have been wont to slip along upon a skate.

The Theological dangers of our time, therefore, are not those of a coming winter, but of an opening spring. They are the dangers of men not reading the signs of the times, and lingering on the floating ice, and being carried out to sea, drifting they know not whither, because fancying they are safe on the beaten track of some venerable creed, as old at least as the Reformation. But the result is that they are thrown into opposition to the most living, earnest, and progressive men of the times, and a shockingly large part of the preaching of the present day is taken up, not as was that of our fathers, with simple, earnest, living views of spiritual truths, elevating the soul, and thus purifying the life and deportment, but in trying to make the old track still answer, or in cutting a fresh one as close by the side of it as possible on a sheet of ice floating out to sea. Thus we hear unscientific replies to scientific difficulties, and witness the useless combat with objections. It is like a battle of ship-wrecked sailors with enraged seals that rise up hydra-headed on every side, or an iceberg, where all are drifting together further and further from the solid shore.

This is the true cause of that deadness so much complained of in the pulpit. Intelligent Christians of the most earnest piety, both young and old, complain that they cannot find food in the sermons; that educated preachers seem to lack the warmth of former years, or that the spiritual life of a Church is found, if at all, in the prayer meeting. The style of preaching is borrowed too often from the Theological Education, one half and more of which in many of our Divinity Schools, is taken up in meeting or anticipating the suppositions objections of infidels, objections not against Christianity in any of its essential features, but against modern ideas and statements of plenary verbal Inspiration, remote questions of chronology or geology or history or criticism. These discussions indeed exercise great learning, great ingenuity, research and dialectic skill, and are so far perhaps useful. But, not exercising these on the spiritual truths that bring God and the soul together, they become utterly useless as the food of hungry Christian men, or for the development of moral and religious power in the churches. And exercising this ingenuity sometimes in subtile and tricky evasions and dishonest conclusions, they beget a disingenuous habit arising out of the exigencies of supporting an exploded theory. All the pernicious effects of this, experience shows to be growing up amongst us, so that as such ministers become more orthodox, they become less true and simple, less sincere and honorable as men of God.

About twenty years ago, a pastor commenced a course of lectures on the Evidences of Christianity. They were fresh and living, because drawn from the truths that had convinced and moved his own heart. He dwelt on the marks of authenticity and credibility, external and internal, in St. Paul's Epistles and life, — on the Divine humanity stamped on the character of Christ, the Divine authority of Christianity as a system, and there he stopped, not feeling quite clear as to many of the common views on Inspiration. A lawyer who attended the course, and had been much interested, expressed a desire to hear the pastor's views on that subject. Fearing to concede too much, and his own mind being in doubt and obscurity, there was a confusedness in his dealing with the theme, which more than undid all that his former lectures had done. The lawyer abandoned the church, and the minister travelled and studied for six months, until this at least became clear to him,—that he would no more preach dogmas taken merely from theological education, but from what had become obvious to his own living consciousness and experience of Christian truth. In doing this, he by no means rejected or taught others to reject all that his or their experience might not yet have taught them. But he dwelt chiefly on those truths of religion to which he could be a witness from having felt their certainty; while all beyond that, he spoke of as the opinions of Christians, or of the church, or as resting on the authority of Scripture. Thus many of the dogmatic phrases of other generations died out from his preaching, and technical terms gave place to the language of the present age as it came from his heart. Those who loved the forms and phraseology of a party better than the truth itself, considered him heterodox and unevangelical; but others listened to his words, feeling his sincerity, and were converted or confirmed in a living faith in the Divine authority of Christianity, who had not so felt its power before.

There are many preachers and more private Christians who have passed through a similar experience, and come round to this higher faith in the Divine authority of the Christian religion, who yet, were you to ask them for an explanation or proof of their views on Inspiration, would have to acknowledge the mystery to them of the whole subject. They see and feel in the writings, especially of the New Testament a mysterious and unique power, a something that guides the lives of those who follow them in heart with a superior and unearthy knowledge and wisdom. Without seeming to consult the interest of any individual, but making him renounce all for Christ, — father, mother, houses and lands, — these writings yet give him back all these and a hundred-fold more in the present life. While not directly inculcating patriotism, and in some cases opposing much that goes by that name, they enjoin principles which are the blessing, glory and source of the exaltation of all states, just in proportion as the citizens walk according to them. Indeed, their effects on nations are most remarkable. All history seems to centre in Christianity, and the present hopes and future greatness of mankind to be more dependent upon carrying out the principles of the New Testament and bringing them home to the masses of mankind, than all other things put together.

In church history, these stand quite alone. The writings of the Fathers, even the Apostolic Fathers, nearly the contemporaries of the Apostles, though highly useful and written by deeply pious men, how jejune and trifling are they compared with the Epistles of Paul. The First Epistle of Clement indeed exhibits much of an apostolic spirit, and but for its occasional defacement, by such stories as that of the Phœnix, gravely told as a fact and proof of the resurrection, might be read as a part of Scripture; but who would compare the Epistle of Barnabas of the first quarter of the second century, with one of those by Paul in the first? And who is not shocked with the hierarchical and inflated tendencies of the so-called Ignatian Epistles? And the shepherd of Hermas, how puerile is it, compared with the sublime visions of the book of Revelations!

It may be safely said, that the superiority of Protestant nations, as a whole, over those governed by Papacy, is entirely owing to the difference between the Christianity of the New Testament and that of the Fathers as the religious and intellectual guide of mankind. As an eloquent divine recently remarked, the New Testament is to Christianity what a *written* constitution is to civil government. It secures freedom from tyranny and abuse.

The probable effects of the Bible upon the future history of the world suggest that it has so far not lost power, but gained it. Since the year 1800, it has probably been translated into more languages, and circulated to the extent of at least twelve times as many copies, as in the whole eighteen hundred years preceding. Let no man think this a mere temporary result of Bibliolatry; but rather let all these things, put together, assure him of an Inspiration of some kind belonging to this book, even though no two writers should agree as to the solution of every difficulty that exists, or in regard to the precise degree of its influence or the mode of its communication. In fact, each Christian feels for himself at times, an influence exerted upon him by the truths of Christianity as a system of authority over his conduct, giving him an Inspiration to a new and better life, that he knows and feels to be Divine.

There are hundreds, nay thousands, of most sincere and highly educated young men who know all this, and yet cannot reconcile their feelings with their understandings. The real efforts of most of the various modern schools of theology are to reconcile these. Doctors Newman and Pusey, a few years ago, at Oxford, rebounding from the temporary scepticism which the study of German theology had introduced into the Universities, returned to the edge of Roman Catholicism, and advocated an infallibility for the Inspiration of the Church, which they failed to find in that of the Scriptures. This mistake, in spite of the purity and zeal of many who held it, soon drove a large number of the more intelligent and honest students at Oxford into such a state of doubt, that they abandoned studying for the Church by wholesale, and entered other professions instead, and the Bishops had to sanction theological schools for the instruction of pious men, too old, too poor, or too ignorant to pass a University examination. These went through a rough course of evangelical theology, without the doubts of educated men and without the ability to meet them, and were pushed forward into all offices of the working clergy, to supply the exigencies of the times. The proportion of such clergy was steadily increasing in England a few years ago, if indeed it has been stopped even now by the introduction of broader views of Christian teaching.

The experience, however, of F. W. Robertson, of Brighton, himself so earnestly evangelical at first, opens up a view of his progress through scepticism to a higher faith in Christianity and its Inspirations, that makes his life well worth study; because it shows that such views need not end in the individual, and will not end in the Church at large, in producing a cold and heartless indifference, but, in a new impulse of commanding power, a living, earnest, glowing love, and more extended usefulness.

The great object which has impelled the author to write this work has been the hope of aiding young men of sincere piety, brought up in evangelical faith, but who are prevented from exerting their energies as Christians, from that sort of secret doubt and dread which arises from a misconception of the requirements of Christianity, induced by modern teachings, as distinct even from the ancient creeds, and from the writers of the New Testament itself on the subject of Inspiration. I wish to show that they can move forward with a firm and practical faith in Christianity as a Divinely authorized and inspired system, although the human element may be palpable in the records. It appears to me that the time has now arrived to correct a popular error or superstition into which large sections of the Church have fallen more or less profoundly, especially since the Reformation, consisting of a too mechanical and verbal view of Inspiration. This mistake, which was clearly seen by many of the most intelligent Protestants at the Reformation, was not brought forward at the time, only lest harmony should be disturbed, and the faith of the masses needlessly distracted. But now that the logical sequences of this error have begun to appear, and the masses of Christians are better able to study their Bibles, while many divines esteemed orthodox have become less and less studious of the great fundamental principles of universal religion, it is necessary that the error which has occasioned this Bibliolatry, on the one hand, and neglect of even natural religion, on the other, should be corrected, at least so far as the Christian ministry is concerned. Like all other errors of this sort, the attempt to clear it away will for the moment arouse great prejudices. It will seem to many as a new form of infidelity, or at least as undermining and unsettling the foundations of the Christian faith, where it is in fact only uncovering the *true* foundations, to show how much deeper and more solid they are, and imbedded in the very being of humanity. And all this process will end in putting faith in Christianity on a firmer basis, purifying our conceptions of it from many errors, strengthening our faith in Christ, enlarging our charity, and building up the universal Church instead of pulling it down.

In 1752, in order to correct the Calendar, which had drifted into error, the 3d of September, old style, was by act of Parliament declared to be the 14th, new style. Even so small and unimportant a change as this of twelve days, made to put us really right with antiquity, and in correspondence with other nations, was esteemed by many an impious innovation. It was thought to be unsettling the foundation of all our computations of time, rendering dates uncertain, and all who adopted it guilty of falsehood. Many made adherence to the old a point of conscience, and never would use it. Yet now it is established universally; no one is deceived, and no evil has come to the world. Who would think it proper to go back to the old style? We are right with the year as it was in the days of the Cæsars and of Christ, and an error has been thus corrected.

In the same way, the Church has innocently drifted, especially the Protestant branch of it, into a popular misconception of the simple word Inspiration. By most, it is considered to imply, in regard to Scripture, what it certainly does not even now in regard to any other utterances or writings, i. e. the idea of absolute and theoretic infallibility. The mistake has grown up not unnaturally from the fact of their *practical* infallibility for the purposes for which they were written, namely, that godly men may be thoroughly furnished unto every good word and work. When indeed we have sought and obtained the most perfect knowledge upon any subject, which lies within our means, and the time for exertion arrives, we have to act on the best light, as if it were infallible. It is so *to us*, although we may know it is not so absolutely.

At the Reformation, when Luther denounced the infallibility of the Pope, he seemed to the masses of the unreflecting to be attacking Christianity. Pious people expected the birth of Antichrist, and emperors and princes the loosening of all civil and social ties. Even the learned Erasmus stood aloof, remarking satirically, that he had no vocation for becoming a martyr. Yet the result was the formation of a new school of simpler but severer piety, and all the superiority of Protestant nations has sprung from the contest. Even the Roman Catholic Church was much purified, and many abuses have been ever since abated. And now, at the end of three centuries, a higher, purer, stronger Christianity is visible where that Reformation has spread. Even the triumphs of Prussian armies over Austrian may in part illustrate this superiority.

But the Protestant world must now open its eyes upon another Reformation, and learn not only that the Church is fallible, but that the Scriptures, especially of the Old Testament, though truly and properly to be venerated as holy, inspired and sacred documents of the Christian faith, are not therefore to be esteemed, especially in matters of current opinion, as science and history, absolutely infallible, but as having partly received their color from the ages in which they were produced, and from the sincere yet fallible opinions of the holy men, moved by the Holy Ghost, who wrote them.

In fact, my object is to show that fallibility, such as this in the sacred books, does not impair their claim to Christian faith as inspired guides, but is necessary to the credibility of the whole, *the Inspiration of the sacred writings being precisely equivalent to the Divine authority of the Apostles.* For as the latter did not prevent them from falling into individual errors, or take away the need of being corrected by that presence of the Paraclete, animating the whole body, so the Inspiration resides not in each passage alone, but rather in the spirit of the whole book, taken in connection with the purposes for which it was written, with the other sacred teachings, and with the principles of universal religion.

CHAPTER I.

ON THE USES OF THE TERM INSPIRATION.

I.

THE term "Inspiration" occurs but twice in the English Bible, — Job 32: 8, and II. Tim. 3: 16; and in this, the English fairly represents the originals. In the proper place, the whole Scriptural doctrine of Inspiration will be examined; at present we want simply to ascertain the use of the term. In Job 32: 7–8, Elihu, as a young man, apologizes for speaking before his elders, and says, "I said, days should speak, and multitude of years should teach wisdom, but there is a spirit in man, and the *inspiration* of the Almighty giveth them understanding." *   The mean-

* The Hebrew word נְשָׁמָה means literally *breath*, and is so translated in the almost parallel passage, Job 33–4. In the Septuagint, we have in both of these cases πνεῦμα corresponding to spirit, and πνοή answering to "inspiration" or "breath." " πνοή conveys the impression of a lighter gentler breath of air than πνεῦμα" says Trench, (Sy-

ing of the passage would seem to be, that while age and experience give one kind of wisdom, there are also other sources of knowledge; there is an abiding presence of the Divine spirit in the soul of man, which teaches, and there are Divine impulses or breathings from the Almighty, which inspire suitable thoughts. On this account he will show his opinion. In all this, Elihu, while recognizing, with Plato, abiding Divine intuitions, as one source of knowledge, and with Socrates, special Divine inspirations as another, never dreamed of claiming *infallibility* for his utterances; or if we should say he did, it must at least be owned, that in making this claim he was mistaken. All he asserts is, that there are certain Divine in-breathings from the Almighty, for which our English word *inspiration* (from *in* and *spiro*, to breathe) has become the natural and proper representative.

The other passage, — II. Tim. 3 : 16, — reads in our English version, " All Scripture is given by inspiration of God ($\theta\epsilon o\pi\nu\epsilon\upsilon\sigma\tau o\varsigma$), and is profitable for doctrine, for reproof, for correction, for instruction in righteousness." Dr. Pye Smith, in company with the Douay and almost all the ancient versions, translates thus the 15th and 16th verses : " From a child, thou hast known the holy writings, which are able to make

non New Test. Part 2, Sec. 23,) following in this Seneca and Augustine. It is perhaps more occasional and less abiding.

thee wise unto salvation, through the faith which is in Christ Jesus. Every writing Divinely inspired is also profitable for instruction," &c. That this is the proper translation, will be shown below.*

* His remarks on this much disputed text, appear to me so conclusive, that little more can be said after quoting them. "It has been supposed impossible to establish from the Greek text alone, so as to preclude objection on either side of the agitated question whether θεοπνευστος agrees immediately with πασα γραφη or is as it is translated in the common version and in many others, a part of the predicate. Yet I cannot but think the fairest way of rendering πασα γραφη is *every writing*, so that the adjective is necessary to qualify the term, and must therefore be its attributive. This is clearly included in the rule laid down by Middleton (On the Greek Article Part I, Chap. 7,) though the good Bishop seems to shrink from the application in his Note to this text. Every one acquainted with the Greek idioms in the use of και is aware that to convey the meaning of *all Scripture*, as we use the phrase in English, would have required πασα ή γραφή. The form without the article used here by the Apostle, *necessitates* our taking the substantive in its most universal signification, and consequently that the adjective annexed must be a qualifying or distinguishing epithet. The exegetical use of και in the sense of even and also, is very frequent. I. Cor. 2: 24. II. Cor. 1: 3. Eph. 5: 10. Acts 3: 24. Heb. 4: 13. Gal. 4: 7. The Syriac, the Vulgate, nearly if not all the ancient versions, and most of the Fathers, Origen six or seven times over, Clement of Alexandria, Theodoret, and others, thus interpreted this passage. (See Smith on the person of the Messiah, Book I, Chap. 2, notes.) When however, we come down to the times of Luther, Beza, and the Protestant translators, the text seems to have been regarded as too important theologically against the Catholics, not to have been pressed into service in the translation, although Wyckliffe, Tyndall, and the Bible of 1551, had rendered it like the earlier versions. The

Do these two passages, then, properly translated, decide that the terms "inspiration," or "given by in-

use of the καὶ alone leaves the slightest doubt. De Wette in his last revision adopts the present English translation. So does Gaussen. The former of these goes further, and asserts that no matter which translation we adopt, it all amounts to the same thing. To us the matter seems different. Of course this passage refers entirely and exclusively to the Jewish Scriptures. To say that all the sacred writings are Theopneustic or God-inspired is one thing, to say that all Theopneustic or God-inspired writings are profitable is quite another. It gives us a clue and a safeguard as to what is to be the proof of Inspiration, — an internal sense of profitableness as well as external evidence. The importance of all this to Timothy is easily made clear. He was the son of a Jewish mother, by a Greek father, brought up probably out of the range and influence of the Palestine Jews, he had never been circumcised until Paul met him, and was probably therefore only acquainted with the Alexandrian or Greek version, which contained the Apocrypha mixed up with the Old Testament. It is true the Hellenistic Jews like Josephus and Philo, who visited the Palestine Jews, did not fully admit these as a part of the Canon. De Wette, quoting Berthold says: "It is certain that the Egyptian Jews never considered the Apocryphal books as a part of the Canon, properly so called, but it is equally certain they regarded and used them as an appendix to the Old Testament before the time of Christ. They were read as valuable, religious and moral writings, and were neither placed in the Canon, nor treated as common books. They were deemed holy but not perfectly holy, and so placed beside the Canon, not in it, as until the time of Antiochus the Hebrew Hagaiographa had been. The ancient Christians who were not acquainted with the Hebrew, and therefore were dependent on the Egyptian Jews for their knowledge of the Scriptures, considered all books of the Alexandrian Codex as genuine and sacred, and accordingly very soon made the same use of the Apocrypha and the Old Testament.

spiration of God," necessarily include absolute and verbal infallibility? or is it not at least an open question, whether the man inspired of God is not yet a man, giving his own characteristics to the writings, and a human element that is more or less fallible? The Church, whose history as a whole is that of an inspired body, is yet also one whose frailty in all its individual parts is obvious.

But this practice was founded on a mistake, for the Alexandrine Jews themselves never viewed these writings in that light." Nor did the better informed of the Christian Fathers always. The Apostle Paul used both the Hebrew and the Alexandrine Versions, and neither he nor any other New Testament writer ever quotes the Apocrypha. To a Greek Jewish Christian like Timothy, St. Paul never could have intended to say that every writing was God-inspired and profitable, that was found in the Greek copies of the Old Testament Scriptures as he was accustomed to see them. Yet nothing is more consistent, than that St. Paul wishing to warn him against the old wives' fables of the Apocryphal writings, mixed up with, and added to the books of the Old Testament he was in the habit of reading, while yet encouraging the study of the valuable and divine portions of them; should say, "every divinely inspired writing is also profitable," &c. This we in common with nearly all antiquity (where nothing special was to be attained from the other view) may take to be the sense of this passage. We are not here however discussing the question, what are the books of the Old Testament Canon, or whether the Apocrypha was included in it or not by any portion of the Alexandrine school, indeed we regard it as certain that if any did so, these words of St. Paul would afford a proof that he reprobated such an idea; but Dr. Pye Smith's interpretation gives the true rendering as Coleridge further agrees in his Confessions of an Inquiring Spirit, Letter 6.

II. The Lectures of Dr. William Lee, of Dublin, written to show the actual and absolute infallibility of the Inspiration of the Scriptures, yet fully admit that "the term *Inspiration* has been assigned to that *ordinary* actuation by the Holy Spirit," which does not render the recipient infallible. Indeed, he complains of Dr. Arnold, for having continued to regard as *identical* such operations of the Holy Ghost, with those under which Scripture was written, while he considers them specifically different. In illustration of this, he quotes from Dr. Arnold, who, enumerating certain erroneous inferences relating to Inspiration, says that it is an unwarranted interpretation of the term Inspiration, to call it a communication of the Divine perfections. Surely, many of our words and many of our actions proceed by the Inspiration of God's spirit, without whom we can do nothing acceptable to him. Yet, does the Holy Spirit so inspire us, that our best words or works are utterly free from error or from sin? All Inspiration, then, does not destroy the human and fallible part in the nature which it inspires. It does not change man into God. Dr. Arnold is also quoted as saying, "If a single error can be discovered in Scripture, it is supposed to be fatal to the credibility of the whole. This has arisen from an unwarranted interpretation of the word 'Inspiration,' and by a still more unwarranted inference. An inspired work is supposed to mean a work to which God has communicated his own perfections, so that the slightest error or defect of any kind in it is inconceivable, and that which is other than perfect in all points cannot be inspired. This is the unwarranted interpretation of the word Inspiration." Yet, even Dr. Lee still admits that the Inspiration of the Bible "contains a human as well as a Divine element." He says, "On the one hand, God has granted a revelation; on the other, human language has been made the channel to convey it, and men have been chosen the agents to record it." On this account, he disclaims what he terms "the mechanical theory" of Inspiration, because "it practically ignores the human element of the Bible, and fixes its exclusive attention upon the Divine agency." "On its principles the sacred writers, on receiving the Divine impulse, resigned both body and mind to God, who influenced and guided both at his sole pleasure, the human agent contributing meanwhile no more than the pen of the scribe. In a word, he was the pen, and not the *penman* of the Spirit." * This mechanical idea Dr. Lee professedly repudiates in regard to the Bible, as not accounting sufficiently for difference of style, &c. Enough this to show, then, that Inspiration does embrace a human as well as a Divine element. But he adds, " While I can by no means accept this system as correct, it will be my object to establish in

* Lect. I.

the broadest extent all that its advocates desire to maintain, namely, the infallible certainty, the indisputable authority, the perfect and entire truthfulness of all and every part of Holy Scripture." How far Dr. Lee succeeds in doing this, we shall see hereafter. At present it is sufficient to learn that the idea of inspiration is not necessarily the same as dictation, that it involves a human as well as a divine element, so that the common prejudice, which sets aside all argument, by supposing that the admission of Inspiration precludes necessarily every sort of error, is quite erroneous. That idea may be proved true, or it may be proved false in regard to Holy Scripture. But the simple admission that any writing is given by inspiration of God, does not determine the fact that it is therefore infallible. Elihu did not claim infallibility if he thought that the inspiration of the Almighty gave him understanding. Yet it is here that there is the greatest confusion. The idea is that all who doubt the absolute infallibility of every scientific or historical difficulty, necessarily so far question the Inspiration of the writer, and indeed of the whole Bible.

III. Inspiration is a *positive* and not a *negative* term. It *asserts* a fact, and not merely *denies* one. It means literally a breathing into, and indicates a spiritual power imparted or infused into the mind, of a superior and elevating character, above all that belongs to the individual in his purely and natural state. Such is certainly the meaning of the term in its ordinary use, apart from any particular theological sense. Thus Bacon speaks of "an instinct *inspiring* not only the hearts of princes, but the pulse and veins of the people, and leading them to anticipate the happiness to ensue in time to come from certain courses of conduct." *

Blair, also, speaking of the Christian, says, that "when he looks up to heaven, he rejoices in the thought that there dwells that God whom he serves and honors, that Saviour in whom he trusts, and that spirit of grace from whose *inspiration* his piety and charity flow."

When the poets, ancient and modern, invoke the inspiration of the muse, it is not infallibility, but *elevation* of thought and heart they seek. Not the absence of error, but the presence of truth. Thus Milton seeks the inspiration of that Divine Presence that had filled the soul of Moses under the Jewish, and been the chief light of the Christian dispensation.

> " Sing, Heavenly Muse, that on the secret top
> Of Oreb, or of Sinai, didst *inspire*
> That shepherd who first taught the chosen seed.
>   *   *   *   *   *   *
> And chiefly thou oh Spirit that dost prefer

* Bacon, Henry VII.

> Before all temples, the upright heart and pure
> Instruct me, for thou knowest   *   *
> *   *   *   What in me is dark
> Illumine, what is low, raise and support,
> That to the heighth of this great argument
> I may assert eternal Providence
> And justify the ways of God to man."

The negative view, the absence of mistake has never formed the chief thought in regard to Inspiration among any class of men except our modern Theologians. Positive expansion, enlargement and elevation best keep the soul of the good man free from error.

The proper conception of the inspiring spirit, is not that it destroys the true man, or any of his powers, or individualities, so far as *they* do not destroy *it* within him. It may, indeed, be said that by so much as man is a sinner, is he less than a man, and he is only wholly a man, inasmuch as wholly possessed of the spirit. By so much as any man is a Christian, is he an *inspired* man, and this was the doctrine fully held and felt in the early Church, as might be easily illustrated from the prayers accompanying the laying on of hands in the Apostolic Constitutions, and the titles given to the newly baptized in early Church history. Every Christian was, indeed, taught so to consider himself. "The Holy Ghost gives us the gift of spiritual wisdom, by which we are illuminated, edified, instructed, and consummated to perfection. This is the account which the ancients generally give of the original of the laying on of hands," says Bingham.[*] Inspiration is, so far as it goes, the restoration of man's normal state, the realization of man's destined condition. The Inspiring work of the Holy Spirit is not so much to destroy, as to elicit into distinct manifestation, and to quicken the individual·powers of the inspired one, causing him to outgrow the wrong uses of them by putting them all into employment in a full and sanctified use. And this is the true and positive view of the Inspiration of the Holy writings as well as that of holy persons. Have not the liturgies of all ages besought the Lord to inspire within the souls of his servants, all good thoughts and holy desires? In most Communions, each Christian Minister in some set form, declares that he believes himself inwardly moved by the Holy Ghost to enter the office of his Ministry. Does the term *inspire*, so far as it is used in these cases, refer to a *negative* or not rather a *positive* impulse? Is the idea one of absolute sinlessness, or of inward living energy, pressing towards a higher, nobler life, yet not ensuring the absence of all imperfection?

Why, then, should these proportions of thought be all inverted, or rather altogether changed by most, when they speak of the God inspired Scriptures of the

* Book XII, Chap. 4, Sec. 6.

3

old and new Testament. Whether the Inspiration of Scripture implies a total exemption from every kind of fallibility, or whether this is simply a Pharisaic incrustation of superstition which the Christian Church has not yet altogether risen above, we will consider hereafter. But assuredly this is not the chief or positive idea in regard to it. The Inspiration of Scripture is a divine inbreathing and animating power resting upon its authors, human beings as they were, so that holy men of God spake as they were moved by the Holy Ghost.

IV. Mr. Morell in his philosophy of religion, considers that it is the *intuitional consciousness*, as distinct from the sensational, the perceptive, and the logical powers of our nature, that alone is susceptible of religious inspirations or impressions. Yet it seems to me that the elevation of any one part of our spiritual nature elevates the whole, and that when God gives to a man that is good in his sight, that intuitive spiritual wisdom, which is true inspiration, it quickens in turn, any and all the perceptive, the reasoning, and even at times the sensational powers, *super*-naturally, that is not in a manner contrary to nature, not perhaps what would be commonly called miraculously, but to a degree above what is natural through any other agency. The mathematical genius of a Newton may be termed an inspiration; the elevation of a Milton in his poetry, as well as that of a Bazaleel* to design and work in brass for the service of the temple. Did not Pericles and the most eloquent of ancient orators pray for inspiration in their speeches, and have not the supremely wise and good of all ages sought for it in their daily work, and found therein a new and original wisdom leading to the loftiest success? Much of this is, indeed, of a different kind from simply religious inspiration, even where originating in it. But who shall say that all kinds of inspiration, that of poetry and of the reasoning powers, have not contributed their quota to make our Bibles fit to furnish all men so thoroughly to every good word and work? Nothing has ever kindled the abstract reasoning powers, as religion has done, and supplied that patience of exact, clear and earnest thinking, coupled with correctness of feeling of which the Bible is so full. And is not the influence reciprocal?

The elevation of the Scriptures as a whole, is of course of a higher and nobler kind than the mere inspiration of genius, as it is also higher in *degree*, though not different in *kind*, as I apprehend from that of the Christian, when inwardly moved by the Holy Ghost to consecrate himself as a Minister or Missionary or translator of the Bible for the heathen. It is, therefore, more truly *super*-natural, although the Church of God

* Exodus 36: 1-2.

is now and ever shall be instinct with spiritual life, a holy and a truly inspired body. This is promised to it by the master, aud asserted of it by the Apostles. The distinction between the authority and inspiration of the living Apostle in his teachings, and the deceased Apostle in his writings, a distinction drawn in favor of the latter, is wholly an invention, a sort of canonization of saints after their departure, which they strenously resisted while living, and which has been only paralleled by some of the superstitions of the Romish Church.

CHAPTER II.

MODERN VIEWS OF INSPIRATION STATED AND CLASSIFIED.

BEFORE proceeding to settle what that view of the Inspiration of the Bible is, which will best meet all the facts of the case, or even to give an historical development of present opinions on this subject, it is proposed in this chapter to present a simple statement of what are the chief and distinct opinions now held by Christians of different denominations and schools in this country, and in Europe, classified not historically, but according to their natural affinities and resemblances.

Dr. Lee of Dublin, in his profound lectures on Inspiration, very properly suggests that such views should be classified according to the two leading systems in this department of theology, the one suggested by the prominence assigned to the Divine element, the other resulting from the weight attached to the

Human.* The former, so far as it alone is followed, makes every thing of *Authority*, the latter of *Reason*. The former unchecked tends towards blind superstition, the latter alone, to Rationalism. The one makes Inspiration entirely Objective, the other Subjective.†

I. There is one class of views on Inspiration now current, which takes into account the Divine element, but ignores practically the Human. We include here, not alone as Dr. Lee does, what he calls the mechanical theory of plenary *verbal* Inspiration, but also what he distinguishes from it, as the Dynamical ; in fact, all that make the Divine element so overpowering as to leave no room for human frailty or errors to creep in, and no work for human reason to perform, when it once understands the meaning of the writing. We include in a word, those systems which profess to establish an *infallible* scheme of religion by means of the words of the Bible.

1. The Roman Catholic system, though extremely variant in proportion as the authority of the Council of Trent is or is not regarded as of binding authority, amounts to this: that without distinctly asserting or denying the absolute infallibility of the Scriptures alone, ‡ it supposes the Church an infallible interpreter of Scripture, without which the Bible is a sort of lock

* Lect. I, p. 32-3.　　　† Wescott's Introduction, p. 31-2.
‡ See Mochler's Symbolism, Sec. 38.

without a key, but with which the whole possesses infallibility. Thus in the Douay Bible, after translating II Tim. 3: 16. " All Scripture inspired of God is profitable to teach, to reprove," &c.; a note adds, " Every part of Divine Scripture is certainly profitable for all these ends. But if we would have the whole rule of Christian faith and practice, we must not content ourselves with those Scriptures which Timothy knew from his infancy, that is the Old Testament alone; nor yet with the New Testament, without taking along with it the traditions of the Apostles, and the interpretation of the Church, to which the Apostles delivered both the book and the true meaning of it." The Council of Trent* decrees that the truth and discipline of the Gospel " are contained in the written books, and unwritten traditions which, received by the Apostles from the mouth of Christ himself, or from the Apostles themselves, the Holy Ghost dictating, have come down even unto us." " One God is the author of both (the Old Testament and the New,) as also the said traditions dictated either by Christ's own word of mouth, or by the Holy Ghost."

The Roman Catholic believes, therefore, in the Inspiration of both the Church and the Bible, but the Church first and most important. It does not regard the Bible as a sufficient or perhaps infallible guide,

* Session 4.

independently of the interpretations of the Church. Indeed it was perhaps one object of those who decreed the equal authority of the Vulgate with the Greek Text of the New Testament, and the canonical authority of the Apocrypha as a part of the Old; to keep alive the ancient view that Inspiration is not the same thing as Infallibility.

2. The Modern High Church view of such Episcopalians as Dr. Pusey, or such members of the Reformed Churches, as Dr. Tholuck in Germany and possibly Dr. Nevin in this country, does not differ very greatly from the Roman Catholic view as to the relations of the Church and Bible, though widely differing in other respects especially as to who compose that church which is the interpreter of the written word.

It varies from the Roman Catholic view also in this respect, that while as asserting that both the Church and the Bible are inspired, it does not absolutely declare or deny that *either* of them are *infallibly* inspired. This modern view originated in a re-actionary movement against a Rationalism approaching that of Strauss. It asserts that the Church and the Bible are, however, inspired in such a manner, that from the combined influences of the two, faithful souls shall receive a fully sufficient and divine guidance for each exigency, one of practical infallibility to those who have faith in it, if not theoretically infallible for all mankind.

There are many shades of this opinion, and its depth and force are but little understood. Robertson of Brighton, though opposed to many of. the High Church views, ably remarks that there is a certain incorrectness that is not only consistent with, but necessary to Inspiration, as where the sun is said to rise and set, or where the geological, or other scientific statements are clothed according to the age and knowledge of the writer or reader, not in words of absolute scientific accuracy.*

3. Opposed to these, though in some respects in the same great division, stands the *mechanical* view, which with slight modifications of expression, is found in the bulk of almost all the Orthodox Protestant Articles of Faith, to this day, whether Calvinistic or Armenian. "When the first act of the Reformation was closed, and the great men had passed away, whose presence seemed to supply the strength which was found in the recognition of one living body of Christ, their followers invested the Bible as a whole, with all the attributes of mechanical infallibility, which the Romanists had claimed for the Church. Pressed by the necessities of the position, the disciples of Calvin were contented to maintain the direct and supernatural action of a guiding power, on the very words of the inspired writer, without any regard to his personal or national posi-

* Vol. II, p. 148.

tion."*   " All the written word is inspired of God even to a single iota or tittle," says Gaussen, as the " conclusion " of his whole discussion, the object of which is to show that the Scriptures are given and guaranteed by God, even in their very language, and contain no error."   Dr. Lee in his work on Inspiration, complains of this as too mechanical a theory for him, because he says, " it practically ignores the human element of the Bible, and fixes its exclusive attention upon the Divine agency, exerted in its composition ;" — because " in fine, each and every point has not only been committed to writing, under the infallible assistance and guidance of God, but is to be ascribed to the special and immediate suggestion, embreathment and diction of the Holy Ghost."

4. But we fail, as Coleridge did, to find that the difference is of any practical moment, between the above and Dr. Lee's own, or what he calls the ' Dynamical ' theory of Inspiration, especially when he says, " It will be the object of the present discourses, to establish in the broadest extent *all that the supporters of the mechanical theory desire to maintain,* namely, the *infallible* certainty, the indisputable authority, the perfect and entire truthfulness of all and every part of Holy Scripture." On the next page, he disclaims, as ascribing undue prominence to the human element of the Bible, all

* Wescott's Introduction, p. 31.

theories like those of Bishop Wilson, of Calcutta, which assume various "*degrees* of Inspiration."

In a confession known as the New Hampshire Confession of Faith, originally written by Rev. John N. Brown, and extensively adopted by Baptist Churches and Associations throughout the country, the Holy Scriptures are described as having "*God for their Author*, salvation for their object, and truth without any mixture of error for their contents," — yet this really conveys, and is only intended to convey, a belief either in the mechanical or dynamical theories, as may suit the subscribers. Even those who hold to degrees of inspiration, whether but two degrees like Stapfer, or five, or even *eight*, so long as the possibility of error was excluded, believe what amounted substantially to the same thing.

All these theories I consider really the same. They seem more or less to "ignore the human element," and "fix the exclusive attention on the Divine agency," insisting upon the absolute *infallibility* of every portion of the Old and New Testaments.

Dr. Dwight, for instance, insists that "while each writer was so left to his own manner of speaking or writing, as that the style was strictly his own," yet that "each inspired man was as to his preaching or his writing, *absolutely preserved from error.*"

Dr. George Hill, Principal of St. Mary's College,

does not go quite so far, but draws a distinction between the inspiration of *suggestion* and that of dictation. He thinks that Paul distinguishes between counsels that he gives in matters of indifference upon his own judgment, and the commandments he delivers with the authority of an Apostle, speaking in the one case by permission, in the other by commandment; that he sometimes discovered a doubt or a change of purpose as to the time of his journeyings and other incidents; and that there is an imperfection and obscurity which at times remains on the style of the sacred writers, especially of Paul. But these he thinks not at all inconsistent with the *Inspiration of direction*, through which, however, the writers were, by the superintendence of the Spirit, *effectually guarded from error while they were writing*, and were at all times furnished with that measure of inspiration which the nature of the subject required."[*]

Dr. Henderson, who objects to verbal inspiration, says that there is "no material difference" between himself and those who hold to the other view, as they were "always secured, by celestial influence, against the adoption of any forms of speech or collocations of words that would have injured the exhibition of Divine truth, or that did not adequately give it expression."

Dr. Leonard Woods also thinks they "were so

---

[*] Lect. p. 333–8. Edinburg, 1825.

guided by the Divine Spirit, that in every part of their work they wrote just what God willed they should write."

We may therefore regard all these views as substantially one. Dr. Lee, and many before him and since, draw a strong distinction between *Revelation* and *Inspiration*. Revelation he considers "the manifestation" of a truth, Inspiration "is the record of it." It is, he thinks, the Logos that reveals, the Holy Ghost that inspires. All this may be true, and yet at last I do not see that it is of any particular moment. Indeed, Stapfer, a theological Professor at Berne, who died in 1775, and is quoted by Dr. Pye Smith, says, " We must distinguish between those parts of the Sacred Scriptures which were written by the *immediate* inspiration of the Holy Spirit, and those which have been consigned to writing by his direction only. To the former class belong the peculiar discoveries of revelation, respecting the way of salvation, predictions, &c. To the latter class belong truths already known from Natural Religion." But it is added, " Nor was any error permitted to creep in with regard to even the minutest fact or circumstance. All alike comes to us through Inspiration, and is of equal precision, whether it be by revelation or observation or reasoning, if we follow the letter, there can be no error in our conclusions, except by not properly applying the laws of Interpretation."

II. We turn next to exhibit some of those theories in regard to Inspiration which ignore the Divine element altogether, or to so great an extent exalt the human reason as to overthrow in every way the *Divine Authority of Scripture.*

1. The first of these that we will here mention is that of Strauss, who in 1835 first published his Life of Christ, and has lately re-written it in a more popular form. Following the Hegelian Philosophy, and denying the existence of a personal God, he could of course believe, in no proper sense, in Divine Inspiration. But yet, regarding *Humanity* as God manifest in the flesh, even the Gospels seemed to him as a mythical exhibition, a sort of inspired and dream-like picture of that idea portraying itself by degrees in the shape of stories and legends. The Gospels with him are popular legends, and the miracles significant poetry. That Jesus was a real historic personage, he believes, a popular rabbi and teacher, but an innovator and an enthusiast who fancied he had a Divine mission. After his death, exaggerations naturally took place, of his teachings, and these gradually grew, not by design, but as the natural growth of the poetic and philosophical imaginings of the early Church. After about fifty years, these myths began to resolve themselves into the

Gospels.   The meaning of this mythical life of Christ is thus explained at the close.   The career of Christ symbolizes the moral history of mankind.   The narrative is therefore true, yet not of the individual, but of the race.   The teachings of Christianity are true, though its professed facts are fables.   So early as 1802, G. L. Bauer had published a " Hebrew Mythology of the Old and New Testament," while Niebuhr had reconstructed Roman history by regarding its early records as a collection of myths.

As to miracles, Strauss says, " No just notion of the true nature of history is possible without a perception of the inviolability of the chain of finite causes, and of the impossibility of miracles."   So far he was Anti-supernaturalist.

Already before Strauss began his wholesale work of destruction upon the New Testament, several had applied that system to the Old, and had, he tells us, divided off its myths into *three* classes, — historical, philosophical and poetic.

Historical myths are narratives of real events, colored by the light of antiquity, which confounded the Divine and the human, the natural and the supernatural.

Philosophical myths are those which clothe in the garb of historical narrative a simple thought, a precept, or an idea of the time.

Poetical myths are historical and philosophical myths partly blended together, and partly embellished by the creation of the imagination, in which the original fact or idea is almost obscured by the veil which the fancy of the poet has thrown around it. Where no object, for the sake of which the legend might have been invented, is discoverable, it is to be pronounced *histori-cal*. But if the principal circumstances combine to symbolize a particular truth, this undoubtedly was the object of the narrative, and the mythus is *philosophical*. When the account is so wonderful that it cannot be a detail of facts, and when it discovers no attempt to symbolize a particular thought, it may be suspected that the entire narrative owes its birth to the imagination of the poet. Schelling thinks this last was done because, deficient themselves in clear abstract ideas, and in ability to give expression to their conceptions, they sought to illumine what was obscure in their representations by means of sensible imagery.*

Thus a myth may have *no historical* basis of fact, and in the absence of explicit evidence we have no right to assume any. Mr. Grote has tried to show this in regard to the History of Greece. But then it differs from the fable in being a *spontaneous* and gradual growth; not a work of any one mind, but of many minds successively moving forward in one given direc-

* Strauss' Life of Jesus,—Introduction, Sec. 8.

tion of thought. The fable and parable are works of conscious invention. But the myth differs from these, in being an unconscious production, never of deliberately perpetrated untruth. This it is that probably reconciled Strauss, as it has done many others, to the mythical theory in preference to the Naturalistic, which involved the idea of wilful falsehood. Asserting that he believed the ideas thus mythically represented to be truth, Strauss supposed that his theory of the Gospels would be received as coming nearer to the old views of Inspiration than the Naturalistic explanations that had preceded.

Before Strauss, some efforts had been made to explain parts of the Gospels on the mythical theory. Thus Baur, though he says that a history which was altogether mythical was not to be sought in the New Testament, yet believed that there might be single myths transferred from the old religion to the new, or springing up spontaneously in the latter. Thus, in the details of the infancy of Jesus, much seems to him to require this solution. Usteri had on this theory explained the temptation of Jesus. It is not, however, to be imagined, he says, that any one individual seated himself at his table to invent these scenes out of his own head and write them down as he would a poem; but these narratives, like all other legends, were fashioned by degrees, which can no longer be traced, acquired consistency, and at length received a fixed form in our written Gospels.

Dr. Strauss was not, therefore, breaking altogether new and untrodden ground. But he thought the application of the notion of the mythus too circumscribed and says, " we are prepared to meet with both legend and mythus in the gospel history, and when we undertake to extract the historical contents which may possibly exist in narratives recognized as mythical, we shall be equally careful neither on the one hand by a rude and mechanical separation to place ourselves on the same ground with the natural interpreter, nor on the other, by an hypercritical refusal to recognize such contents, where they actually exist, to lose sight of the history."

Dr. Strauss supposes that about fifty years after the death of Jesus, the oral Gospel which formed the basis and cause of the great similarity of the three first gospels, was produced, being after a while committed gradually to writing by several, under the guidance of some Apostle, or Apostolic man, and that from these writings our present gospels were compiled, especially the synoptics, not being written by the evangelists, but only " according to " their supposed views and teachings, as he after Schleiermacher considers the term κατα to imply. But he will not admit that even Luke's Gospel was written until early in the second Century, but together with the Acts, composed or edited from earlier manuscripts.

He lays down some rules, which he thinks will assist us to determine what is historical, and what unhistorical, but he concludes by saying that "the boundary line between the historical and the .unhistorical in records in which as in our Gospels this latter element is incorporated, will ever remain fluctuating and unsusceptible of precise attainment. In this obscurity, the author wishes to guard himself in those places where he declares he knows not what happened, from the imputation of asserting that he knows that nothing happened."

Such were the views of Strauss when he penned the first edition of his work in 1835. But thirty years later, he re-wrote the whole in a more popular style. He still calls his a *mythical* theory of the Life of Jesus, and notwithstanding the many replies that have been written to what he wrote, and the complete revulsion of public opinion against his theory, contends that he has been unanswered, and that he was only so far mistaken, as a man is in error, who, having supposed that his neighbor owed him forty pounds, finds that the debt is much greater. So he says that he now discovers so much intentional falsification, that he abandons his former ground, in which he professed to acquit the Gospel authorities of this, and instead of being devout enthusiasts mistaking fiction for fact, he considers them as artful theologians, bent on establishing their views, and using pious frauds for this purpose.

He, therefore, wishes to extend the meaning of the term mythical, and strains it still more than in his former edition so as to include *all narratives that spring out of a theological idea.* He considers the Gospel of John as not written till between 160 or 175 A. D., and thinks that it purposely misdates the time of the crucifixion for a theological purpose.[*] In a word, Strauss becomes more and more skeptical as he grows older.

2. From Strauss we turn to Baur, a much more reasonable critic. He is or has been considered a follower of Hegel, even to Pantheism, but it is said, on the other hand, that he has only employed Hegel's philosophical analysis of the inner life of history, without identifying himself with the theological deductions at which Hegel aims, and in his system, claims to have found a counterpoise against the negative and destructive philosophy of Strauss. His desire seems to be to establish Biblical Criticism on the same platform as the philosophy of history. As a critic of this kind, his fame is unequalled among those of the Tubingen school, at the head of which he stood. Indeed, his ability, originality and fairness have been fully recog-

* See Essays on the Supernatural origin of Christianity by G. P. Fisher, p. 428–9.

nized even by Professors like Dorner, opposed to him on the most vital matters, so that his history of the doctrine of the Atonement is perhaps most admired by those who would least agree with his philosophical or even his theological opinions.

He, like Strauss, restricts his attention to the New Testament, but he stands in direct opposition to Strauss' inclination to undervalue the historic element. The great problem he undertakes, is to re-construct the history of early Christianity, to re-investigate the genesis of the gospel biographies and doctrine. Declining to approach the books of the New Testament with dogmatic preconceptions, he breaks with the past Judaism, and interprets it by the historic method, proposing for his fundamental principle, to interpret Scripture exactly like any other literary work.

" Pretending that after the ravages of criticism, the Gospels cannot be regarded as true history, but only as miscellaneous materials for history, his school takes its stand on four of the Epistles of St. Paul, i. e. I and II Corinthians, Romans and Galatians, the genuineness of which it cannot doubt, and finds in the struggle of Jew and Gentile, its theory of Christianity, which is not regarded as miraculous, but as an off-shoot of Judaism, which received its final form by the contest of the Petrine, or Judæo-Christian party, and the Pauline or Gentile, which contest is considered by it, not to have been decided, till late in the Second Century. By the aid of this theory, constructed from few books which it admits to be of undoubted genuineness, it guides itself in the examination of the remainder, traces them to party interests which determined their aim, pronouncing on their object and date, by reference to it. In this way it arrives at most extraordinary conclusions in reference to some of them. Not a single book except four of Paul's Epistles is regarded as authentic. The gospel called that of St. John is considered as a treatise of the Alexandrian philosophy, written late in the Second Century, to support the theory of the $Λόγος$. It will thus be perceived that the enquiry of his school, though it professes to be objective, yet has a subjective cast."*

Hasé, in his Life of Jesus, Fourth Edition, gives the following summary of the conclusions of Baur, and of the Tubingen school. "That the Canonical Gospels were written in the Second Century, that the Gospel of Matthew is the most genuine, and is a comparatively faithful translation of the Gospel to the Hebrews, that the Gospel of Luke is a compilation of the materials already existing, proceeding from the stand point of Paul as a balance against the Ebionites; that the Gospel of Mark consists of extracts from the two others, with the purpose of taking middle ground

* See Farrar's Critical History of Free Thought, p. 277–8.

between them, and so forming a stepping stone from one to the other; and that the fourth gospel was composed subsequently as a spiritual romance about the Logos, out of materials taken from the synoptics — which assumes that its ideal contents are necessarily opposed to historic truth." But all this criticism of the sources comes back at last to rest for its foundation upon a criticism of the gospel narrative itself. Bauer himself says "the principle argument for the later origin of the Gospels must forever remain this, — that separately and still more when taken together, they give an account of the life of Jesus which involves impossibilities." * Elsewhere Hasé says, "the Revelation of John and the four great Epistles of Paul are alone regarded as genuine monuments of the apostolic Church, and the first gospel is looked upon as a collection of apostolical traditions made very near the same period." †

But, in fact, this school has been so variant in its conclusions, that it has lost much of the importance at first attached to it. Indeed, at Tubingen, it has entirely died out. Bruno Bauer, of Berlin, though he cannot be called a Tubingen man, has pushed matters further, so as to abandon even the four Epistles of St. Paul; while many of the present Professors at Tubin-

* See Clarke's Translation of Hasé's Life of Jesus, p. 35–6.
† Hist. Christian Church, Sec. 458.

gen, taking their stand on these four Epistles as un-questionable, have reconstructed a faith in the early history of Christianity and its writings, so closely approaching to Orthodoxy, that many of them have become pietists of the most strictly symbolical kind.

Perhaps this has been in part the effect of a political feeling; and not only of intellectual conviction, but such as induced Niebuhr to educate his son Marcus with the determination to make him "believe in the letter of the Old and New Testament." " I shall nur-ture in him," he said, "from infancy, a firm faith in all I have lost, or feel uncertain about." This seems a sad but most natural termination of merely sceptical criticism, that is, of reasoning negatively alone, and without any fixed basis of authority from which to begin, or any great practical effort in life at which it aims. Its highest attainments at last seems to be doubt in the correctness of its own disbelief, and a hatred of it even more intense than its doubt.

There have been, however, many in whom, as we shall see, the re-active movement against excessive dis-belief has been of a most sincere and positive kind. Indeed, now, not alone at Tubingen, but elsewhere, the tendency seems to a return, not merely to the Medi-ation views of Schleiermacher, but to a pietism the most intense. How, indeed, could it be otherwise? If any of Paul's writings are admitted to be genuine, then the parenthetic and other peculiarities of the style readily assure us of the genuineness of much of the rest. But even taking only the four admitted Epistles to be genuine, they evidently take for granted all the important facts of the life and character of Christ as believed and taught by all, sometime before the death, if not before the beginning of the reign of Nero. Whatever may be thought, therefore, of particular Epistles, or parts of Epistles and books, the substance of the New Testament, so far as the life of Christ and the conduct of the Apostles is concerned, must have been at that time believed by the great body of the Church, as given us by the Evangelists and the Acts, from the time say of the conversion of St. Paul. The tendency of the historico-critical school in Germany has been of late years back increasingly towards admitting the very *early* authorship of some of the New Testament Scriptures. The Apocalypse is now placed back in the first year of the Vespasian, and all the Gospels are considered by Tischendorf as of the first century. The substance of Matthew's Gospel is regarded as in existence, though not perhaps in its present exact form, at the close of the first century, and as having been considered authentic and authoritative by the Christian Church, Gentile and Jewish, by Dr. Frederick Bleek.

3. The next writer whose opinions may be said to

4

belong representatively to the present day, is Renan, who, early destined for the Church, renounced it after he had pursued the study of Hebrew, Syriac, and Arabic, became distinguished as a philologist, was sent by Napoleon to Tyre, Sidon, and Lebanon in 1860; there he made some excavations and discoveries, and drew up a report to Napoleon, and was appointed a Professor in the University of Paris, to the disgust of the Roman Catholic Priests, whose profession he had abandoned, and who now had their revenge by getting him silenced in consequence of some sceptical remarks in his opening lecture. He then produced that Life of Jesus, which has had a large sale in France. There, very little close Biblical study goes a long way, as in Roman Catholic countries generally. Indeed, his work produced quite a large sale of the New Testament, from the sort of new interest it threw around the study of the Life of Christ.

He is also a Pantheist, and his work is full of the most extreme exaggerations and all the results of a vivid imagination, asserted with all the confidence of the most certain fact. The very ten commandments, were, according to him, written on tables, not of stone, but of brass, in spite of the Hebrew, the Septuagint, and the Vulgate. In his work on the Semitic languages, he declared the whole Semitic race naturally Monotheistic, instead of confining his remark to the family of Abraham, to apologize we suppose for the failure of the Jews and Christians to attain to the wisdom of Pantheism.

In some respects he is, however, much less sceptical than the school of Bauer, though in critical sagacity he is behind him. He thinks that " all the books" of the New Testament " had become fixed very nearly in the form in which we read them, before the year one hundred," — " the composition of the gospels having been one of the most important events which occurred during the second half of the first century."

" Matthew and Mark are impersonal compositions," he says, " in which the author totally disappears." The words " *according to*," Matthew or Mark or Luke or John do not imply that the gospels were written from one end to the other by these authors. It only signifies that these writings embody the traditions coming from " these apostles," and covered by their authority. " A proper name written at the head of such works does not mean much." ·But he thinks the third gospel is certainly by Luke, the companion of Paul. " It is," he says, " beyond doubt that the author of the third gospel and of the Acts, is a man of the second apostolic generation, and it was written after the siege of Jerusalem, and soon after." He esteems it certain, also, that Matthew and Mark wrote before Luke. In regard to John's gospel, " there is," he says, " no doubt that towards the year 150, the fourth gospel was in existence, and was attributed to St. John. Formal texts of St. Justin, Athenagoras, Satian, Theophilus of Antioch, and Irenæus, show that from that time, this gospel was used in all controversies, and served as a corner stone for the development of doctrine." Indeed he seems pretty fully persuaded that the Gospel, except the twenty-first chapter, and the first Epistle are both the genuine work of John the Evangelist, written, however, after the year A. D. 68. Still the style of the discourses given by John is so different from the Synoptics, that while he entirely dissents from Bauer and his school, who suppose this gospel only a theological thesis, without historical value, he regards these records as the memories of an old man, sometimes of marvellous freshness, and sometimes having suffered strange mutilations. But the discourses reported are not, he thinks, historic, but intended to cover with the authority of Jesus, certain doctrines dear to the compiler, and especially to oppose the Gnosticism then arising. "Considering Jesus as the Incarnation of Truth, John could not but attribute to him what he had come to take for truth." The narrative of John he thinks to be preferred to that of the Synoptics, but the discourses of John are put into the mouth of Jesus, as Plato has done with Socrates in his Dialogues. Yet, after all this, Renan will not pronounce upon the material question, what hand traced the fourth gospel, and inclines to believe the discourses are not by the son of Zebedee. He admits that "this is really the gospel *according to* John." "Upon the whole, I accept the four canonical gospels," he says, "as authentic. All, in my judgment, date back to the first century, and they are substantially by the Authors to whom they are attributed, though in historic value, very unequal."

In nothing does Renan more differ from the German authors, to whom we have referred, than in the contempt he feels for all the apocryphal gospels now left to us, and the fragments of those lost, which are in his view, but flat and puerile amplifications, based on the canonical gospels, and adding to them nothing of value.

4. The opinions of Theodore Parker have been presented to the public in such various ways, that I close the view of this class of Theologians with those held by him. In this country he has been looked upon as a social reformer, but it is as a laborious if not consistent and patient theological thinker on the subject of Revelation, that we have to do with him here. He was, beyond doubt, one of the most indefatigable students, and though not minutely accurate, he finally became one of the most learned men on the American Continent. But he was chiefly self-taught, always growing, and so far changing his views that the most

contradictory opinions have been formed of his character. Even Professor Fisher, of Yale College, de-
scribes his position as one of uneasy equilibrium
between Pantheism and Theism, though he admits that
there are other expressions decidedly Theistic in their
purport. The article in the American Encyclopædia
also gives as his scheme of theology, that "God is
infinitely wise and good, impersonal because not com-
prehensible in any human conception, but personal,
because containing all his attributes in a unity of will
and essence." However erroneously he may at mo-
ments have expressed himself as to what is required in
order to personality, yet by those who believe that
wherever there is a Will guided by intelligence, there
is personality, Theodore Parker must be regarded as
one of the most thorough and intense Theists the
world has often seen. The volume of his prayers
published since his death prove this. "Few nobler
attacks on atheism or defences of the Benevolent
character of the Divine being exist, than those he
supplied."* In this respect, he rises with a manly and
vigorous feeling of the Divine Personality, that places
him, if a thinker of less delicacy at times, yet one also
of greater vigor and thoroughness than many of those
intellectual idealists so common in Germany, who
have refined away all clear conceptions of what Per-

* See Farrar's Critical History of Free Thought, p. 324-5.

sonality really consists in, or the proofs of its existence anywhere.*

The position of this Philosopher towards Christianity was clear and well defined. With an admiration and love for the character of Jesus, unrivalled in sceptical literature, and with an enthusiasm for the Scriptures themselves viewed from his stand point, he became by degrees, a settled and stern opponent of the Supernatural as distinct from the Natural in every form and shade. Without declaring the impossibility of miracles, he utterly denied any proof of them. He there-

---

* The *intellectual* nature of man alone, never can perceive proofs of the Divine Personality directly or immediately. It is his intellectual united with his moral nature, his own consciousness of power as a being of Will, that assures him of *another power*, outside of himself, vast and infinite, who possesses like him that combination of Intellect and Will in a single consciousness, which alone demonstrates the personality of God. Prof. Maurice has shown in his admirable essay on the History of Intellectual and Moral Philosophy in the Encyclopedia Metropolitana, that the full clear certainty of one personal God, first announced among the Greeks so far as we know by Anaxagoras, after ages of mental struggle and conflict, was, from the time of Socrates through the Platonic Philosophy that which gave to the best Grecians their great step in advance, and carried them to the point that forever separated them from the Indian Pantheism. Jewish Prophets and Psalmists had indeed announced this truth hundreds of years before the Greeks at least. But this healthy feeling of personality and trust in a personal God, which has of late been again lacking in many through the fear of receiving it merely as a Christian tradition, because no thorough history of Natural Religion had traced it out, was not wanting in Theodore Parker.

fore, of course held to the fallibility of the Scripture Records. Inspiration he was far from denying, but did not confine it to any religious sense, and considered works of intellectual genius also as produced by its influence. While regarding Christianity thus, as an inspired system (and the best yet exhibited of man's moral and religious nature,) he considered it subject to improvement and not final. The religion he .thirsted after and taught was "the absolute religion." Hence he thought that holy and good men of old, who were striving after truth, spake according to the light which was in them. He had on the one hand an earnestness of nature, that made him capable of the most true and lofty eloquence ; and on the other, a sarcastic and malignant spirit at times against the faith of his opponents, that provoked much bitterness against himself. Yet his friends ever felt that his love of the truths he knew was more valuable, than his hatred of what he supposed erroneous was hurtful, and even thought that it was this love of what he considered positive and eternal truth, that made him impatient and bitter against what he supposed to stand in its way.

Thus have we given a sketch of the opposite extremes of opinion as held at the present moment respectively by Supernaturalists, and Anti-supernaturalists ; by those who look upon the Bible as infallible and alone authoritative, and by those who not only look upon it as fallible, but deny any special authoritative Revelation.

CHAPTER III.

MODERN VIEWS, CONTINUED.

THE various opinions framed to mediate between the two extremes we have presented, must now occupy our attention.

Some years ago, M. Cousin came out and avowed himself an Eclectic Philosopher. Afterwards, Mr. Morell wrote a History of Philosophy, in which he followed closely M. Cousin's method, and divided all possible systems into five great classes: 1. That of *Sensationalism*, in which all our knowledge is supposed to arise simply from sensations: 2. *Idealism*, in which our volitions, desires, and the subjective laws of our reason and intelligence become separated from the whole region of sensation: 3. *The Sceptical Philosophy* which arises from the apparent contradiction of the two former modes of obtaining knowledge, and aims, by doubting, to destroy error and all that is false: 4. *Mysticism.* The mind never rests long content with a system of negation, but seeks some *positive* ground, and hence it re-acts towards a Mysticism which resolves the basis of all knowledge finally to the voice of God, speaking and stirring within us, and teaching us to know what is true. But this system leads to superstition and error, men mistaking their own fancies for the inward voice: 5. Hence, finally arises the *Eclectic* Philosophy, which perceiving that these four preceding systems owe their origin to some correct idea, and all succeed in eliciting some fragments of knowledge, that would otherwise have probably remained neglected or concealed, proposes to follow one or other of these four directions, as the case may be, to a certain extent, but rejects in each what may appear absurd or extravagant.

Cousin and Morell seem to think this a sort of ultimate philosophy, partly on account of its catholic plan of embracing *all* that is true in others, but chiefly on account of its supposed cautious and safe results.

There are several systems aiming at eclecticism on this subject of Inspiration. In the life of F. W. Robertson, of Brighton, he thus replies to a lady who asks him what *he* is. "Not an eclectic, certainly. An eclectic is one who pieces together fragmentary opinions culled out of different systems on some one principal of selection. I endeavor to seize and hold the spirit of every truth which is held by all systems under diverse, and often in appearance, contradictory forms. * * * * I get a truth not by eclecticism, taking as much of each as I like, *but that which both assert.*" The points in each really opposed to each other he rejects as false, that in which both agree he esteems true. Accordingly in giving the basis on which he taught, he lays down as three of his fundamental principles, "first, the establishment of positive truth, instead of the negative destruction of error. Secondly, that truth is made up of two opposite propositions, and not found in a via media between the two.* Thirdly, that spiritual truth is discerned by the spirit instead of intellectually in propositions, and therefore truth should be taught suggestively not dogmatically."†

---

* Hegel assumed that the law of logic was the law of the Universe, according to which all opposites are elevated, until they become lost in a higher unity. — (Hasé, Sec. 450.)

† That there is much that is valuable in all these suggestions, few will doubt. Indeed all who have ever felt that there was justice in the eclectic system as a practical method of arriving at truth on any subject, must also have felt that it was a most unscientific way of doing so, as nothing was decided as to the principles on which the selection of methods should be made, or the degree to which any one system should be followed, or where the pursuit of it should stop. All, too, must have felt that it is a method, which, if it ever accidentally leads to right conclusions, has often led to false ones, that it is as it were, mere guess work, and more often a cowardly and compromising system, which is

We turn therefore, to look at some of the different systems which are now proposed, and popular in several circles, for uniting the claims of Authority and Reason in regard to Inspiration.

1. In Germany the difficulty has been most openly and intensely discussed, and Schleiermacher may perhaps be regarded as the leader of those who after a long season of religious deadness, guided the learning and

convenient chiefly for those who are afraid of avowing an unpopular truth, and therefore divide it, and mix it up with so much of popular error as shall make it palatable to the age. Mr. Robertson's system would however be claimed by the true Eclectics as fairly embraced within this method, and only a more precise statement of their system. As such we are disposed to regard it. It is this which makes the historical development of any truth so convincing. Mr. Lecky says truly, that there is an increasing tendency to this, and if so, it must be because thus amid a thousand contradictory circumstances, the opposite *poles* of every great truth will show themselves in history, and the synthetic point of their union.

There is little doubt that Coleridge meant what Mr. Robertson has described more fully, when he said "all power manifests itself in the harmony of corresponding opposites, each supporting the other." The two poles, and the point of harmony belonging to every truth, constitute that tri-unity that he thought the most clear and necessary method of comprehending any subject. But Coleridge the *Mystic*, got this thought from Plato the *Idealist*. And, indeed, all the Trinities of the ancients are older far than the Alexandrine School, older than Plato; they belonged to the Druidical systems, to the early Greek Philosophy, to the Egyptian, and back of them to the Indian methods of thought. Thus the oldest philosophy and newest meet and agree, and the two poles of highest antiquity and most severe modern thought unite.

wisdom of Germany from a cold and dead rationalism to religious faith and earnestness, while infusing into the pietism of other classes a proper respect for their own intellectual powers.

Born in 1768, his father a German Reformed Pastor, and his mother the daughter of a minister of the same Church, educated under the instructions of the pious Moravians, to which Communion his sister devoted herself, he became in his own experience a strange mixture of opposite tendencies. Before he was fourteen, a teacher had inspired him with an enthusiasm for classical literature. With it had sprung up what he calls, "a strange scepticism," "a peculiar thorn in the flesh," and which made him doubt the genuineness of all the early ancient authors. The innocent orthodox piety he met with among the Moravians, made a great impression on his whole after life, for he was one easily influenced by all around him, and possessed the wonderful faculty of drawing all the good, true and beautiful from even the most seemingly opposite sources. The age was sceptical, German theology peculiarly so, while he was going through the University at Halle, and he was constitutionally of that turn, so that he left without any fixed religious system, yet with the hope of "attaining by earnest research and patient examination of all the witnesses to a reasonable degree of certainty, and to a knowledge of the boundaries of human science and learning."

This was the man, who in after years at Berlin, became the most remarkable preacher and Professor of his day, lecturing on Philosophy and Theology daily, and without founding a distinct school, yet giving an impulse to the religious life of Germany similar to that which Coleridge afterwards gave to the thinking classes of England; an influence which *now* at a period of ninety years from his birth, has retained its hold upon the wisest and most mature minds, as that to which they return from the extremes of Strauss and Bauer with fresh satisfaction. In 1799, he published his " discourses on Religion, addressed to educated men among its despisers," which appears to have had a wonderful effect upon the rising generations of Theologians. His piety at that time, very dreamy and tinctured with the pantheism of Spinoza, ripened gradually into a feeling of absolute dependence upon God, and direct conciousness of him. His translation of Plato in six volumes, placed him in the front rank of critics upon those wonderful thoughts, which, ages before, had prepared large bodies of men to enter the Christian Church through the gate of the Alexandrine School. Both he and Neander, with many others were thus led most fully into Christianity. Yet he digested all he read into a system thoroughly his own.

" He can be ranked neither with the Rationalists nor with the Supernaturalists of his generation, but sought a higher unity of both these opposite systems." " In the aim of his life, in his mixture of reason and love of philosophy and criticism, of enthusiasm and wisdom, of orthodoxy and heresy, or considering the transitory character of his work, and the permanence of his influence, church history offers no parallel to him since the days of Origen." *

He produced one of the most important theological systems ever conceived. Religion was with him placed on a new basis, a home was found for it in the human mind distinct from reason. He made it clear that Religion is the feeling of the Infinite, the particular felt to be part of the universal, to view God in all things, and all things in God. The old rationalism was shown to be untrue, because radically defective in its psychology. Truth in religion he felt was not to be attained alone by reasoning but chiefly by a direct insight which he calls Christian consciousness answering to what evangelical men have been wont to call Christian experience. Piety he makes to consist in the emotional feeling of dependence on the Infinite, not on mere morality, while the intellectual basis of Theology, he lays, in a faith or intuition which apprehends God and

* Farrar, Lect. 6.

truth and critical faculties which act upon the matter presented and thus form the *Science* of Religion.

Christianity he considered as a feeling of dependence upon Christ, and an intellectual appreciation of Christ's work. The Church existed before the New Testament Scriptures which are the records of Christian truth, and a witness to the religious consciousness of Apostolic times. They were written for believers. Although thoroughly a Protestant, he was so far Catholic as to make the collective Christian consciousness the ultimate standard of faith, just as in art or in morals, he regarded the intuitions of human nature the final appeal.

He denied the infallibility of the Inspiration of the Bible, yet not reducing it to genius, but an awakening and excitement of the religious consciousness, different in degree rather than in kind from the pious inspirations or intuitive feelings of holy men. He held firmly to the historical verity of the Life of Christ, and made faith in him as one with the Father, the brightness of his glory, and the express image of his person in the Sabbelian method of conception, essential. At the same time, as the ideal of humanity was actualized in his life on earth, to attain to the realization of this, was to be the great Christian aim and struggle.

On the Old Testament he never lectured, regarding it as containing the history of the growth of religious

life among the Jews, and a Preface so far to the stock
on which Christianity was at first grafted. But he
develops in his "Dogmatics" the whole system of
Christian faith as a description of the religious consciousness or experience determined by a vital union
of the soul with the sinless and perfect Saviour. He
made less of miracles than doctrine as an evidence of
Christianity, yet drew attention to it as something
more than a single republication of natural religion,
just as Christian consciousness of the Redemption of
the soul, by a union of man with God, through one-
ness with the Redeemer, is more than mere moral
experience.

2. Of the coadjutor of Schleiermacher, De Wette,
less need be said here. His views of Inspiration were
quite as free as those of Schleiermacher, and perhaps
rather more fully developed in his Criticisms on the
Old Testament and on the New. In regard to the
former, he first carried the documentary theory of the
Pentateuch to practical and positive results. About a
century ago it had been proved by a Frenchman,
Astruc, that the use of the term *Elohim*, God, in the
first chapter of Genesis, and to the end of the third
verse of the second chapter, followed by the use of
Jehovah Elohim, Lord God, through the rest of the
second, was due to the fact, that our book of Genesis
was composed of at least two pre-existing documents.

As, however, he supposed that Moses produced the book in its present form, this occasioned no greater necessary shock against the most verbal theory of plenary Inspiration, than other extracts inserted into the Old and New Testaments. But De Wette pushed the investigation of this subject much further, aiming to get positive proof from it, as to the age in which the Pentateuch was written. In many points, he was mistaken, but the result of the whole has been a general conviction among competent scholars, that the Pentateuch was called by the name of Moses, not in the sense of his being the author of it, but because his labors were its chief subject. The Psalms in like manner are some of them Jehovistic, and some Elohistic, consisting, indeed, of five collections no doubt of different dates. The first collection, Psalm 1 to 41 has the word Elohim 15 times, and Jehovah 272, while the second collection, Psalm 42 to 72 has Elohim 164 times and Jehovah 30. In one case Psalms 14 and 53, the same psalm substantially has been bound up with both collections, only that one has Elohim, God, in most instances, where the other has Jehovah, Lord.

In his criticisms on the New Testament, De Wette is equally free. The third Gospel, and the Acts of the Apostles, he considers as the production in their present state, of one author or editor, but as written in the early part of the second century, though compiled especially so far as the Acts of the Apostles is concerned, from documents pre-existing and contemporaneous. Thus he supposes that Acts 16 and 21, where the first person is used, — "*we* that were of Paul's company," was part of the journal of Timothy or Luke or some other companion of St. Paul, incorporated into the narration of the correspondent of Theophilus.

It must be remembered that De Wette wrote at the dying out of the old school of Rationalists, the impress of whose opinions upon him is very marked. Yet he himself did much to destroy them, for although he did not believe in miracles, he loved and revered Christianity intensely, and led others to go much further in that direction than he himself went, and even in Biblical Criticism, to advance nearer to Orthodox views. De Wette in fact seems to study the whole Bible more for the sake of its literature, and as a witness of the opinions held by the writers, than with the feeling of its *authority*. He prepared the way for a race of critics more reverend of Christianity than himself. Such a man, for instance, was Neander.

3. This noble Christian, a Jew by birth, a follower and admirer of Schleiermacher, approached the Christian religion from the Platonic philosophy. He was led by the Christian consciousness to rely on Christ as the head and centre of his faith, even more implicitly

and devoutly than Schleiermacher. And this seemed to enable him to receive even the most miraculous portions of the life of Christ with reverence and faith, not indeed so much as evidences of Christianity, but as those wonders which must naturally be expected to attend the advent of such a character. His Life of Christ, written really in answer to the mythical theory of Strauss, and his Planting and Training of the Christian Church, show how closely one approaching Christianity from the stand point of the Platonic reason, and led by the Spirit, could unite at last in heart with those who viewed it from the stand point of authority alone.

On the subject of Inspiration, he is remarkably decided. " Of this I am certain," he says, " that the fall of the old form of the doctrine of Inspiration, and indeed of many other doctrinal prejudices, will not only not involve the fall of the essence of the Gospel, but will cause it no detriment whatever. Nay, I believe that it will be more clearly and accurately understood." But I have already alluded sufficiently to his views.

4. If from Germany, we turn now to England, we shall find that at the beginning of the present century, Dr. Priestly the Unitarian, stood alone and attracted great obloquy by denying the infallibility of some of the Scripture reasonings of St. Paul, while yet, so great was his faith in the Divine Authority of the New Testament as containing a Revelation from God,

that though as a philosopher, he was a Materialist, and of course denied the immateriality or natural immortality of the soul, yet through faith in Scripture, he died most firmly believing in a resurrection. "Return unto thy rest oh my soul, for the Lord hath dealt bountifully with thee. I will lay me down and sleep *until I awake in the morning of the Resurrection;*"— such was the epitaph prepared by himself. The author of these pages has often read and pondered over it, and copied it from his tombstone in the grave yard at Northumberland, Pa.

5. Dr. Pye Smith in his work in opposition to his views, complains of Priestly's opinions on Inspiration as self contradictory. But the fact is that Dr. Pye Smith lived to be complained of by his Orthodox brethren on precisely the same account. He rejected the Song of Solomon at one time, and the universality of the deluge at another. And while in some parts of the first edition of his work, he contends against Priestly for what he calls a "complete inspiration," he subsequently says, "I must confess that this hypothesis of universal verbal inspiration does appear to me to be clogged with innumerable difficulties;   *   *   *
it deprives all translations of their claim to the authority of Inspiration. Hence it would follow that the general body of Christians who are under a necessity of depending on translations, are in fact destitute of any

inspired Scriptures."   And with a general approval, he even quotes from Stanley's Life of Arnold, the assertion that any accurate, precise, and sharply defined view of Inspiration, Arnold had not.   In fact he seems to have wavered much, and even abandoned in the latter part of his life the strictness of his earlier views.   The destruction of five hundred thousand men, II Chron. 13: he regards as incredible, and speaks of "the numbers as not being objects of inspiration as they stand." " These facts he adds, must fearfully affect the theory of a servile literality of Inspiration."*

6. But it was Coleridge who may be said to have first broken ground fully and fairly on this subject in England.   During his life, in his most wondrous conversations, he did this, hinting it in his writings.   He would pour out his deep convictions that the line of demarcation between the primitive gifts of Spiritual Inspiration and the Inspirations of the Spirit now, was a line drawn without authority.   Edward Irving, from these views gathered from his conversations, started off into absurdities that disgusted him.   Another went, after his death, into opposite yet greater extremes.   Yet he ever used to maintain that a deep religious insight into causes was the true prophetic foresight of events, thus aiming to elevate the natural, and so unite it with the supernatural.   After his death, the Confessions of

* Book I, Chap. 2, Notes Appendix.

an Inquiring Spirit gave the true key note of harmony to the theological efforts of his whole life. This has proved the most potential of all his writings, producing a vital change among the English clergy, in many cases improving in the highest degree.

His seven letters on Inspiration, left in manuscript at his death, are intended to solve this question, " Whether it is expedient to insist on a belief of the Divine Origin and Authority of all and every part of the Canonical Scriptures, as a first principle of Christian faith, or whether the due appreciation of the Scriptures collectively, may not be more safely relied on as the result and consequence of the belief in Christ." " I have perused, he says, books of the Old and New Testament, and have found words for my inmost thoughts, songs for my joy, utterances for hidden griefs, and pleadings for my shame and my feebleness. Whatever *finds me*, bears witness for itself that it has proceeded from a Holy Spirit. Here, perhaps, I might have been content to rest, if I had not learned that, as a Christian, I cannot, must not stand alone, or if I had not known that more was required by the churches collectively ever since the Council of Nice." In the second letter, he says that there is more in the Bible that finds him than he has experienced in all other books put together, and at greater depths of his being; and that whatever thus finds him, brings with it an irresistible evidence of having proceeded from the Holy Spirit,—dictated by an infallible Intelligence. Thus he receives the essential truths of Christianity from an inward conviction. But as to the book, he believes that the word of the Lord did come to Samuel, Isaiah and others, and says, " I believe the writer, in whatever he himself relates of his own authority, and of its origin." But he cannot find any such claim as the doctrine of universal and verbal infallibility made by the Scriptures explicitly or by implication, but, on the contrary, they refer to other documents, and express themselves as sober minded, veracious thinkers. The passages on which this sort of plenary inspiration is based are few and incidental, referring, with perhaps one exception,— II Peter 3: 16,—only to the Old Testament. The conclusion so obviously involves a *petitio principii,* that he does not think the doctrine proved even in regard to the whole of the Old Testament, especially as we know not the time of the formation and closing of the Canon.

He says, that at no period was it the judgment of the Jewish Church respecting the Canonical books of the Old Testament, that they were all equally or infallibly inspired. It was from the Jewish Rabbis, he thinks, who strained their fancies in contending for a perfection in the Revelation given by Moses in the Pentateuch *alone,* that the Christian founders of this doctrine have borrowed their notions and phrases in regard to the entire Bible. Between the Mosaic and the Prophetic Inspiration, they asserted such a differ- ence as amounts to a diversity. And between both the one and the other, and the remaining books of the Old Testament, called the Hagiographa, the interval was wider still, and the inferiority in *kind*, and not only in degree, was unequivocally expressed. " The language of the Jews respecting the Hagiographa will be found to differ little, if at all, from that of religious persons among ourselves, when speaking of an author abounding in gifts, stirred up by the Holy Spirit, writing under the influence of special grace and the like." Mr. Coleridge feels that there is every distinc- tion between saying, " the Bible contains the religion revealed by God," and " whatever is contained in the Bible is religion, and was revealed by God." The Bible is the appointed conservatory, an indispensable criterion, and a continual source and support of true belief, but not the only source, not that which consti- tutes the Christian religion. " I prize and reverence this sacred library as of all outward means and con- servatives of Christian faith and practice, the surest and the most reflective of the inward Word. I hold that the Bible contains the religion of Christians, but dare not say, that whatever is contained in the Bible is the Christian religion, and shrink from all questions

5

respecting the comparative worth and efficacy of the written word, as weighed against the preaching of the Gospel, the discipline of the churches, the continued succession of the ministry, and the communion of Saints, lest, by comparing, I should seem to detach them."

He thinks that "in all ordinary cases, the knowledge and belief of the Christian religion, should precede the study of the Hebrew Canon. Indeed, with regard to both Testaments, I consider oral catechismal instruction as the preparative provided by Christ himself in the establishment of a visible Church. To make the Bible, apart from the truths and doctrines and spiritual experiences contained therein, the subject of a special article of faith, I hold an unnecessary abstraction which in too many instances, has the effect of substituting a barren acquiescence in the letter, for the lively faith that cometh by hearing. Who shall dare enjoin aught else as a matter of saving faith, besides the truths that appertain to salvation? The imposers take on themselves a heavy responsibility. They ante-date questions and thus in all cases aggravate the difficulty of answering them satisfactorily. They convert things trifling or indifferent, into mischievous pretexts for the wanton, fearful difficulties of the weak, and formidable objections of the enquiring."

It is, he thinks, quite out of time to put the

affirmation after enumerating all the articles of the Catholic faith, "and further you are bound to believe with equal faith, as having the same immediate and miraculous derivation from God, whatever else you shall hereafter read in any of the sixty-six books collected in the Old and New Testaments. — I would never say this. But where I saw a desire to believe, and a beginning of love of Christ, I would say, there are likewise sacred writings, which, taken in connection with the institution and perpetuity of a visible Church, all believers revere as the most precious boon of God, next to Christianity itself, and attribute both their communication and preservation to an especial Providence. In them you will find all the revealed truths which have been set forth and offered to you, clearly and circumstantially recorded, with examples, maxims, hymns and prayers, in all which you will recognize the influence of the Holy Spirit, with a conviction increasing with the growth of your own faith and spiritual experience."

" We assuredly believe that the Bible contains all truths necessary to salvation, and that therein is preserved the undoubted word of God. Besides these express oracles, and immediate revelations, there are Scriptures which to every soul and conscience, bear irresistible evidence of the Divine Spirit assisting and actuating the authors. And if in that small portion of the Bible which stands in no necessary connection with the known and especial ends and purposes of the Scriptures, there should be a few apparent errors, resulting from the state of knowledge then existing, errors which the best and holiest men might entertain uninjured, and must have entertained without miraculous intervention,— be it so, what then? The absolute infallibility of the inspired writers in matters altogether foreign to the objects and purposes of their inspiration, is no part of my creed, and if a professed divine should follow the doctrine of the Jewish Church so far as not to attribute to the Hagiographa the same height and fullness of Inspiration, as in the law and prophets, I feel no warrant to brand him a heretic. If I say, use the Old Testament to express the affections excited, and to confirm the faith and morals taught you in the New, and leave all the rest to the students and professors of Theology and Church history,— you profess only to be a Christian,— am I thus misleading my brother in Christ?"

" This I believe of my own dear experience, that the more tranquilly an inquirer takes up the Bible, as he would any other body of ancient writings, the livelier and steadier will be his impressions of its superiority to all other books. And all other knowledge will be valuable in his eyes, in proportion as it helps him to a better understanding of the Bible. Would I then withhold the Bible from the cottager and the artizan? Heaven forefend. The fairest flower that ever clomb up a cottage window, is not so fair a sight to my eyes as the Bible gleaming through its lower panes. Let it be but read, as by such men it used to be read, when they came to it as a ground covered with manna, even the bread which the Lord had given for his people to eat; where he that had gathered much had nothing over, and he that gathered little had no lack. *They gathered, every man according to his eating.*"

The main error of Bibliolatry, Mr. Coleridge thinks, consists in the confounding of two distinct conceptions: Revelation by the eternal Word, and actuation of the Holy Spirit. In this way, he remarks, the term Inspiration has acquired a double sense. " Between the first sense, that is Inspired *Revelation*, and the highest degree of Communion with the Spirit, that every Christian is instructed to pray for, there is a positive difference *in kind*. Of this first kind are the law and the prophets, no jot or tittle of which can pass unfulfilled, for they wrote of Christ, and shadowed the everlasting Gospel. But with regard to the second kind of Inspiration, neither the so called *Hagiographa*, or holy writers themselves, nor any fair interpretations of Scripture · assert any such absolute diversity from that of the pious Christians of all ages, or enjoin the belief of any greater difference of degree than the experience of the Christian world, growing out of the comparison of these Scriptures with other works holden in honor by the Churches, has established. And *this* difference I admit."

" 'This cannot, he thinks, but be vague and unsatisfactory to those to whom the Christian religion is wholly objective, to the exclusion of all its correspondent subjective.   *   *   *   But as all power manifests itself in the harmony of correspondent opposites, each supposing and supporting the other, so has religion its Objective or historic and ecclesiastical pole, and its Subjective or spiritual and individual pole." In the miraculous parts of religion, he thinks we have the union of the two.

Mr. Coleridge concludes by expressing the belief that modern theologians too often, instead of enquiring after truth in the confidence that whatever is truth must be fruitful of good to all who are in him who is true, seek with vain precautions to guard against the possible inferences which perverse and distempered minds may pretend, whose whole Christianity, do what we will, is and will remain nothing but a pretense.

I have thus given, almost in his own words, the substance of those seven remarkable letters of Mr. Coleridge on Inspiration. Few will consider them complete, or consistent, much less as a satisfactory finality upon this subject. But as a means of breaking ground on it, as Dr. Arnold well said, as one of the most suggestive and many sided treatises on this subject in the English language, it seemed due to give his views, even at this length. Nearly all who have since written, whether Professor Lee in his work on Inspiration, Rev. Edward Garbett, author of God's Word Within, or any one else, have derived their best germs of thought from this work, even where trying to refute large portions of it. The learning and boldness and breadth of its speculations, together with the humble and submissive piety of its conclusions, have made it the key to all that has been written since. Few will agree with the High Church views, in which it would seem to have led him to take refuge, so far at least as a necessary line of Apostolic succession is concerned. But, as we shall see, the Broad Church views of Dr. Arnold, to whom we now turn, will show how little necessary are such opinions to the support of Coleridge's chief thought.

7. Few men have been more influential in forming the present state of religious thought in England, than the late Dr. Arnold, of Rugby. A thorough scholar, a profound thinker, and a man of most earnest religious feeling, he hesitated long before receiving holy orders, just because he did not and could not believe in the doctrine of plenary Inspiration, especially in regard to

certain portions of the Old Testament. The Archbishop of Canterbury, however, knowing his scruples and respecting them, because also well aware of his earnest faith in Christianity as a divine system, after a full ascertainment of his opinions, and perhaps sympathizing with them, offered him holy orders. He was soon after chosen Master of the Rugby School, where he died at the age of forty-six, after having laid the foundation of greater changes and progress in the Church of England, than perhaps any man of his day. He carried his love of Christianity with him so earnestly into the School, that he sent up to Oxford year after year large bodies of young men who proved to be the best scholars, and at the same time, students not afraid intellectually to defend and earnestly to carry Christianity with them even at Oxford. They were, as a class, opposed to the mixture of scepticism, pietism and shams of several of the Puseyites, then rising into power; and were distinguished by their broad scholarly views of Christianity in its relations to Universal Religion. Soon they formed a conspicuous party at Oxford, hated and yet dreaded alike by the Evangelicals on the one side, and the Puseyites on the other. In the life of F. W. Robertson, are some hints of what he then, an Evangelical Churchman of the strictest kind, saw and felt of the influence of this party while an Oxford student. For he heard Dr. Arnold deliver the beginning of his lectures on Roman history there amid every kind of derison and contempt, yet saw him walk up to his desk with the quiet, self possessed energy of a man who knows what he is about. He even lived to see his work crowned with the highest success, and the admiration of the whole University, as the honor of his age and country. The friend of Niebuhr and his follower in the criticism of Roman History, he possessed even a safer judgment as a literary critic, and a warmer, sounder heart in Biblical matters and love of Christianity.

The following extract from a letter of his on Coleridge's Confessions of an Inquiring Spirit, will best show his views on this subject of Inspiration:

"Have you seen Coleridge's letters on Inspiration, which I believe are to be published? They are well fitted to break ground on that momentous question, which involves in it so great a shock to existing notions; the greatest probably that has ever been given since the discovery of the falsehood of the Pope's infallibility. Yet it must come, and will end in spite of the fears and clamors of the weak and bigoted, in the higher exalting and more sure establishing of Christian Truth."*

In a letter from Rev. B. Price to Dr. Stanley, the

* Life of Arnold, p. 239.

Editor of Dr. Arnold's life, the following is the account given of Dr. Arnold's views. He "approached the human side of the Bible in the same real historical spirit, with the same method, rules and principles as he did Thucydides.   *   *   *   The Bible announces an historical religion,—and the historic element Arnold judged of historically by the established rules of history, substantiating the general veracity of Scripture, even amidst occasional inaccuracies of detail, and proposing to himself the reproduction in the language and forms belonging to our own age and therefore familiar to us, of the exact mode of thinking and feeling and acting, which prevailed in days gone by.   But was this all?   Nothing could be further from Dr. Arnold's feelings.   In the Bible he found and acknowledged an oracle from God, a positive and super-natural revelation made to man;—an immediate inspiration of the Spirit.   But he came upon it *historically*.   He did not start with any preconceived theory of Inspiration, but rather in studying the writings of those who were commissioned by God to preach the gospel, he met with the fact that they claimed to be sent from God, to have a message from Him, to be filled with the Spirit.   Any accurate, precise or sharply defined theory of Inspiration, to the best of my knowledge, Arnold had not, and if he had been asked to give one, I think he would have answered that the subject did not admit of one. I think he would have been content to realize the feelings of those who heard the Apostles. He would have been sure on the one side that there was a voice of God in them, whilst on the other, he would have believed that probably no one in the apostolic age, could have defined the exact limits of inspiration. Never did a student feel more his positive faith, his sure confidence that the Bible was the word of God, than in Arnold's hands." Such was the impression of his views left on the mind of a pupil.

Dr. Arnold's views on this subject are partly given in his Sermons on the Christian Life. He says, " If a single error can be discovered in Scripture, it is supposed to be fatal to the credibility of the whole. This has arisen from an unwarranted interpretation of the word " Inspiration," and by a still more unwarranted inference. An inspired work is supposed to mean a work to which God has communicated his own perfections, so that the slightest error or defect of any kind in it is inconceivable, and that which is other than perfect in all points, cannot be inspired. This is the unwarranted interpretation of the word " Inspiration." * * * Surely many of our words and many of our actions are spoken and done by the inspiration of God's Spirit, without whom we can do nothing acceptable to God. Yet does the Holy Spirit so inspire us as to communicate to us his own perfections? Are our best words or works utterly free from error or from sin? All inspiration then does not destroy the human and fallible part in the nature which it inspires. It does not change man into God."* Dr. Arnold, therefore, says what may illustrate his view of St. Paul's Inspiration. " This great Apostle believed that the world would come to an end in the generation then existing. * * * Shall we then say that St. Paul entertained and expressed a belief which the event did not verify? We may say so safely and reverently in this instance."

Notwithstanding the many great names that have given in their adhesion to this opinion in Germany, i. e. that Paul had mistaken views of an approaching millenium, and the many passages which may be quoted in favor of it, it may be doubted whether any fair interpretation of the Second Epistle to the Thessalonians can be framed on such a supposition. For it seems entirely to have been written for the purpose of correcting a wrong inference as to his views drawn from his peculiar mode of speaking in the fourth and fifth chapters of the First Epistle. In the fifth verse of the second chapter, Second Epistle, he tells them to remember that when he was with them, he declared that the day of the Lord was *not* at hand. Unless therefore,

* Sermons on the Christian Life, p. 486–7. Edition, 1841. *Jude.*

what he meant by the prior falling away, and the revelation of the man of sin, could all take place in that generation, he could not have believed as Arnold and many others have supposed.

On the other hand, Dr. Lee's criticism on Dr. Arnold, that " his statements are embarrassed by his having continued to regard as identical, specifically different phases of the Holy Ghost," are unjust. Whether his views are right or wrong, there is no embarrassment about them. They are clear, consistent with themselves, and represent the views of Prof. Maurice and several others beside.

8. From this view has sprung the school of Broad Churchmen, of whom perhaps Dean Stanley may be considered one of the best representatives. His opinions of the Hebrew Scriptures have been judiciously stated in his History of the Jewish Church.

A few years ago, Dr. Temple, the successor of Dr. Arnold at Rugby, Drs. Williams, Jowett, and Baden Powell found themselves brought into great notoriety by the accidental conspicuousness, which certain Essays and Reviews assumed in English Theological Controversy. These Essays had stated the Broad Church views of Inspiration openly, and pushed them to consequences that Dr. Arnold would have been far from allowing; some of their number denying miraculous interferences and the Supernatural in toto.

Such was the position of Rev. Baden Powell, since deceased.

9. To counteract the influence of these Essays, Dr. Thompson, now Bishop of Gloucester, procured the writing of another Series of Essays, called Aids to Faith, in which every effort was made to support higher views of Inspiration. Many of these writings are of great learning and value. While arguing for the " plenary inspiration" and the " complete inspiration" of the Old and New Testaments, and in some places seeming to maintain that this rendered the writers absolutely infallible as to all religious topics, they yet allow that errors. in the scientific and miscellaneous matter included in the Bible may be admitted as possible and perhaps as actual. Where, however, the line is to be drawn, they do not say. In fact, what is intended is for a practical and specific object, and all not tending to it is pushed aside. It would be a great mistake, however, to suppose the Authors of these " Aids" assert a belief in the infallibility of the Inspiration of all parts of the Scripture, though they undoubtedly would have done so, had they believed such a doctrine tenable.* Thus viewed, their language proves nothing so much to a thoughtful mind, as that in the English Episcopal Church, the leaders of the most learning, and earnest tendency towards Ortho-

* See Essay VII on Inspiration.

doxy, silently give up as hopeless, the attempt to maintain the old views of Scripture infallibility.

.Indeed, matters would seem to have arrived now at the point, that when men of this general class come to examine the Scriptures from the stand point of sacred criticism and science, they naturally find and avow a much greater effect produced upon the language of Scripture through the human element, than those who read it simply for religious purposes, are generally willing to concede.

10. Thus Bishop Colenso, at first an Evangelical man, when he sat down to translate the Bible into the Tulu language, and to explain to the docile natives, for example, how all the birds, beasts, and reptiles from hot and cold countries came to Noah into the ark, and how Noah gathered food for them all, was guided he says, to those examinations which led him to differ from the common view, as to the time at which the Pentateuch was written, and its strictly historic character.

11. Dr. Davidson, after being the eminent Professor of Biblical Literature among the Congregationalists, in his most recent Introduction to the Old Testament, protesting that "personal religion does not lie in the reception of intellectual propositions or dogmas, but in the emotions of the heart toward God and man," declares that his sole ambition is to be the humble

expositor of God's word in the Bible, and to cultivate
in his Master's service the one talent given him. Perhaps it is to be regretted that both of these eminently
learned men, accurate in their scholarship and no
doubt sincere in their apparent purposes and piety,
provoked by shallow, ignorant and sometimes insincere
criticism, have allowed themselves unnecessarily to
wound the feelings of many excellent Christians, by
the use of language needlessly offensive in regard to
sacred things. At the same time, they both come to conclusions of nearly the same import, i. e. that the Elohistic portions of Genesis were not written until about
the time of Samuel and perhaps by him, and that
the most of the Pentateuch, particularly Deuteronomy
was written about the time of Manasseh, and published when found in the cleaning out of the rubbish
in the temple, in the days of Josiah. Both, however,
" sincerely believe that the Holy Scriptures contain
everything necessary to salvation, and to that extent,
have the direct sanction of the Almighty." Dr.
Davidson, moreover, is fully convinced that Moses
committed to writing not only the ten commandments,
but nearly all the laws of the Tabernacle contained in
Exodus, such as Ex. 21 to 23, 19; and 25 to 31; Lev.
1 to 7; and 11 to 16; with some portion of the Book
of Numbers. These he ascribes to Moses, not, indeed,
in precisely their present state, but as incorporated

(perhaps by Samuel,) into the Elohistic document, and thence included by the Editor of the whole. "It is now an acknowledged result of scientific criticism, that Moses did not write the Pentateuch as it is. The authority of the work is not impaired on that account, though persons ignorant of the true learning of critical theology may think so. * * * Those who regard the record as the depository of the early religious traditions of the Hebrews, and the revelations vouchsafed to their wisest men, who look upon it as embodying the divine truth possessed by that race, and preparing the way for a higher and purer dispensation do not destroy the authority of the Pentateuch. They do not undermine the pillars of Christianity. To affirm that they do, is mischievous absurdity. They do deny the infallibility of written books, as well as the infallibility of the persons that composed them. They do hold the Mosaic books to be faithful records of the ancient Jews, containing sublime views of the Almighty Creator and his works, showing a pure Monstheism to have been the faith of the highest minds among the old Hebrews, yet with imperfect notions on their part of theology, science, art, and civilization. Christianity stands on another and better basis than the Mosaic composition of the Pentateuch. It has nothing to do either with the question of its authorship or documents. It is *not* injuriously affected by the discrepancies observable in the traditions it embodies. Moses was emphatically a law-giver, not an historian, a grand spiritual actor in the life drama of the Israelites, who founded their theocratic institutions under the direct guidance of the Supreme." Such are the latest views of Dr. Davidson in his Introduction to the Old Testament.

It must be confessed, however, that in proportion as men of this class look at the question of Inspiration for merely critical purposes, their labors seem to end in a comparatively negative work, i. e. in pulling down our reverence for the accuracy and infallibility of Scripture. But those who take up these subjects practically, seem to find views more positive, encouraging and elevating. Even while admitting all that Davidson or Colenso would desire in theory, they produce a widely different effect upon the mind. We have already seen that Dr. Stanley no less than Bishop Colenso or Dr. Davidson, admits that "the Pentateuch, the books of Samuel, Kings, Chronicles and Ezra are now universally acknowledged in their present state to be the work of several hands," and that "the books of Moses, Joshua, Samuel and Job are so called not because these works were necessarily written *by* but *of* them and their deeds." And yet the first effect of a constructive work like Stanley's or Milman's History of the Jewish Church, is very different from the analytic writings of Davidson or Colenso. Yet all of these would have seemed very strange a few years ago.

12. In like manner, F. W. Robertson, of Brighton, in the third Sermon of the first Series, "On Jacob's Wrestling," although he is quite as candid and outspoken in regard to the local, narrow Jewish, and even mythical character, which he considers the narrative of Jacob's wrestling to assume, yet elevates our conception and makes us feel the *reality* of the scene which then and there took place. His views of the shadow and substance of the Sabbath in the sixth Sermon, may not be such as most Christians have been accustomed to, but all must feel that there is a spiritual life in them, and a positive earnestness tending to build up and not to destroy the Christian life and faith.

In addition to what I have already quoted from his writings, there are in his Life and Letters, passages which show the positive and constructive quality of his views on Inspiration in connection with a freeness and boldness of speculation which are quite rare. Comparing the "Excursion" of Anaxagoras with the writings of Moses, and with the Epistles of St. Paul, he says, "The Excursion reveals some beautiful truths of our moral being, but by how much our spiritual life is higher than our sensitive and moral, so much are the Epistles above the Excursion higher in kind, and high-

er also in degree of Inspiration, for the Apostles claim
in matters spiritual, unerring power of truth.   Newton's
revelation of the order of the heavens, grand as it was,
is inferior to that which we technically term Inspiration,
by how much one single human soul transcends the
whole material universe in value.

"I think it all comes to this; God is the Father of
Lights, the King in his beauty, the Lord of love.   All
our several degrees of knowledge 'attained in these
departments are from Him.   One department is higher
than another; in each department the degree of
knowledge may vary from a glimmering glimpse to
infallibility, so that all is properly inspiration, but
immensely differing in value and in degree.   If it be
replied that this *degrades Inspiration*, by classing it
with things so common, the answer is plain; a sponge
and a man are both animals, but the degrees between
them are incalculable.

"I think this view of the matter is important, because in the other way, some twenty or thirty men
in the world's history, have had special communication, miraculous and from God.   In this, *all have it*,
and by devout and earnest cultivation of the mind and
heart, may have it increased illimitably.   This is really
practical." *

Of miracles, and their value as evidences, Mr.

* Life of Robertson, Letter 53, p. 271.

Robertson says: " In John 14: 11, two kinds of proof are given, and one is subordinated to the other. It is quite consistent with God's wisdom to reveal himself to the senses as well as to the soul.   *   *

*   When the Eternal Word is manifested into the world, we naturally expect.that Divine power shall be shown, as well as Divine beneficence. Miracles, therefore, are exactly what we should expect, and I own a great corroboration and verification of his claims to sonship. Besides, they started and aroused many to his claims, who otherwise would not have attended to them. Still the great truth remains that they appealing only to the natural man, cannot convey the spiritual certainty of truth, which the spiritual man alone apprehends. However, as the natural and spiritual in us, are both from God, why should not God have spoken both to the natural and spiritual part of us, and why should not Christ appeal to the natural works, subordinate always to the spiritual self-evidencing of Truth itself.   *   *   *   Men try, you say, to find Evidences for Faith in Reason, rather than for Reason in Faith. If there has been a single principle which I have taught more emphatically than any other, it is that not by Reason, (meaning by Reason, the understanding,) but by the Spirit, that is the heart trained in meekness and love by God's spirit, truth can be judged of at all. I hold that the attempt to rest

Christianity upon miracles and fulfilments of prophecy, is essentially the vilest rationalism, as if the trained intellect of a lawyer, which can investigate evidence, were that to which is trusted the soul's salvation, or as if the evidence of the senses were more sure than the intuitions of the spirit to which spiritual truths, almost alone appeal.   It is not in words, though they are constant, but in the deepest convictions and first principles of my soul that I feel the failure of intellect in this matter." *

13. Mr Westcott in his admirable Introduction to the four-Gospels, has a Chapter on Inspiration, which, while defending the " completeness " and what he terms " plenary " character of it, objects equally to what he terms the Calvinistic and some modern views of it. He thinks a medium can be found between them: While earnestly contending for the " real existence of such an influence," he also thinks that the Divine and human elements cannot be separated, but that it is Dynamical and not Mechanical.   His statements are guarded, and require to be carefully read to be appreciated.   He shows by quotations, that while the early Christians all believed fully in the Inspiration of the Scriptures, that so they did also, and perhaps equally, in that of the Church; although no one supposes them to have considered the Church theoretically infallible.

* Vol. 2, Letter 53, p. 146-9.

14. In Note fifty, at the close of the Critical History of Free Thought, its learned author Rev. Mr. Farrar, says that the different Theories that have been held in regard to Inspiration, may be arranged under three heads: I. The belief in a full Inspiration. II. A disposition to admit that the Inspiration ought to be regarded as appertaining to the proper material of the revelation, i. e. religion, but at the same time to maintain firmly the full inspiration of the religious elements of Scripture. III. To admit that the book does not even in its religious element, differ in kind from other books, but only in degree. Under the second head, he makes a subdivision, i. e. that while maintaining the full inspiration of the religious element, some go so far as to avow that its revelation would not be lessened if errors were admitted in the scientific and miscellaneous matter which accompanies it, while others seem to say nothing about this last. For himself, he only says that he " dissents entirely from the third of these views," from which I suppose it may be inferred that he holds to the second.

There is, however, a great want of clearness in this arrangement, and especially in the *statement* of each class of views, unless it be the last. For our purpose, a much simpler and better arrangement of the views which have been here alluded to, is as follows:

I. There are those who hold that the Inspiration

of Scripture secures its absolute infallibility in every part, as to its science, its history, and its theological or religious elements.

II. There are those who consider the scientific and historical matter of the Bible, as colored by the age and opinions of the writer, and therefore not rendered infallible by Inspiration, while yet the religious portions are thus absolutely and entirely infallible.

III. There are those who look upon Inspiration as a positive and not a negative Divine power; as not destroying but elevating the human element in man; as not conferring a necessary or absolute immunity from all error or infirmity, but as guiding the authors and quickening their writings with a divine life, and clothing them with a Divine authority similar precisely to that with which the Apostles themselves were endowed, when commissioned to institute and establish the primitive Church. That is to say, their inspiration gave them certain Divine powers as a whole, leaving their individual and human errors to be eliminated by degrees as necessary for the life of truth, just as St. Paul said of himself: "We have this treasure in earthen vessels, that the excellency of the power may be of God and not of us."

All the views now held by those who regard Inspiration as any real power, may, we think, be classified under one of these three heads, although in regard to the last, some would like more and some less to trace the analogy of this Divine power in Nature or in Grace, natural or supernatural.

This appears to be as close a classification as it is necessary or possible at present to make of the various opinions current, at least until we have determined which of these views must command our assent. Having been led myself from an adherence to the *first* gradually and steadily to the conviction that the *last* alone is tenable, I proceed though with much reluctance to point out some of the difficulties attending the two former theories of Inspiration. They may be considered as either External or Internal.

G

CHAPTER IV.

THE EXTERNAL DIFFICULTIES AS TO INFALLIBILITY OF THE OLD TESTAMENT INSPIRATION, CONSIDERED.

I.

THE Chronology made use of in the present Hebrew Old Testament Scriptures, and, indeed, the whole subject of its numbers afford strong indications of important alterations and mistakes, so that they cannot be depended upon as being infallible now, or in fact ever having been so. We need not here go into the profounder or more difficult points of this subject, but touch only on those plainer difficulties admitted by all. Those who wish to follow out some of these matters more minutely, can take up Colenso, or Ewald, or De Wette. But it is well known, that the present Hebrew Bibles, which form the basis of Archbishop Usher's system of Chronology, would make the birth of Adam to have taken place 5874 years ago from the present time (1867,) or 4004 years before our present Anno Domini. But Dr. Hailes following the Septuagint, makes the birth of Adam 7281 years ago, or 5411 years B. C., a difference of 1407 years. This difference is after all not a serious matter for us as Christians. It is nothing to the new Chronological difficulties opened up by science, but the manner in which it has been brought about, gives it an importance in regard to the question on hand, it would not otherwise possess. Exactly six hundred years of it occurs between the time of Adam and of the flood, in this way: If we suppose, (as I do,) that the Septuagint Chronology is the more correct, or original, then in six places in the fifth chapter of Genesis, one hundred years has been taken from the lives of the Patriarchs, before the birth of their eldest son, and the same number of years has been put on to the length of their lives afterwards, thus making the whole amount of years that they lived, precisely the same. But the age of the world at the time of the flood becomes so much less. The object of this alteration, as well as the time of it, will be shown in a little while; the fact and the manner of the change, is what we must first of all point out.

In Gen. 5: 3–5, the Hebrew Text corresponds with our English translation: " Adam lived *an hundred* and thirty years, and begat a son," — Seth, "and the days of Adam after he had begotten Seth, were *eight* hundred years, and he begat sons and daughters. And all the days that Adam lived, were nine hundred and thirty years, and he died."

But the Septuagint reads, " Adam lived *two* hundred and thirty years and begat a son," — Seth, " And the days of Adam after he had begotten Seth, were *seven* hundred years, and he begat sons and daughters. And all the days that Adam lived, were nine hundred and thirty years, and he died." Here, it will be observed, is a *purposed* alteration of the text, of one hundred years either in the Hebrew or the Septuagint Chronology. Two changes are made, each of one hundred years, that counterbalance each other so far as the age of the Patriarch is concerned, but make a purposed difference of a century in the age of the world.

Precisely the same change is made in the account of five other of the Patriarchs, i. e. Seth, Enos, Cainan, Mahaleel and Jared. Thus in Gen. 5: 6–7, Seth lived *an hundred and five years*, and begat Enos, says the Hebrew; — *two* hundred and five years, says the Greek. Eight hundred and seven years afterwards he died, says the Hebrew; while the Greek reads seven hundred and seven years, and thus both are made to agree in the total length of Seth's life, i. e. nine hundred and twelve years. Precisely similar changes occur in verses 9, 10, 12, 13, 15, 16, 21, 22, and produce the alteration of six hundred years in the ante diluvian chronology.

The same system has been carried on in verses 25 and 26, 28, 30 and 31, and in parts of the chronology after the flood, especially Gen. 11. In verse 10, Shem's age is left untouched on account of the flood. But in verse 12, the Septuagint makes Arphaxed one hundred and thirty-five years when he begat his first born instead of thirty-five years according to the Hebrew, while in this latter, in verse 13, the one hundred and thirty years of Cainan before he begat Sala, are omitted, that is a whole generation is here struck out of the Hebrew text, though it remains in the Septuagint, and *is also inserted in Luke*, 3: 36, which thus contradicts the Hebrew Chronology. Sala's life before he begat Eben is also shortened a hundred years in the Hebrew text, and so the work goes on, until the whole makes up fourteen hundred and seven years difference.

It is evident that this is not an *accidental* difference, but one of design. Either the Hebrew text was altered from what it originally was, or the Septuagint text was purposely altered after the translation was made. The Chronology of the Deluge according to Josephus, corresponds substantially not with the Hebrew, but with that of the Septuagint, and as he could read both versions, we may be pretty sure that up to the destruction of Jerusalem, the two texts generally agreed. This literary fraud was adopted at a later date. Indeed, both Josephus and Philo agree in asserting the strict correspondence of the two chronologies, in their time, and the Christian Church for the first four hundred years, steadily adhered to that of Josephus and the Septuagint.

But the Jews had long had a belief in common with some other nations, that as the world was six days in being created, but the seventh was the day of rest, so the world should experience six thousand years of sorrow, and then a millenial or seventh thousand year of peace. In proportion as sorrows multiplied around their nation, they looked forward with longing to this period of rest, and there was a general belief and prediction that about the middle of the sixth thousand period, or A. M., 5500, the Messiah should appear. This belief, no doubt, formed the basis of the Chiliastic views, which commencing even in St. Paul's time* created great excitement amongst the Christians of the second century. The year 5500 of the world, would have brought the Messiah about A. D. 85, or fifteen years after the destruction of Jerusalem. The Christians, therefore, taunted the Jews, and said, your time is up, your Messiah has not come; ours has.

About A. D. 125–8, Aquilla made a new Greek translation of the Hebrew text, avowedly to correct

* II Thes. 2.

the well known errors of the Septuagint. He first
introduced into the Greek language, these chronological curtailments, which the Jews had probably already
made in the Hebrew text. Very few of the Christians
could read Hebrew, and the Jews therefore, could
easily, and must actually have altered the text to suit
their own purposes, and destroy this argument of the
Christians. But as late as the time of Eusebius, it
would seem that some of the Hebrew copies read one
way, and some the other. Ephraim Cyrus A. D. 387,
says, " The Jews [have subtracted six hundred years
from the generations of Adam, Seth, Enos, Cainan,
Mahalcel and Jared, in order that their own books
might not convict them concerning the coming of
Christ, he having been predicted to appear for the de-
liverance of mankind after five thousand five hundred
years."

Of course hardly any two persons agree on the
matter of Chronology, and these views will be disputed. But none will, none can dispute that there has
here been a purposed alteration of figures, making a
difference of fourteen hundred years in the age of the
world, and making the Hebrew genealogy Gen. 11:
12, conflict with that of Luke, 3: 36, by a whole
generation.

It will of course be said that this alteration of the
text has been clearly made since the Canon of the Old

Testament Scripture was completed, and that it is an objection only against the *infallible preservation* of the Scriptures from subsequent alterations, (for which no one contends,) rather than the infallibility of their Inspiration. But it does show this, that infallible certainty as to the accuracy of these dates cannot be necessary to Christian faith now, since if cannot be obtained. It is surely vain to say, you must believe that every word and letter was correct once, but you may and perhaps must believe that it has been subjected to such corruptions and alterations since, that we cannot tell what the correct reading was.

Having seen these alterations, is it necessary, is it possible for us to believe that all of those numbers in the Old Testament, even in which both the Hebrew and Greek copies do agree, are certainly correct?

Dr. Kennicott, in his first dissertation, acquits the Jews of " willfully corrupting the Old Testament." "But twenty-five years afterwards," adds Dr. Pye Smith, " accumulated evidence compelled him to adopt the opposite opinion, and he complains heavily of the craft and dishonesty of the Jewish transcribers." Dr. Pye Smith also thinks national pride led them to exaggerate. " Very remarkable are the numbers which occur in some places of armies and men slain in battle. Abijah has with him an army of four hundred thousand men, and Jeroboam double that number, picked troops on both sides, and *half a million* of the latter army fall in battle. II Chron. 13. Let it be considered that the territory of Judah did not exceed in extent the two English counties of Norfolk and Suffolk, and that of Israel was not equal to Yorkshire and Lancashire; both mountainous countries, though the valleys and hill tops were permanently fertile. Let it be asked whether from the most dense population conceivable upon such an area, a number of fighting men could be raised, which would give a selected body out of it, at all approaching to those numbers. Xerxes was three years raising, some say, one million seven hundred thousand, others one million, and Pliny, seven hundred thousand. All the ancient historians are full of astonishment at this extent of armament. Yet the little country of Palestine furnishes so many troops as to allow a *selection* to be made, which brings one million two hundred thousand fighting men. I might remark upon the incapacity of the plain of Jezreel or any other part of the country to be the field of battle, unless it were a pell mell massacre. Napoleon's largest army that of 1812 against Russia was only half a million, the very number here said to be slain in a single battle. How could such a number be buried? But if not, a dreadful pestilence would ensue in that climate." The numbers he firmly believes have been altered.

A similar remark, he thinks, might be made upon the numbers of animals offered in sacrifice on various recorded occasions in the Temple at Jerusalem. " If the blood flowed away in sewers, it would have choked up the channels and overflowed the receptacles, for there was no great river to carry it off. The pool of Siloam and the Brook Kedron would have been as nothing for the purpose. Even a river equal to the Thames would scarcely have sufficed, not to mention the waters being rendered unfit for drink. Such a quantity of blood, and the rejected matter from the viscera in the hot country of Judea, would have bred a dire plague." " I am speaking only of the *numbers* as not being the objects of Inspiration *as they stand.* How can we escape the suspicion of their having been altered by an enormous multiplication ? * * * These questions affect not any part of doctrine or of duty. All religious truth stands up in peerless majesty, unaffected by these little shoals of accidental sand. But these facts must fearfully affect the theory of a servile literality of Inspiration. It is that theory which has put the most ostensibly powerful arms into the hands of the foes of God and man." * Such is the language of Rev. Dr. J. Pye Smith, one of the most learned, pious and Orthodox Dissenting Ministers of England, recently departed, and whose work

* Book I, Chap. 2, Appendix to Note 5.

on the Person of Christ was for many years considered the book on that subject for the Divinity Students in one of the Universities.

II. The Geological Statements of the early chapters of Genesis while not preventing the high Inspiration of the writer for the great religious purposes intended, i. e. exhibiting a pure and lofty Theistic plan, purpose and power as lying at the back of all the progress manifest in the work of Creation, yet cannot be re-regarded as a literal and infallible record of the facts of the case. They supply just the element that science is most apt to leave out in its statements of these things. This is their purpose. But to him who will believe nothing of science but what can be fairly made to square with these statements, so far from proving a store house of scientific knowledge, they must become insuperable obstacles to progress.

Rev. Dr. Pye Smith took up the subject of the Deluge. He felt the difficulty of supposing the whole dry land of the globe to have been covered fifteen cubits with water at one time, and produced such arguments as have forever settled the question with all men of thought, that the Deluge could not have been simultaneously universal, but only simply over that part of the globe then the abode of men. We may take it for granted that no person who has read his lectures on this subject, published more than twenty years ago, now claims more of extent for the Deluge than this. Geologists at least know that such a deluge as the illiterate suppose, (without another greater miracle to obliterate all traces of it,) must have left marks that are not to be found. They know that there are rocks and mountains of an older date covered with pummice-stones that must have been washed as they are not, had such a deluge occurred. They know that such an additional mass of water on the surface of the earth, if created for the occasion, must have been annihilated when its work was done, and would have thrown the relations of our globe to the planetary system into hopeless disorder while it lasted. It is, therefore, now admitted by all earnest and enlightened Christians that Noah's flood was only partial.

But this though quite true, and not in the least inconsistent with the Inspiration of the Old Testament in that only vital sense that makes it full of *religious* truth and instruction for the pious mind, is yet quite incongruous (notwithstanding all the explanations of Dr. Pye Smith) with the literal infallibility of the records of Genesis. For the language of a writer always means what the writer thought and intended the reader to understand by it. Now Gen. 7: 17–23, expressly declares, that "all the high hills *that were under the whole heaven were covered*, and *all* flesh died that moved upon the earth, both of fowl and of

cattle, and of every creeping thing that creepeth upon
the earth, and every man. All in whose nostrils was
the breath of life, and all that was in the dry land died.
Noah only remained alive, and they that were with
him in the ark." There can, I think, be no doubt but
that the writer of this passage must have intended to
convey his belief both that all men were destroyed, and
all living land animals, and that the deluge covered
every part of the earth at one time. The only fair
solution of this difficulty is that the author recorded
what was universally believed in his day, that he reported the history as he had received it from his
ancestors. His object was to show how sin brings the
Divine wrath and leads to destruction. He uttered a
great religious truth, one that had inspired his own
breast, and there entwined itself round the imperfect
history he had received from the tradition of the past.
His knowledge and belief of facts was human and
imperfect, though his holy thought was Inspired and
Divine.

Eusebius A. D. 338, has given us from the writings
of Berosus, a Priest of the Temple of Belus about B.
C. 275, another version of the same history preserved
among the Chaldean annals as follows: " In the
second book was contained the history of the ten kings
of the Chaldeans, and the periods of the continuance of
each reign, which consisted collectively of an hundred

and twenty sari, or four hundred and thirty-two thousand years, reaching to the time of the Deluge.   *
*   *   After the death of Ardates, his son Xisuthrus reigned eighteen sari. In his time happened a great Deluge, the history of which is thus described. The Deity Cronus appeared to him in a vision, and warned him that upon the fifteenth day of the month Dæsius, there would be a flood, by which mankind would be destroyed. He therefore enjoined him to write a history of the beginning, procedure and conclusion of all things, and to bury it in the city of the Sun at Sippara, and to build a vessel, and take with him into it his friends and relations, and to convey on board everything necessary to sustain life, together with all the different animals, both birds and quadrupeds, and trust himself fearlessly to the deep. Having asked the Deity whither he was to sail, he was answered, " To the Gods," upon which he offered up a prayer for the good of mankind. He then obeyed the Divine admonition and built a vessel five stadia in length, and two in breadth. Into this he put everything which he had prepared, and last of all conveyed into it his wife, his children and his friends. After the flood had been upon the earth, and was in time abated, Xisuthrus sent out birds from the vessel, which not finding any food, nor any place whereupon they might rest their feet, returned to him again. After an interval of some days,

he sent them forth a second time, and they now returned with their feet tinged with mud. He made a trial
a third time with these birds, but they returned to him
no more, from whence he judged that the surface of
the earth had appeared above surface of the waters.
He therefore made an opening in the vessel, and upon
looking out, found that it was stranded upon the side
of some mountain, upon which he immediately quitted
it with his wife, his daughter and the pilot. Xisuthrus
then paid his adoration to the earth, and having constructed an altar, offered sacrifices to the gods, and
with those who had come out of the vessel with him,
disappeared. They who remained within, finding that
their companions did not return, quitted the vessel with
many lamentations, and called continually on the
name of Xisuthrus. Him they saw no more, but they
could distinguish his voice in the air, and could hear
him admonish them to pay due regard to religion, and
likewise he informed them that it was on account of his
piety that he was translated to live with the gods; that
his wife and daughter and the pilot had obtained the
same honor. To this he added that they should return
to Babylonia, and as it was ordained, search for the
writings at Sippara, which they were to make known
to all mankind; moreover, that the place wherein they
then were, was the land of Armenia. The rest having heard these words, offered sacrifices to the gods,

and taking a circuit, journeyed towards Babylonia.
The vessel being thus stranded in Armenia, some part
of it yet remains in the Corcyrean Mountains of
Armenia, and the people scrape of the bitumen with
which it had been outwardly coated, and make use of
it by way of an alexipharmic and amulet. And when
they returned to Babylon, and had found the writings
at Sippara, they built cities, and erected temples, and
Babylon was thus inhabited again." *

" Other notices of the flood may be found in the
Phœnician Mythology, where the victory of Pontus
(the sea,) over Demarous (the earth) is mentioned in
the Sibylline Oracles, partly borrowed, no doubt, from
the Biblical narrative, and partly perhaps from some
Babylonian story. To these must be added the
Phrygian story of King Annakos or Nannakos (Enoch)
in Iconium, who reached an age of more than three hundred years, foretold the flood, and wept and prayed for his
people, seeing the destruction that was coming upon
them. Very curious as showing what deep root this
tradition must have taken in the country, is the fact
that so late as the time of Septimius Severus, a medal
was struck at Alpamea, on which the Flood is com-
memorated. As belonging to this cycle of tradition,
must be reckoned also the Syrian related by Lucian,
and connected with a huge chasm in the earth near

* Eusebius 5-8. Cory's Ancient Fragments, p. 26.

Hieropolis, into which the waters of the flood are supposed to have drained, and the Armenian quoted by Josephus. Another cycle of traditions is that of Eastern Asia. To this belong the Persian, Indian, and Chinese. The Persian is mixed up with its cosmogony, and hence loses anything like an historical aspect. The Chinese story is in many respects, singularly like the Biblical. The Indian tradition appears in various forms. Of these, the one which most remarkably agrees with the Biblical account is that contained in the Mahabharata."*

The only question is, did the writer of Genesis receive his account of this event from some one or more of these sources, or they from the writer of Genesis, or both from the same common source. The whole formed probably a part of some widely extended tradition of a flood that occurred perhaps on the banks of the Euphrates or the Oxus, of which men have been periodically reminded by great floods since as they have travelled westward. This is not the place to discuss the authorship of the pentateuch. But that it was composed of pre-existing documents, especially Genesis is now beyond all doubt. Berosus appears to have drawn his account of the flood from the same sources as those from which parts of Genesis are also derived. All this we shall see as we proceed.

* Smith's Bible Dictionary, Art. Noah.

But parts of Genesis are avowedly from pre-existing documents;— Gen. 5: 1. "This is the book of the generations of Adam," that is, the Sethite family record down to the thirty-second verse, (as chapter four gives us the Cainite.)* Gen. 6: 9, commences another; the family record of the life of Noah and the flood. Chapter 10: 1, begins another, and chapter 11: 10, yet another of these family records, which seem first to have been put together by the Elohistic, and finally edited by a Jehovistic author, whose religious feeling leads him to put the whole narrative together.

We may not pretend to speak accurately upon points on which all sorts of theories are afloat, but rather to show how without intending to utter any-thing not according to fact, a really holy man may have mistaken accounts of some local and partial deluge which swept over all *they knew* of the earth and its inhabitants, for one strictly universal. All great calamities are God's messengers of glorious truths, bringing to the survivors their own moral lessons and renovations of character. Looking back to these, and considering the deeper corruption that reigned before, a truly religious man would be most anxious that the improvement of the world thus obtained should not be lost.

There are at this time in Belgium, bone caves being

* See Davidson on the Pentateuch, Vol. I, p. 135.

ransacked, that tell a marvellous story of a deluge that must have inundated the whole of that country, and much of the northern part of France, caused by the melting of Swiss glaciers and which is thought to have swept away a whole race of men, dwellers in caves, of whom very ample proofs and relies have been preserved owing to the falling in of the tops of one or two of the caves, crushing down and burying their flint arrow and spear heads, their bone needles for sewing garments of skin and all the debris of daily life. The whole country has been covered with a dense yellow clay, the deposit of this inundation. Had any one or two or three survivors been able to have written out an account of this event after the subsiding of the waters, it might have seemed to them, as *they saw* no place but what gave evidence of having been submerged, as if the deluge were universal, and such a description as that of Genesis would most faithfully record the truth *to them* though not the absolute geological fact. Now it is truth to the human heart and perception and experience, rather than to philosophy and fact, that is the truth we need in these addresses to the religious experiences of man. And one who is no philosopher, may be as truly inspired of God to give religious instruction, and his very imperfections and ignorance may make him more ready in his access to the hearts of multitudes than if he had a more precise knowledge of all the facts.

But the chief Geological objection against verbal and scientific exactness being included in the true idea of Inspiration, arises not from the Deluge, but the much controverted subject of the six days Creation. Here it all turns upon this question whether it is possible for us to believe that in what the writer of the first chapter of Genesis intended to convey to us of information as to the history of Creation, he is consistent as to time and circumstances, with what we now know through Geology to be the facts of the case. The point is not whether the words used are *capable* of being explained away, so as not absolutely to contradict scientific truth. In this case, there is not merely a casual allusion to creation, as where we speak incidentally of sun rise and sun set, but there is a professed *narrative* of it, and that narrative is in words which would leave no doubt on the mind of a scientific man that the writer did not understand things consistently with the facts now made known to us by science. We do not say that the author may not manifest a degree of scientific knowledge very wonderful, but he certainly understood himself and intended to convey to his readers as facts, some things not as they really are, though as he conceived them to be. He believed, for instance, if we may rely upon Gesenius, upon the

Septuagint, the Vulgate, and even our English version in the existence of "*a firmament*," that is, a firm and solid hemispheric arch over the earth, answering to the στερέωμα or solid hemisphere believed in by the Greeks. In it, according to that ancient opinion were the fixed stars, and above it was the celestial ocean with windows in the firmament through which the water fell as rain upon the earth.*

It will of course be said that this is a matter of no consequence, a sort of thing like alluding to the sun rising and setting, and other cases where we speak truly, while uttering what we all now know to be philosophically contrary to fact. Neither is it a matter of the least practical importance to the pious Christian, but that is because the Inspiration of the Bible writers was never intended to enable them to teach or conceive of matters of scientific knowledge with absolute infallibility. It would have injured their religious instructions, and made them too far beyond their age, or probably our age, had they written thus. Their

* Gen. 1: 7; and 7: 11. The original word רָקִיעַ has been thought by these, the best authorities, to involve this belief, being derived from רָקַע to beat or stamp down, and so render solid. To avoid this idea of a firmament, some, like Prof. Stuart, have taken the term in the sense simply of *expanse*, since the root contains the thought of beating *out* (like gold) and so extending, expanding it. The best authorities however, ancient and modern, are against receiving this latter as the fair signification of the term used.

very imperfections rendered the divine truths taught, such as the unity of the Divine Being and his agency in Creation the more useful and easily received. Thus the philosophical mis-conceptions of their age were permitted to remain, because (as in this case) when the natural philosophy of future ages went beyond that then current, belief in the antiquated would be sure to cease and do no harm to the great theological truths taught. So far, indeed, as a mistaken view of Inspiration causes an attempt to be made to claim infallibility for the scientific imperfections in Scripture, it by thus uniting too closely, things really quite distinct, destroys faith in both.

The above will be a key to the proper interpretation of the *six days* of the first chapter of Genesis. The ideas recorded there were to a great extent the current views for ages from the Oxus and the Indus across the Tigris and the Euphrates, to the Nile, and to Phœnicia that is through forty degrees of longitude at least. The origin of the notion so wide spread of the six milleniary ages of the world is explained by the learned Gregory of Oxford, " Because God was six days about the creation, and a thousand years with him are but as one day,* therefore after six days, that is six thousand years dura- tion, there shall be a seventh day or milleniary Sabbath of rest." This early tradition was found also in the

* Ps. 90: 4. II Peter 3: 8.

Sibylline Oracles, in Hesiod, in the writings of Darius Hystaspes, the old king of the Medes, derived probably from the Magi, and among the Egyptians.

The belief then of the Creation in six days, was probably wide spread *before* the book of Genesis was committed to writing, and the object of the writer was not to teach a new and unknown cosmogony, but adopting that, because it.was universally believed traditionally, his intention was to exhibit and inspire his own faith in One only living and true God as the real author of the visible universe, — a theological truth in which inwardly inspired of the Almighty, he anticipated the later belief of the same by Socrates, or Anaxagoras, who, born about B. C. 500, was the first to proclaim the doctrine of a Supreme regulative Intelligence among the Greeks.

Even Mr. Cory in. his Ancient Fragments, though refusing to believe that one cosmogony was borrowed from another, considers it " manifest that the circumstances of the Creation and the Deluge were well known to all mankind previously to the dispersion. And the writings of Moses give to the chosen people, *not so much a new revelation,* as a correct, authenticated and inspired account of circumstances, which had then become partially obscured by time, and abused by superstition. The formless watery Chaos and the etherial substance of the heavens, enfolding and passing over its surface as a mighty wind, are the first principles both of the sacred and profane cosmogonies, but they are reclaimed by Moses as the materials, created by the immediate agency of an Almighty power. The subsequent process of formation so completely corresponds in both systems, that if they were not borrowed the one from the other, *   *   they must each have been ultimately derived from the common source of revelation."

When the earlier parts of the book of Genesis were first committed to writing, it is not possible to determine precisely. This we shall see more clearly in the next chapter. As Dean Stanley has said, it is to be regarded as an anonymous work called at a later period after the name of Moses, not because he was its author, but rather because he is the chief *subject* of it, and uttered many of the sayings it records. Dr. Spiegel considers that it is clearly written after the Rig-Veda, and after the earlier part of the Avestas. All three show considerable affinities in the religious customs and laws and theological opinions exhibited. But if any one after reading the Avestas (a translation of which has been published in England,) turns to our Pentateuch, he will see that progress towards a loftier, purer, simpler faith that will best exhibit the inspiration of its author, while yet he will also see the striking connection of pre-existing and wide spread religious opinions of a similar character.

The Elohim document of Genesis may have been committed to writing about the time of Samuel, although it, no doubt, contains many laws written by Moses, and other documents perhaps older than that.

With such a view as this, of the chapters of Genesis, it seems almost incredible, the amount of theological labor that has been expended in trying to prove that they are in no-wise contrary to the dates and ideas that science gives us as to the creation of the world. The great theological lesson which they were intended to teach, and which the other accounts had ignored, i. e. that one personal and Infinite Intelligence had formed the Universe, and given the laws that govern it, is true and Divinely Inspired. All the rest is merely circumstantial. This is the sole idea it was written to unfold, nor need we doubt that it would and did inspire closer observations of nature and gave further insight into many scientific truths than others at that time possessed. Hugh Miller and others supposed they found proofs of much of this sort of knowledge in Genesis, and we need not stop to doubt or to discuss that. It all seems possible and probable enough. But to say that the whole of this account is fairly reconcilable with all that is given by Science, must

7

make good men of future ages astonished at our credulity and superstition.

Let any candid man of science consider what is involved in the reconcilement of these things as attempted by Hugh Miller and others. The six days, they say, are *six periods*. Because the word day, is sometimes used figuratively, and does not *always* mean in the Bible or in common language, a literal period of twenty-four hours, therefore it is supposed we are at liberty to take it figuratively in this case, and make it mean any unlimited period we require. Let be granted that in Gen. 2: 4, the word "day," means more than twenty-four hours. But is it not a law of Interpretation that "every word can have but one meaning at the same time and place, and that although each word may have several distinct significations in different connections, the sense cannot be diverse and multifarious at the same time and in the same expression." And what that meaning is, is to be found from the general manner of speaking or from the proximate words or context.*

Can any one suppose that when the writer or Editor of Genesis wrote the first chapter, he knew of or intended to convey to his readers, anything but six literal days? If he intended "periods," what is the Seventh on which the Creator is said to have rested?

* See Stuart's Ernesti, Sec. 17–19.

It must be the present period ever since the Creation of man. But what if it shall be proved that man has been in existence ever since, or at least just after the passing away of the great glacial period, which clothed all Europe and most of America in ice for thousands, or hundreds of thousands of years? Are not the evidences of Divine activity as truly manifest in the changing and improving aspects. of creation since as before that period? Truly "the Father worketh hitherto." There is progress every where.

Let any one now read Hugh Miller's Lectures on the six days or periods of Creation. "They are first, the Azoic day or period, second, the Silurian or Old Red Sandstone day or period, third, the Carboniferous day or period, fourth, the Permian or Triassic day or period, fifth, the Oolitic and Cretaceous day or period, and sixth, the Tertiary day or period; seventh, the present period.

To say that Genesis and Geology *cannot* thus be reconciled, would be very much beyond my present purpose. But yet on the same principles of interpretation, one might reconcile the Bible with any thing, and Geology with Ovid's Metamorphoses. We have "an evening and a morning," as well as a day of rest to explain away figuratively, and the non-appearance of the sun and moon until the fourth day, (by enveloping it in fog) with the direct intimation they were *then*

"made" and "set in the firmament;" and the represen-
tation is that this was *the great* work of the fourth day
or period.   Can this fairly be done?   Is it right, wise
or religious to attempt it?   I think not.

That is to say, according to this mode of reconcilement, until the fourth day or period, the sun never
shone on this earth.   But long before that, it shone,
they admit, upon the mists and clouds that encom-
passed the earth, clear, bright and warm as now, and
the moon and stars would all have been visible to
the eye of one who could have ascended to a sufficient height, but not to one standing on the dry land.
Why there should be so much particularity to adapt
this statement to the eye of man standing on the
earth, when no man was yet created, is not apparent.

But would it seem scientifically probable that there
were *no* bright and sunny days until the fourth great
geologic period, that is until after the great Carboniferous period?   Let us compare now for a moment
the first three days of Genesis with the first three
periods declared by Hugh Miller to correspond with
them, as these latter are described not by him but in
a treatise on Geology, simply scientific, — the article
on that subject in Appleton's Cyclopedia.   The first
day's work in Genesis is simply the creation of land,
water, and light, and the separation of the light from
the darkness.   This is the grand Azoic period accord-

ing to Miller. It takes no cognizance of any long duration in which the whole planetary system was a vast fire-mist, — of its cooling down and breaking up into so many worlds of molten mass, rotating and still cooling until the surface fell below two hundred and twelve degrees, so that deep waters could cover as now, portions of the globe, and mighty winds sweep over their surface.

Commencing then just there, and supposing, as Hugh Miller did, vapors to obscure the sun, moon and stars from the eye of man, (if there had been a man to see them,) the first question for science to consider is whether during the vast ages, in which we suppose this globe must have been revolving in a molten and more heated state, there must not have been corresponding to the revolutions that fixed the shape of our globe, diurnal changes of light and darkness ? In this period geologically, we find nothing but rocks, which we call azoic, simply to designate that there are no remains in them indicating organic life.

. The second great day or period of Genesis, records only the formation of a firmament, dividing the waters above it from those below. Geologically, this embraces, we are told by Mr. Miller, two distinct periods or series, the Silurian and Devonian, with many subdivisions in each. Hugh Miller says, " the broad seas of the lower Silurian Epoch stretching over large portions of the globe, contain their peculiar types of marine life, crustacea, cephatopoda, and algæ, all perfect in their kind, and as admirably constructed as their representatives found in modern seas on which now tropical suns shine. To these invertebrata, next appeared in the deposits left by the waters of the Devonian period, the first vertebrated animals in the form of fishes." "Fishes not with bony skeletons, but of cartilagenous structure," the American Cyclopedia tells us, first appear in the upper members of the Silurian. "Some land plants are also met with in the same group." "Fishes with bony structure, true vertebrata, first appear in the Upper Helderburg; in these land plants too are first met with," i. e. about the middle of the Devonian division. But in the upper Devonian,—that is in the Catskill and Upper Red sandstone, we have genera of fishes that have been described minutely by Hugh Miller himself and thus immortalized the Old Red sandstone.

In Genesis fishes are the creation of the fifth day, yet here we find them on the second, according to Hugh Miller's reconciling attempt; together with coniferous plants which are in Genesis the work of the third day. This third day is distinguished by nothing but the creation of plants and trees, and therefore Hugh Miller reserves for that the Carboniferous period when the earth, or at least those parts of our continent where the coal measures are found, had a tropical climate, stimulating the growth of what are now small ferns to trees of a heighth of sixty or seventy feet. In this period we find not only gigantic forests, however, but " Aquatic reptiles and those forms of animals adapted to moist tropical districts, scarcely elevated above the sea level." " Reptiles related to the batrachians on the one hand, and the so-called saurord fishes on the other." Indeed, some of the genera of fishes are wearing out at this period, and giving place to higher forms. "The trilobites which form the Silurian, had gradually lessened in number, as compared with other fossils, disappear, and their places are supplied by the kindred genus, limulus or crab king, a family still represented in our seas. About one thousand and fifty species of this group have already been described."

" Insects are detected here too, as extinct species of beetles, crickets, cockroaches, &c., and the vestiges of marine mollusca, coral and fishes preserved in the sandstone." Thus far we have only quoted the description given of things up to the end of the third period, when according to Genesis, we ought not to expect any thing but herbs and plants and fruit trees! True we have all these, but we have *more* than ought then to have been created. We have fishes the creation of the fifth, and reptiles that of the sixth day already anticipated!

But the point of most importance is that though fishes and reptiles and insects *with eyes* exist, it is not until after this in the fourth period, that the sun and moon and stars are made and set in the firmament. In the second great period (and these periods mean hundreds of thousands of years) we have, it will be observed, fishes, vertebrate fishes in the ocean, and plants on the land, showing that its temperature and light could not have been greatly different from that of our Southern oceans and lands now. In the third period we have a tropical climate, and a picture left to us of enormous ferns and trees and reptiles, and can it be that no ray of sun light had ever yet stolen through the supposed mist. The oceans were seemingly as large and sweeping then as now, the water was cool enough for fishes, why then should we suppose no sun? Is the supposition possible? Let it be observed that in these coal measures, we have only pictures of the low swampy ground. If cloudy steaming mists pervaded these, can it be supposed that no ray of sun light came down on the mountain peaks and hill tops of the globe in this period? There certainly is no geologic fact that confirms this view.

In like manner, we have clear traces of birds, who

have left their foot prints in the mud of this fourth period. And the reptiles are all of a higher type. No doubt all these brought forth more abundantly in the fifth period. And this would be the authority of Hugh Miller, perhaps, for thus arranging the days or periods. But then on the same principle, we should have to place the creation of man in the seventh period instead of the sixth, and that would put the whole manifestly into confusion, even to his mind.

Still it will be said, although the days may not be precisely marked, or exactly fitted yet by modern science to the book of Genesis, there is enough to show that essentially the same order was preserved, and that this proves supernatural knowledge in scientific matters. But as this is not the point at issue, we need not discuss it. Perhaps it might be said all scientific indications would lead us to believe in the existence of fishes at least as early as land plants, and certainly not to place one in the third, and the other in the fifth great period, but we have no desire to discuss geological questions further than to show that if Geology and Genesis are to be harmonized, it is not by this system of periods for days in the manner proposed by Hugh Miller, or any thing like it. And yet in many of our colleges this attempt to harmonize what cannot be reconciled, seems the chief point of geologic study with many. I have taken a simply scientific compendium, written without a thought of aught, but giving a faithful record of creation as it presents itself to the eye of the geologist, and creation as it presents itself to the man who is resolved to construe the days of Genesis into given periods. Whether there is any other way of reconciling them or not by ingenuity, this at least is clear, that there is no such revelation of scientific truths in Genesis as could be of service to the scientific man. There is nothing that has assisted geologists in their science, but much in the whole scheme so apparently different from well known facts, that geology has suffered great prejudice, opposition and retardation from a mistaken idolatry of the letter of Scripture. This has led many to conceive it necessary as Christians to believe in Genesis at the expense of the geological strata as containing the Divine revelation not only of religious but of scientific truth.

A more plausible method of reconciling the first chapter of Genesis with Geology, would be that suggested by Dr. John Pye Smith, by drawing a line between the first and second verses, and saying that the former belongs to the period before the fitting up of the earth for the residence of man, and the rest to six literal days, with real instead of mythical mornings and evenings, as many thousands of years afterwards as the facts may demand. But this would involve so many difficulties and conflicts with science on account of the creation of an entirely new flora and fauna at the commencement of the residence of man on earth, that Dr. Pye Smith finally proposed to confine all the statements of this chapter (Gen. 1.) to that small portion of the globe first, fitted up for the residence of man; admitting thus that it *cannot* be fairly applied to the whole habitable globe at. *any* period. But with the difficulties of this last interpretation, we need hardly trouble the reader, as it in fact gives up the literal accordance of the record in Genesis with the geology of the globe.

To us it appears that Genesis has a higher use to serve in regard to our faith as Christians, i. e. to check our tendency to Bibliolatry and to prevent our resting in the letter instead of the spirit and power of that which the Bible expresses. It is more safe, truth loving and Christian, to give up our ideas of Inspiration as being identical with infallibility, especially in matters of science, and own that the writer wrote according to the best and truest knowledge he then possessed, and sought to sanctify the science of his age as we must do that of ours, neither being perfect. The writer of Genesis dreamed not of being thought infallible, but taught earnestly and religiously with the best light then attainable, and for our practical guidance. If we love the letter of Scripture, we must love its spirit better, and confess that more cannot be claimed for the writer of this book than sincerity, and as most inspiring because inspired and pious recognition of God in science. Faith in this, is the great lack of our age, and every age. We get lost in minuteness of detail and fail of a sufficiently comprehensive view of God's supreme relations to us, as the author, architect, and therefore controller of the Universe.

III. There is another and more specific external difficulty to maintaining the infallibility of the Old Testament inspiration which has been already alluded to, and which will, I feel sure, appear more and more insurperable every year from the direction in which scientific enquiry is advancing. It is *the Antiquity of the race of man* upon the earth. We have seen already our present Hebrew Scriptures have been tampered with on the subject of the Chronology and that our systems now depend upon whether Seth was one hundred and five years old or two hundred and five, when he begat his first born, and questions of that nature. But all of these dwindle into insignificance compared with those now opening up from the great stone leaved book of nature, and which seem to render it probable that the race of man so far from having inhabited this earth only for six or seven thousand years, cannot well have lived in it for less than sixty or seventy thousand, or more probably six or seven hundred thousand.

Thus far, it has been generally said that in one respect at least, Geology has verified Scripture chronology by showing clearly that the race of man has only existed in recent periods. And this is unquestionably true. Even after the vast ages of the primary and secondary formations, the Tertiary has been divided into *three* periods by the proportion of the fossil shell contained in them being recognized as identical with those now found living in our waters. In the lower tertiary strata, there were about three and a half per cent identical with recent; — in the middle tertiary about seventeen per cent and in the upper tertiary from thiry-five to fifty per cent. Hence they were named by Lyell, *Eocene* from ἠώς and καινός *the dawn* of the recent, *Miocene* or *less recent*, and Pliocene or *more* recent. Yet the Miocene and older Pliocene deposits contain the remains of Mammalia, reptiles and fish, exclusively of extinct species. In *none* of these strata do we find any traces of man. It is only in the *post-tertiary* that we find proofs of his existence. But this latest grand division is still to be divided into two groups, the Post-Pliocene which is earliest, and the Recent or most modern, in which we have no extinct races of mammals, (of the least consequence.) But in the Post-Pliocene, those strata are found in which the shells being recent, a portion and often a considerable one of the accompanying fossil quadrupeds, belongs to extinct species, the land having undergone more changes than the temperature and quality of the water.

So long as our knowledge of human remains extended only to the most Recent or modern periods, Geology did not appear to contradict, but to confirm the account of Genesis as to the chronology of man, though not of other animals. I have mentioned a circumstance which more than twenty years ago, in spite of the somewhat careless statement of Dr. Koch, led me to doubt if some races of man might not be proved to have existed in the Post-Pliocene period in Missouri along with the Mammoth, the Missourium, and other gigantic but extinct animals.

In the same period, Sir Charles Lyell has now become well satisfied that in Europe, arrow heads of flint and other works of rude pottery and art, together with human bones and bone needles and other implements attest the existence of human beings, some dwelling in caves, some who must have existed for ages in pretty populous settlements, judging by the size of the mounds of oyster shells and other remains left by them.

The pre-historic races have been now found to classify themselves according to their progress, men always seeming to advance in art, thus: At first they use stone implements of war and the chase, — stone arrow heads like those of our own Indians of the most barbarous races, stone hammers and hatchets and spears. In the course of ages (for improvement moves *very* slowly at first, and until they get to the point of reading and writing records of their knowledge,) they learn to chip and prepare these more and more carefully, and to use bone needles seven or eight inches long. One of these found imbedded with human remains and the bones of a rhinoceros in a cave near Liege, is a polished and jointed needle shaped bone, with a hole pierced obliquely through it at the base. With these they clearly used to sew the skins of the animals they slew for clothing, some of the skin " with the hair off" having been recently found in one of these Belgian caves. Huge elephants, suited to a cold climate, were their game, and the reindeer, the extinct horse, with the cave bear, were animals they killed. The bones of many species now extinct, and many more common to us are found in such connection with those of man, as to show that they were contemporaries and formed his prey. He even cracked their bones to get out the marrow. The teeth and the skulls of these men are found, and their bones, one of the most ancient, the Neanderthal bones indicating enormous strength and muscular development, with a skull the most brutal ever discovered. Instead, therefore, of beginning with a golden age, from which there has been gradual deterioration, physically, morally and intellectually, the indications of science would all show that even the age of stone must have been one of great progress. It is succeeded at length by an age in which bronze implements superceded those of stone, and much higher degrees of refinement were attained. That period in turn was followed by one of iron from which all historical progress must be dated.

In the Cabinet of the Scientific School at Cambridge, on shelves one above another, are carefully arranged specimens from each of the three stages found at the bottom of the Swiss Lakes, out in which are still to be seen when the waters are low, the charred remains of piles on which three successive races of men have lived, and from which the last have been driven by fire, but of none of which history furnishes us with record.

The Belgian Caves have been very carefully explored by Sir Charles Lyell, the bones of some hundreds altogether of human beings have been examined, and the results are condensed by him thus: "I may conclude by quoting a saying of Professor Agassiz that whenever a new and startling fact is brought to light in science, people first say, 'it is not true,' then that 'it is contrary to religion,' and lastly, that 'every body knew it before.' If I were considering merely the cultivators of Geology, I should say that the former co-existence of man with many extinct mammalia, *had already gone through these three phases* in the progress of every scientific truth towards acceptance. But the grounds of this belief have not yet been laid before the general public."

Since the above extract was written, (in May, 1865,) a cave was discovered on the banks of the river Lesse in Belgium, opposite the hamlet of Chaleux, upon which M. Dupont recently made an instructive report to the Minister of the Interior. It appears from it, that all the bone caves of this vicinity furnish indisputable evidence of this fact, that the cave dwellers were destroyed by a sudden inundation which covered the whole of Belgium and the north of France. The evidences of this, M. Dupont finds in the *limon* of Hesbarge, and the yellow clay of the fields, and in the peculiar debris in the caverns. The number of objects found in this cave is greater than that obtained from the whole of those previously explored. Of worked flints in various stages of manufacture, thirty thousand have been collected. Fossil shells perforated, are some from Rheims, some from the department of Seine et Oise. A few shark's teeth were found, and those of horses and bones of the water rat. "These ancient people and their customs re-appear, after having been forgotten for thousands of years, and like the fabulous bird in whose ashes are found the germ of a new life, antiquity becomes regenerated from its own *debris*. We see them in their dark subterranean dwellings surrounding the hearth, which is protected by the supernatural power of immense, fantastically shaped bones, engaged in patiently making their flint tools and utensils of reindeer horn, in the midst of pestilential emanations from the animal remains, which their indifference allowed them to retain in their dwelling. The skins of wild beasts, having the hair removed, were stitched together by the aid of their sharpened flints and ivory needles, and served as clothing. We see them pursuing wild animals, armed with arrows and lances tipped with a barb of flint. We take part in their feasts, where a horse, bear or reindeer, replaces on days when their hunting has been successful, the tainted flesh of the rat, their only resource against famine. Their trading extended as far as the regions now forming part of France, from whose inhabitants they obtained shells, jet, with which they delight to ornament themselves, and the flint which is so valuable to them. But a falling in of the roof drives them from their principal dwelling, in which lie buried the objects of their faith and their domestic utensils, and they are forced to seek another habitation. We know nothing certain of the relation of these people with those of earlier times. Had

they ancestors in this country? The great discoveries
of our illustrious compatriot, Schmerling, and those
which Professor Malaise has made at Engehoul seem
to prove that the men whose traces I have brought to
light on the Lesse did not belong to the indigenous
races of Belgium, but were only the successors of the
more ancient population. I have even met with certain evidences of our primordial ancestors at Chaleux,
but the trail was lost as soon as found. Our knowledge
of these ancestors stops short at this point."

The shells and skeletons found imbeded in the Hes-
bayan mud, show that this Deluge which swept off
the last race of cave dwellers, found the Elephans E.
primigenius, and the Rhinosceros tichorchinus, then inhabitants of that neighborhood. Upon the whole,
therefore, it can hardly be doubted from these caves
alone, that there were races of men in Belgium and all
over Europe from the period soon after the recovery
from the glacial ages that is in the very earliest ages
of the Post Pliocene. This period is indeed Geologically '*recent*,' but yet so remote as to be probably
before the close of the second Continental period,
when there was nothing but solid land, where. now
flows the British channel, and when Ireland even was
still attached to England, to Scotland, and to France,
— a period sufficiently remote to cause all historical

times to appear quite insignificant in duration, when compared with the antiquity of the human race.

The rate of progress in knowledge, and the arts and sciences, proceeds in geometrical ratio. Hence the slow advance of early ages. " The vast distance of time which separated the origin of the higher and lower levels of gravel of the valley of the Somme, both of them rich in flint implements of similar shape (although those of oval form predominate in the newer gravels) leads to the conclusion that the state of the arts in those early times, remained stationary for almost indefinite periods." *　And yet men climbed up by degrees to the civilization of Egypt. The mud of the Nile for sixty feet deep, below the Perystyle of the obelisk of Heliopolis has been penetrated, and is supposed to prove an antiquity of at least twelve thousand years before the erection of that Obelisk, and perhaps thirty thousand. At the lowest of these borings however, while we find traces of burnt bricks and Egyptian art and civilization, while we find the bones of several sorts of existing animals, no bones or traces of extinct species are found of any kind whatever, nor of a stone period of art. When the penetration has gone down to these, we may perhaps get something like a connected view of the history of man's existence on the earth, and be able to begin the conjecture in years, as to how long ago it is since

* Lyell on the Antiquity of Man, Chap. 19.

the latest men of the stone age in the valley of the Somme existed.

Those who would fairly estimate the scientific evidence on this subject, should carefully study the remarkable work of Sir Charles Lyell on the Antiquity of Man. Instead of six thousand years, it is probable man has been on the earth at *least* two hundred thousand. Indeed, Sir Charles appears to suspect that we may yet come across the proofs of human existence in Northern Europe before the Glacial period.

What already appears certain, must render any theory of Inspiration, which suspends our whole faith in Christianity upon the literal and infallible accuracy of Genesis increasingly mischievous. And yet in this book, properly regarded, we may trace an inspired preface to the records of the great struggle between Theism and Idolatry, and perhaps Pantheism. The purpose of it is to teach in the forms of the popular belief as to the history of the origin of all things, that the One living and true God was the Originator of the order of the Universe. Professor Agassiz, indeed, suggested several years ago, that there is no necessary contradiction between the book of Genesis and the supposition of the race of man having been on the earth for any number of thousands of years; provided we are willing to consider

the account of the Creation of Man on the sixth
day in Gen. 1, distinct from and prior to the other
account of the creation of Adam and Eve given in
the second chapter. Nor is there any doubt but that
these two chapters are from distinct documents, drawn
up by distinct writers, though inedited at a later period
by a common compiler. The theological purpose is,
however, one, i. e. to show that the creation of man,
whether in one original pair or more, was the work of
the Allwise God. Further than this, the book of
Genesis was apparently intended to preserve, so far as the
writer was able, the ancestral records of the Jewish
race. The Editor traces them back to *the man*, (for
Adam means simply this,) the earliest he knew, and
gives the best records he could collect, connecting with
him Abraham and the twelve tribes. These records,
from their evident simplicity of arrangement and
truthfulness of intention are, so far as they go, the
most ancient and valuable written records we have
preserved to us in the present time, in respect to the
spread and distribution of the nations of the earth.
While all other nations, when they got back to the end
of their authentic documents, added on others indefinitely, and made up periods of thousands of years,
there does not appear to have been a single geneolog-
ical table *added* in those of Genesis, although much
may have been omitted. The number of years are

not now to be depended upon. But when the historian got back to the end of his data, he placed the first man there, and so cut short a chronology he disdained to fill up from his own imagination, and thus it is that what remains makes his statement of the world's history so short.

CHAPTER V.

THE INTERNAL DIFFICULTIES AS TO THE INFALLIBILITY OF THE INSPIRATION OF THE OLD TESTAMENT, CONSIDERED.

I.

THOSE who most strenuously maintain the infallibility of the Inspiration of the Hebrew text, little consider to what an extent the sense now assigned to that text is the result of faith in the uninspired Jewish traditions and interpretations. Within the last century or two, by degrees, far the largest and most important part of what used to be considered by Christians as the infallible teaching of the Old Testament, has been swept away. The Rabbinical Schools erroneously taught that the words of Scripture mean all that they possibly can mean. Their maxim was that "mountains of sense hung suspended on every letter of Scripture." The early Christians borrowed the allegorizing system from the Rabbins. Origen, following the Alexandrine custom of Philo and others, converted into allegory the whole of the Creation and fall of man. The Jesuits in later ages carried this out, and made 'the greater light to rule the day,' to mean the Pope, and the lesser light and stars, the Catholic Princes! The followers of Cocceius maintained in the Protestant Church, that "all the possible meanings of a word in the Scripture are to be united." Swedenborg went still further. When it is borne in mind that as early as the time of Origen, beside literal and hidden senses, these latter had been divided into moral and mystical, and even the latter of these subdivided into celestial and terrestrial, or allegorical and anagogical, we may think what all this would involve. In addition to this, they believed that "the whole of the Old Testament history was a kind of emblematical fore-shadowing of Christ, that the prophecies of the ancient seers, treated in their literal import of Jesus Christ, and that whatever was to occur down to the end of time was all pre-figured in the Old Testament." It is quite clear, therefore, that within the last two hundred years, a more critical, literal and confined interpretation has by degrees swept from the faith of the present generation far more than half of what used to be considered essentially taught by the Old Testament. This vicious system of allegorizing seems to have sprung up before hand among the Jews, and even before that

8

among the Pagan commentators on Homer, and the
sacred books of heathenism even in India. The
whole probably sprung out of a superstitious view of
Inspiration, and was used afterwards as a skillful
means of explaining away contradictions, and much
more that could not well be believed literally true,
adding on the authority of the old and established
new and unauthorized dogmas.

II. Another mass of traditional interpretation of the
Old Testament will surely be swept away from our
ideas of infallible Scripture, in proportion as it is distinctly borne in mind that our present Massoretic
Hebrew text is avowedly only a late interpretation or
writing out, so to speak, of the short hand notes in
which the original text was alone inscribed, until after
the Christian era had set in, and Hebrew become a
dead language. Even to this day, the official Synagogue Hebrew MSS. are written entirely without
any vowel points, the pronunciation being a matter of
traditions and arbitrary rules of the elders, which rules
and traditions though confirmed by the points and by
other translations like the Septuagint, are certainly not
infallible.

The case is briefly this: So long as the Hebrew
language was a spoken tongue, it was written without
vowels or any letters being doubled. This is just the
way our short hand writers now take down speeches,

and is generally sufficient to remind the reporter of a speech, the ideas of which have been distinctly and recently understood. Some years ago, a friend undertook to learn short hand. Hessian boots were worn in those days with little tassels, one in front of each. Going out hastily, this gentleman discovered that a tassel was torn off one of his boots, and to show his proficiency in the new art, he wrote to his teacher in another room to ask: " Have you an old boot tassel?" The vowels being all omitted, and also the doubling of the letters, signs were made for the following letters: " Hv y n ld bt tsl," which his friend not unnaturally read thus: " Have you an old boot *to sell?*" But why his pupil could want to be buying an old boot from him, required more explanation than short hand could well give. Now the difficulty of the ancient Hebrew without points is just this: that although where persons are very familiar with the subject and language, this style of writing was ordinarily sufficient at least to guide the Priests, and remind them of the law, so that they could explain it to the people; yet there would always be left many cases where the meaning was extremely doubtful, without the aid and authority of tradition.

We know, for instance, the important difference in the sense often occasioned by the presence or absence of the definite article. To write a memorial or decree in *a* book is one thing, to write it in *the* book, will mean a particular book, the Pentateuch perhaps in such a place as Ex. 17: 14. But in Hebrew, there are thousands of cases where, although this distinction is expressed clearly enough, if you admit only the pointed text, yet the vowels and doubling by the points having been added since the Christian era, possess only the authority of a later tradition, perhaps against that of an earlier translation.*

Suppose then we give up the infallibility of the vowels, and yet hold on to that of the Consonants, how will the case stand? Take the regular verb קטל, without the points it may mean *nine* different things. It may be a noun, a verb, or a participle. It may be active, passive, or reduplicative. It may stand for any one of nine different words, and will in different places have to be read either *qatal*, he did kill, *qetol* to kill, (infin.) or kill thou, (imp.); *qotel*, killing; *qittel*, he has killed many; *qattal* or *qattol*, to kill many; *qattel*, do thou kill many; *quttal* and *quttol*, to be massacred; or *qetel*, slaughter. It is nearly the same with every verb and noun throughout the whole Hebrew language, especially the more regular verbs and nouns. " How imperfect and indefinite such a mode of writing was, is easily seen; yet during the whole period in which the Hebrew was a spoken language, no other sign for

* See Davidson's Introduction, Vol. I, p. 107.

vowels were employed than the ו and י used also as consonants. Reading was therefore a harder task than with our more adequate modes of writing, *and much must have been supplied by the reader's knowledge of the living mother tongue.*"*

דבר might be read *dabhar*, a word; *debher*, a pestilence; *dibber*, he hath spoken; *dabber*, to speak; *dobher*, speaking, or *dubbar*, it has been spoken.

The fact is, then, that the Hebrew tongue was so imperfect a language, until the vowels were added to it, that the Old Testament, as originally written, was only a sort of *help to the memory and traditionary teachings of the fallible scribes and priests* to whom were committed the oracles of God. ' A word,' and ' a pestilence ' were expressed by the same consonants, and whether it was the one or the other, had to be either guessed out from the context, or determined by some translation, or remembered and arbitrarily received on the authority of the living teacher. It was a language, indeed, capable of handing down to us through these laborious and imperfect processes, the simple, sublime and Divine theology committed to the Jewish nation,—a law the glory of all subsequent ages, hymns the most majestic and sublime the world has ever seen, exhibiting a religious culture a thousand times before that of any other

* See Conant's Gesenius, Sec. 7.

records which Greece or India left to us. But it has been preserved in a language which, while it suggests the loftiest inspiration of *thought* at every line, seems to have been constructed on purpose to render the idea of verbal infallibility peculiarly improbable, — a language which leaned upon the inward inspiration of the living fallible teacher in every line and letter for its support, and intelligibility. Let any tolerable Hebrew scholar, used only to the pointed text, take up a copy of the unpointed Old Testament, and he will find that except so far as his memory of the passage assists him, he has the language of that unpointed original yet to learn.

In addition to this, let any one look over the history of the Old Testament MSS. during the long, uncritical period before the formation of the Massoretic text. During this time of near a thousand years, say from about two hundred years before Christ, to seven hundred or eight hundred after, changes of dates and perhaps other readings could be and *were* interpolated flagrantly into the text. The doctrine of infallibility, therefore, if true in the original unpointed MSS., could not assure us now that the present Hebrew Massoretic text, or any translation from it was infallible, as to such a matter even as the World's Chronology by a thousand years and more.

III. The Documentary and anonymous character

of several of the books of the Old Testament, forms a serious difficulty to the belief of an infallible verbal Divine guidance of the writers. Any good man will find in these documents, a boundless source of reflection, instruction and holy thought, who reads them as the sacred library of that nation who first made faith, worship and obedience to the One only true and living God, the basis of its national life, and who thus became the foundation on which Jesus Christ subsequently built his more spiritual kingdom. Or if a man read these books to trace the onward progress of the religious history of our race, he will find much to excite his adoration by the display of the perpetual presence of God in history, and the growth of our race in the knowledge of Him, the knowledge of whom is life. The psalms and hymns and prayers will be the best instruction for his own worship, and he will find that the more he studies these books, the more important to his faith, comfort and instruction in righteousness do they become. But he who attempts to read them as the utterances of a verbally inspired dictation, will find greater perplexities, misgivings and doubts, the more closely he attempts their study. By claiming for them what they never pretended ·for themselves, and what is not true of them, confusion and contradiction are thrown around the whole, and scepticism is infused into the minds of those who thus study them.

Out of thirty-nine books in all, we cannot pretend to know the names of the authors of more than thirteen or fourteen. These are mostly writers of the least important books of the whole, such as Ezekiel, Haggai, and Zechariah. Ezra and Nehemiah, indeed, exercised an important influence in restoring and perhaps editing several of the most important books of the Old Testament into their present form, if tradition may be trusted, but how much they did we know not. How many of the Psalms were really written by David, or those whose names they bear, none now can pretend to decide. Even the Hebrew and Septuagint are on this quite at variance. As to I and II Samuel, I and II Kings, I and II Chronicles, they are clearly anonymous, as are Joshua and Judges. It cannot now, we suppose, be considered necessary to maintain that the first and second parts of Isaiah were written by the same person, or the Chaldean passages in Daniel by the author of the Hebrew portions of that book. There are no more beautiful, touching and truly inspired passages in the whole of the Old Testament than Isaiah 2: 2–5, and Micah 4: 1–4, but is it therefore necessary to believe that an infallible Spirit dictated twice over almost verbatim, those two passages separately to two different prophets? May we not suppose that one borrowed from the other? Let the reader put the two side by side and determine.

In Isaiah, in Jeremiah, in nearly all the chief books of the Old Testament, we have not a few references to, and compilations from each other, and from other writings. It has been commonly asserted, that all this is no objection to a belief in verbal inspiration, the Holy Spirit being supposed to secure infallibility in the selection. But will the facts in these cases favor a theory such as this? Our book of Psalms, for instance, is a compilation, or rather a binding up together of five distinct collections, some of which were certainly composed for the temple worship. Others contain sacred poems, which the best writers of any age would gladly claim as the noblest literature of the world. No other writings have so elevated, comforted, strengthened and fed the most excellent, re-claimed the most vicious, or so decided the feeble purposes of those seeking the better life. But when we find two Psalms like 14 and 53, (let the reader place them side by side,) are we to say that this *repetition* is by infallible dictation of the Spirit of God? Or may we not rather learn from the comparison, to take higher and broader views of the nature of inspiration? Let us fairly grant that in putting together the volumes of lyrics of the sacred library, two copies of a Psalm, one substantially

Elohistic, and the other, a Jehovistic edition of the same, by human fallibility and mistake, got bound up together in the same general collection, as if they were distinct Psalms. De Wette considers Ps. 1: 41 as the original nucleus. The second book from 42 to 72 was added from various collections. But the large proportion of Elohistic Psalms would show that they may probably be looked upon as the older of the two. Ps. 70 is is the same as 40: 13–17; Ps. 108: 6–13, as 60: 5–12; and Ps. 108: 1–5, is the same as 57: 7–11. So that the whole of Ps. 108 is obtained from two previous ones, the parts differently put together.

It is, however, in the Pentateuch, and especially in the book of Genesis, that this fragmentary character becomes the greatest source of perplexity. It has long been known and admitted by all who have examined the subject, since De Wette's investigation,[*] that at least *two* documents are traceable clearly in the early parts of Genesis. Many have thought that they could prove a larger number of distinct writers, and even follow them through most of the Pentateuch. It is not necessary to go far into these discussions here. Dr. Davidson and others, suppose from authors whose writings appear in the first four books of the Old Testament, — the Elohist who, he thinks, wrote about the time of Saul, and may, therefore, have

* See Ante, p. 56.

been Samuel; the Jehovist who wrote later, about the first half of the eight century, B. C.; the Junior Elohist about B. C. 880, the time of Elisha; and a final Redactor after all these, but before the book of Deuteronomy. But the traditions in regard to Ezra indicate a still later revision.

If any, even English reader, will look over the first chapter of Genesis to verse third of the second chapter, he will find the Divine name, God, — Elohim, given about thirty-six times, that is all the way through. But during the rest of the second chapter, we have the words Jehovah Elohim, (Lord, God.) This distinguishes the Jehovistic document as it is called, and so through the third and fourth chapters, we have Jehovah Elohim, or Jehovah, except that in cases like chapter 3: 1, 3, 5, and chapter 4: 25, Elohim is carefully inserted into the speeches, while Jehovah is put in all the narrative, perhaps to be consistent with what is there asserted, that the name Jehovah was not in use until the time of Enos, chapter 4: 26.

But from chapter 2: 4, there is quite a distinct document from chapter 1, where we have already had an account of the creation of mankind in general "male and female, created he them." (verse 27.) Whether therefore the more minute relation in chapter second of the formation of Adam and Eve, is to be regarded as a later and distinct creation of the first progenitor of the

Jewish race, as Professor Agassiz suggested; or whether this is to be regarded as returning to give only a more specific account of the work of the sixth day, as generally supposed, the careful reader will at once see (if only from the terms used to designate the Divine Being) that it is quite a distinct document. The fifth chapter, (except verse 28,) is Elohistic. But the first eight verses of chapter sixth are Jehovistic. From the ninth verse to the twenty-second, the Elohistic is resumed. `And here it will be observed, that but *two* of every sort of living things, are commanded to be brought into the ark, and the same is asserted in chapter 7: 8–9, 13–16, which are also taken from the Elohistic document. While in chapter 7: 1–5, which is Jehovistic, and written after the establishment of the priesthood and its sacrifices, the command is given (verse 2) " every clean beast thou shalt take to thee by *sevens*," although according to verses 9 and 15, which are Elohistic, but *two* would seem to have actually come. In chapter 8: 20–22, which is a Jehovistic insertion, the offering of the sacrifices was narrated, with their acceptance. This agrees with the Chaldean account of the flood by Berosus.

This will be sufficient for our present purpose. The reader desirous to trace this matter further, will find a careful digest of the whole matter in Davidson's Introduction, Vol. I, p. 58–61, as in the writings of many other modern critics. The above is, however, almost entirely from private notes of my own, made directly from the study of Genesis many years ago, before I had ever seen the results of any investigation of this book. All I have here pointed out, will, therefore, easily become an assured matter to any one who will take the trouble to turn to the references given. When I found them so fully confirmed by Dr. Davidson's more careful, learned and elaborate researches, and those of many others, I felt sure they must be certainly and clearly correct.

There are then at least two accounts of the creation and deluge, with different names for the Divine Being, clearly interwoven to form our book of Genesis, yet not so interwoven but that the seams are easily traceable, and the two are not capable, I think, of being fairly and entirely reconciled with each other.

In addition to this, we have in the writings of Berosus another account, showing such verbal coincidence with Genesis, that there can be no escaping the conclusion, either that one was copied from the other, or all from some more general and common source.

And yet, who that has read the fragments of Berosus or Sanconiath, or looked into the Vedas or Avestas, but can see a beauty, an elevation, and a truthfulness about this book of Genesis, far above and quite distinct from the spirit of all these other accounts. It has been written or edited by some pious redactor, taking the outline of the general history as it stood recorded in more ancient, universally believed accounts, with a desire to infuse into them the thought of One true and living God, with which his own soul was filled. When all this was completed, we may not be able exactly to say. Parts of the law were no doubt begun by Moses. The Elohistic document was probably written about the time of Samuel, but the completion of the whole Pentateuch *must* have been after the use of the terms Elohim and Jehovah had both become so familiar that the most extreme venerators of the latter term to designate the Divine name, had ceased to notice or object to the older Elohim being used in Jewish history; seven hundred years after the time of David at earliest.

IV. The formation and different degrees of sacredness attributed by the Jews to the Old Testament Canon, occasion many difficulties in the way of the common views of the Plenary and verbal inspiration of the Old Testament.

There are in our English Bibles, thirty-nine books of the Old Testament mostly anonymous; but we cannot tell by what authority any of these books were admitted or others excluded. The accounts we have are all traditional and more or less contradictory or erroneous. All agree that Ezra had much to do with the formation of the Canon, but *what* who shall tell? Basil supposed that the whole of the Old Testament had been burned up, *and miraculously restored by Ezra,* Chrysostom thought that "out of the *remains* of the Scripture, Ezra re-composed it." Hilary says that " Ezra had collected the Psalms into one volume," and Thedoret, that "the Scripture having been depraved in the time of the Exile, was restored by Ezra."

Most of the Talmudical writers must be placed at a later date than the above. Their story is that there was a synod of one hundred and twenty men, presided over by Ezra, who restored and reformed the Temple worship after the return. The Jerusalem Talmud, which may have been written any time between A. D. 200 and 650, says that when the men of the Great Synagogue arose, they restored magnificence (i. e. the crown of the law) to its primitive state. In Pirke Aboth, chap. 1, (one of the most respectable of all the treatises of the Talmud,) it is said that " Moses received the law from Mount Sinai, gave it to Joshua, Joshua to the Elders, the Elders to the prophets, and these to the men of the Great Synagogue." In the same treatise it is added that Simeon the just was the last survivor of the men of the Great Synagogue, and is said to have completed the canon by adding the books of Ezra and Nehemiah. In the Babylonian Talmud, it is said that the men of the Great Synagogue wrote Ezekiel, the twelve minor prophets, Daniel and Esther, which a Jewish commentator considers to mean that "they collected the books into one volume, and made new copies of them, knowing that the prophetic spirit was about to depart." Le Clerc, therefore, declares the whole history of the Great Synagogue, and the Recension by Ezra, a Jewish fable.*

That Ezra commenced collecting the Temple Library and deciding on the Holy Books to be kept in the ark, and read in the Synagogues, need not be questioned; that he completed it, is hardly possible, and not even asserted, as Malachi clearly lived after the building of the second Temple, — probably fully fifty years after Ezra had been sent with the second colony of the Hebrews. The Jews, therefore, say that Simeon the just, closed the canon, and lived to the days of Alexander the Great. But this is all the wildest fancy, conjecture and confusion. There seem clearly to have been *three* collections made at different times. The Pentateuch, the Prophets, and the Hagiographa. "The reception of historical and of some prophetical writings into the Hagiographa can only be explained," says De Wette, "on the hypothesis that both

---

* See De Wette, Introduction, Sec. 14, and Kitto, — Articles, — Scriptures Great Synagogue and Canon.

the former collections were closed when this was begun." *

We certainly have no authority in regard to this matter out of the New Testament that pretends to be inspired, or that is at all probably true. *Internal* evidence must be our chief resort beyond the traditions of the early Jews and Christians. There is, therefore, nothing that can be considered reasonably to imply infallibility in the Inspiration of the Old Testament of which we have any evidence, beyond what is to be gathered from the allusions to it by Jesus Christ, or the writings of the New Testament. In fact, the Jews themselves appear to have had no uniform or agreed standard of Inspiration, applicable to all their books alike. Coleridge has suggested, and De Wette asserts that "the Jewish teachers assign to Moses the highest degree of inspiration, for God spoke face to face with him, that is without the intervention of visions and dreams. They ascribe the next degree to the prophets who, either sleeping or waking, without the aid of the senses, heard a voice speaking to them, and in their ecstacy saw prophetic visions. The lowest degree of divine influence which they call the Holy Spirit, they concede to those inspired men who, with their senses remaining in perfect action, spoke like other men. Though they did not rejoice in dreams, or prophetic

* Sec. 13.

visions, they nevertheless felt the Divine Spirit resting upon them, exciting and suggesting words of praise and penitence or thoughts relating to divine or civil affairs, and they spoke or wrote them. All the prophets but Moses, prophesied through an opaque, but he through a transparent glass." Abarbanel, he says, "dwells long in explaining the foundation and reason of the distinction between the writings of the Hagiographa and the other books of the Old Testament, as arising from the different mode and measure of divine influence by which they were composed." * Philo speaks in much the same manner, and considers himself in measure as guided by the Spirit.

The whole of this is a subject of great difficulty and delicacy, requiring a degree of original research with an enlightened mind, such as few are able to give to it, and which might well occupy a volume of itself. But the fact that all is left with so little of true information and certainty, and is obscured by Jewish superstitions and falsehoods, proves that Divine wisdom has not thought it necessary for us to be so sure as many profess to be, or to draw lines of infallibility around certain books, because included in the Jewish canon, throwing them out of the range of analogy with all other pious writings, or even the verbal teachings and daily conduct of the holy men who prepared them, or

* De Wette, Sec. 10.

of the Church that has selected and handed them down to us.

Thus looking at the Old Testament as a whole, though it would seem vain to attempt to prove for it, verbal infallibility, yet far more must we beware of failing to perceive in this very ancient and wonderful collection, transmitted to us through the Jewish Church, the work of holy and inspired men of the olden time who "spake as they were moved by the Holy Ghost." They were still *men*,—fallible men who collected these books, but compared with the writings of Greece and Persia at the same date, their religious value is truly wonderful. Take the book of Psalms as a whole, and then read the Vedas with prayers for thieves that the dogs and men may sleep while they steal! or read Homer. Take the moral laws of the Jews, and then read Grote's History of Grecian laws in similar periods; compare the theism of Isaiah with that even of the noblest and best of all the Greeks. How immeasurably superior in moral tone, sublimity of worship, and the holiness inspired by the conscious presence of God, are the best passages of the Jewish writers to those of any others of their age.

Let any one read together the remains which have come down to us of the Greek philosophers, and the Hebrew Prophets, and how much more of earnestness and disinterestedness do we find in the latter, how much more truth and courage in standing up for God and the eternal right. In all this, can we not see true inspiration giving them, if not all the verbal accuracy, nor perfect scientific knowledge, nor even the subtile reasoning powers of a Socrates, — a piety, loftiness and elevation of soul that even Socrates never attained. The wisdom of the Greeks is soiled and worn "as if from earth it labored up." But the Hebrew books record thoughts that "down from higher regions came."

Even the books of Joshua and Judges, Samuel, Kings and Chronicles, though not free from inaccuracies, are, after all, better and truer models both for the whole history of the world than any histories written since in this most vital particular, that each great prosperity or defeat is traced home to its *moral* cause. Whatever other lessons may be omitted or confused, the connection between the fear of the one true, living and holy God, and national prosperity is traced in broad outline with a clear, bold hand; while the neglect of this principle accompanied with all error, discord and misfortune is equally traced. This after all is the grand clue to history. The religious faith of every nation is, as Grote has shown in his history of Greece, the truest key to the causes of their conduct. So long as a Jewish king remains true to the national faith of Jehovah, which inspired all their prophets and the people, so long he prospers. Second causes are often omitted or mistaken, but the primary cause is never lost sight of, and so far there is Inspiration, a Divinely given and holy feeling, producing an insight into causes which gives the true prophetic foresight of events; an elevation of soul above the mists of the momentary circumstances, giving to one writer a clearness in reasoning; to another courage to resist evil, to another wisdom to select and arrange; to another a holy love to write out those hidden mysteries and treasures known only to the pious heart, but eternally true. The holiest and best men of all ages have ever most loved to read these writings, and so far it is that the Old Testament like the New, is a revelation of truths, growing out of the faith of former generations of holy men, and infusing the same living warmth into those who have already the germs of similar faith within themselves. The Bible is not given either in the Old Testament or the New, so much to *create* faith as to *feed* and refresh it. It is the Spirit quickeneth.

As through all the ages of the world, before man was formed, God seems to have been fitting it up by an increasing richness of soil, and by higher types of living animals for the support of him physically, so in all the ages and dispensations since man entered, but prior to Christianity, God seems to have been preparing and educating him to be increasingly governed by the lofty system of faiths which Christianity exhibits to the heart and mind of man. In the Old Testament, we may see a work of preparatory inspiration without which the purer, higher inspirations of the New Testament saints and Apostles could never have grown to the wonderful degree they suddenly developed. The law was our schoolmaster, says St. Paul, to bring us unto Christ. It was a great general preparation to the Hebrews and Alexandrians, who first united Hebrew and Grecian religious thought.

But the same Lord over all, is rich unto *all* who call upon him, and he had his great work of preparation for the Gentiles going on too, among Greek philosophers like Anaxagoras, Socrates and Plato, and Roman sages and statesmen like Cicero, Plutarch and Seneca. When, therefore, St. Paul was preaching before a Greek audience, he caught up a Divinely inspired thought even from a heathen poet who had sung "we are also his offspring," and taught the Universal Fatherhood of God to idolators. When before the last of the Jewish race of Kings, Herod Agrippa, he appealed to him as a believer in the Old Testament Scriptures; but in presence of the Roman Felix, he *reasoned* of righteousness, temperance and a judgment to come; while on Mars Hill, he honored the latent piety amid confessed ignorance in that inscription "to the unknown God."

It belongs not to the present chapter to carry this subject further. And yet I may remark in passing, that the recent address of Mr. Gladstone, on retiring from the Chancellorship of the University at Edinburg, suggests with a breadth of reasoning, and a warm love and reverence for the loftiest truths of Christianity, some thoughts worthy of all honor on the degree to which the highest inspirations of Grecian speculation and Hebrew holy intuition, were both by a Divine purpose fused and blended in the Christian life developed through the Church of the living God.

CHAPTER VI.

THE NEW TESTAMENT TEACHINGS AS THEY BEAR UPON
THE INSPIRATION OF THE OLD.

IT has been the common custom to settle all doubts
and difficulties as to the plenary nature of the
Inspiration of the Old Testament, by asserting that
Jesus Christ and his Apostles appeal to them as
Divinely inspired, without making any exceptions or
implying any doubt as to their perfection, and that this
must settle the whole question for every Christian at
least. Such a mode of closing the argument is more
sweeping than satisfactory. For it begins by taking
for granted that Jesus in endorsing the general authority of the Jewish Church, and inspiration of the Old
Testament Scriptures, thereby asserted the verbal
infallibility of every book, chapter and verse contained
in them. In applying the *argumentum ad hominem*
to one sect of the Jews, i. e. the Pharisees whose

superstitions he particularly reproves, he does not thereby assert to be infallibly true, all that they may have believed.

But further, this argument as it is commonly put, takes for granted that the Inspiration of the *New* Testament at least, is beyond all dispute in the mind of a Christian, exempt from that law of fallibility, which we have seen so much reason to suppose clear in regard to the Old. We believe most firmly that the New Testament stands in a very much more immediate relation to the absolute and eternal communications of Divine truth than the Old. But though Christianity is given from God as an exhibition of the principles of *Universal* religion, and is communicated most immediately by the Holy Spirit, it was yet given through fallible men and in a certain fragmentary form. Nor was it intended to make other ages independent of that same spirit which animated the Church in its infancy, but *more* consciously and immediately reliant upon its ever living presence, as abiding in it for ever. But the discussion on this point belongs properly to another chapter.

Socrates left behind him *no writings*, and from the fragments and recollections of his disciples, Xenophon and Plato, we have to acquaint ourselves with his ideas and teachings. In like manner, our Saviour has not left us a line of his own writing. The records of the Evangelists are all we have. In some cases, the same teachings of Jesus which appear most clear and plain, when we read them recorded by Matthew are so far differently recorded by Luke, that we are thrown into doubt, whether we have rightly understood their nature and meaning. Compare the Beatitudes Matt. 5: 1–12, and Luke 6: 20–26. In John 21: 25 we are assured that we have only fragments of the personal life and teachings of the Saviour.

Still it will be urged that these fragments are clear and decisive. And as to the Divine authority which he concedes to the Old Testament Scriptures for the practical religious instruction and guidance of his Jewish followers, there is no question. The Pharisees, he says, "sit in *Moses' seat*; whatsoever they say, therefore, observe and do. But do as they *say*, not as they *do*, for they say and do not." That is, rigidly reverence and obey the law as expounded by the Jewish Church authorities, and even where you see inconsistencies and flaws, adhere practically and most scrupulously in obedience to all that has *prima facie* claims to be obeyed. Except your righteousness shall exceed that not only of the law, but of the Scribes and Pharisees, ye shall not enter into the kingdom of heaven. They were not to let one jot or one tittle pass from the law, *even as expounded by those who sat in Moses' seat*, binding men with heavy burdens but not lifting them with their own fingers. But did our Saviour mean thus to say that these traditional teachings of Scribes and Pharisees were infallible, and to be of eternal obligation? Certainly not. What Jesus meant, appears to be this: There is an eternal law of God *underlying* the whole. You cannot safely and suddenly separate the true from the false; obey the whole as the Providentially appointed guide for your lives, until each deviation from the customs in which you have been brought up, shall be clearly manifested to be the Divine will. This view becomes quite consistent with St. Paul's doctrine for the Hellenistic Christians of there being nothing unclean in itself, yet many things unclean to those who so esteemed them. Real conservatism walks in freedom and liberty of thought in proportion as it conforms to every precept and custom, fulfils all righteousness, and ratifies every institution.

The Saviour urges upon his followers, and practices himself an observance of the laws of God, more severe than that of Scribes and Pharisees, as a meet preparation for entering into the new kingdom of heaven. It was not merely to the eternal moralities embraced in the Mosaic law, but to its ceremonial observances, and the still further comments of those who sat in *Moses' seat* for the sake of respect to constituted religious government and holy charity and Church authority that Jesus urged the conformity of others to all the social worship of the synagogue, and exhibited it himself. While Christianity was never intended to bind the Gentile converts, "those other sheep not of this fold," with the heavy burdens of Judaism, there was ever that strict conservatism in the teachings of Jesus, that made Christianity adapt itself as much as possible to Judaism among the Jews, on the principle that men always most easily conform themselves to those institutions to which they have been accustomed. Christianity, as a social religion required conciliation and charity and conformity to established institutions from all its followers.

But it must be a strained interpretation of Matt. 5 : 17–48, that can reconcile it with the absolute infallibility of Moses and his law. Let any one study those verses, and he will see how Jesus distinctly teaches that there were many things in broad contrast between the allowances of Moses and those of the new dispensation. The Saviour, therefore, if on the one hand, he honored the Pentateuchal Scriptures as inspired, regarded them not, therefore, as infallible declarations of eternal truth, but as he said, permitting many things for a time which were, nevertheless, at variance from the dictates of final, perfect and eternal morality by defect, and contrary to many laws which he established as henceforth necessary in the new dispensation. Religion among mankind, (as if he had said,) is progressive. It is a holy growth of conscious conformity to that law of God which, as Cicero had declared, is eternal and universal. Moses had been a burning and a shining light for his day, but not, therefore, a finality.

Something like that was the general aspect in which Jesus taught his disciples to view the Jewish Scriptures and the Jewish Church; — both as inspired teachers and conservators of many divine truths; — neither of them to be hastily abandoned by those who were providentially placed under their guidance; and no further abandoned than absolutely necessary, as the new wine might require new bottles. All the rending away from the old was to come from the action of others, not from them. Hence, Jesus forsook not the temple, and was never even formally excluded from the Synagogue, but remained a Rabbi to the end. The new Church was gathered under the wings of the old. Christianity at first regarded itself especially in Judea as a branch of Judaism. Nor was it through any repudiation by the Christians, but by the Jews that the two ever separated. The Apostolic Church met in a porch of the temple, till expelled by persecution. Circumcision was never forbidden to Jewish Christians for a hundred years. Jews were indulged in all their prejudices in the Christian Church, while much that is Jewish, but not of perpetual obligation, has been retained to this day.

The language of him who was introducing a new dispensation of religion in so wise, careful and conservative a manner to Scribes and Pharisees jealous of their law, must, therefore, be construed in accordance with these principles. Jesus, though ever acting with truth and candor, was desirous not to disturb or destroy any prejudices or opinions not necessarily injurious, and he argues with them in favor of the truths he wishes to establish from their own concessions and stand point, without therefore necessarily endorsing all the views they entertained.

But he also uses a freedom at times in regard to the Old Testament which they accounted blasphemous, and which must be regarded as appealing back of the law of Moses to a higher law, and one both universal and eternal. He quotes passage after passage from the most sacred books of the Jewish Canon, and says, "It was said by them of old time," thus and so, and then he adds, " But I say unto you," and on the same subject utters some truths not only far stronger, or very different, but even quite annulling. When calling their attention to the Scriptures, as predicting a Messiah such as he was, he appeals to the prophets in words like these: " Search the Scriptures, for in them *ye think* ye have eternal life, and they are they that testify of me." This is one of the passages most frequently appealed to, as endorsing the plenary, verbal inspiration of the whole of the Old Testament. It cannot, however, be fairly construed as doing any such thing. It is avowedly an *argumentum ad hominem.* The Jews were not by any means all agreed as to their views of the Inspiration of the Old Testament. The Pharisees, Sadduces, and Essenes all differed, and why we should suppose that he held the Pharisaic view, it is hard to conjecture, except that it corresponds with some of the Pharisaism into which we have also fallen. That he did feel and uphold the divine authority of the Old Testament, on specific subjects, and so far as he quoted it, and in the general sense, though with exceptions as we have seen, there is no doubt. But his language here only proves that according to what *they believed*, he was entitled to their credence. The different sects of the Jews held views as widely diverse as to Inspiration, as the Roman Catholics, Calvinists, and Unitarians of our day, and who shall say from such a passage as this, that he himself held the one view more than the other. He argued with them from *their* views, not always fully and minutely exhibiting his own.

The same thing might be urged in relation to John 10: 35, which has sometimes been quoted as a final proof of the absolute infallibility of Old Testament Scripture; "the Scripture cannot be broken." But the whole passage is *hypothetical.* Charged with blasphemy, and making himself the Son of God, he replies, "Is it not written in *your* law, ' I said ye are gods,' If he called them gods unto whom the word of God came, and the Scripture cannot be broken." This clause is to be taken in a restricted sense, says Bloomfield, — "the Scriptures cannot be taken exception against." The whole passage is an argument from their avowed belief, and not any positive assertion of his own. He thus calls the law "*your* law," and seems to say, " If he called them gods, &c., and if the Old Testament writings ought not to be loosened, (in their moral authority,) how say ye," &c. — Campbell translates it, "and if the language of Scripture is unexceptionable.".

In addition to this, we have recorded a case in which Jesus quotes a particular passage as "*spoken unto you by God,*" (Matt. 22: 31.) but this is in allusion not to Old Testament inspiration in general, but to the words uttered from the fiery bush. No doubt the Saviour frequently alludes to the Old Testament in the general sense in which I have spoken, as of Divine authority, and also as inspired, but not, therefore, of that sort of verbal infallibility which seems to be taken for granted rather than proved. There is nothing in the words of Jesus even as reported by his disciples, in the least staking the truth of Christianity upon the absolute verbal accuracy of the Old Testament.

If, however, it could be asserted and shown that the New Testament *writers* make this claim for the Old Testament, its weight would in some measure still depend upon whether we supposed *them* to be absolutely infallible because inspired. In fact, it would depend on whether we take for granted in the New Testament, what we have pretty well disproved as to the Old.

But without going into that matter very thoroughly just now, we have to weigh with care the language which the New Testament writers do use in regard to the Inspiration of the Old. Such words as these are used by the Apostles: " Lord, thou art God   *   *   *   *   who by the mouth of thy servant David hast said, Why do the heathen rage," &c. — (Acts 4: 24, and in Acts 1: 16,) " this Scripture must needs have been fulfilled, which the Holy Ghost by the mouth of David spake before concerning Judas." In these and similar expressions, it will be claimed that the influence of the Divine Spirit is directly taught to have guided quite supernaturally the minds of the Old Testament writers. St. Paul also quotes from Deuteronomy, thus: " The Scripture saith thou shalt not muzzle the ox that treadeth out the corn," and asks, " doth God take care of oxen, or saith he it not altogether for your sakes," and this will be brought forward as a proof that Paul viewed the Old Testament as infallibly inspired in all its parts.

But then we must bear in mind that similar language is made use of in regard not only to the writings, but the *personal* teachings of the Apostles of the New Dispensation, without any exceptions and qualifications. The Apostle Paul himself makes use of equally strong language to prove that all Christians, and especially teachers are also an inspired body. The latter (I Cor. 3,) are declared "laborers together with (or appointed by) God," to speak hidden wisdom and mysteries such as eye hath not seen, nor ear heard, &c., but which God hath revealed unto us by His Spirit." " Which things also we speak, *not in the words which man's wisdom teacheth, but which the Holy Ghost teacheth.* Who hath known the mind of the Lord, that he may instruct Him? *But we have the mind of Christ.*" Yet this strong language is used, not of Apostles only, but of Christian men, and especially teachers as a class, all of whom were in his view, not excepting himself, exceedingly imperfect in their utterances, — some of them "carnal," "envying," "full of strife and divisions." Indeed, the whole company of Christians is looked upon and spoken of by him as an inspired body, while yet at the same time, he even withstands the Apostle Peter to the face, because he " was to be blamed," and " walked not upright," so that " even Barnabas was carried way with their dissimulation."

In regard to the Old Testament, however, we shall be reminded of II Tim. 3: 16. " All Scripture is given by inspiration of God, and is profitable," &c. But that passage can be adduced to prove as we have seen no more than that " all divinely inspired Scripture is also profitable," &c., making the profitableness the test of the inspiration.*

If the genuineness of the second epistle of Peter be considered sufficiently established to render it canonical (and not a subsequent repetition of parts of Jude, as the language might seem to indicate, and as Eusebius and the Paulicians thought) there is in it a passage, often appealed to in regard to one class of writings in the Old Testament, i. e. the prophetic, which would challenge for them (according to St. Peter's view,) a more immediate divine supervision and approach to infallibility than other portions of the Old, if not of the New Testament, i. e. II Peter 1: 20–21. But for the reasons above alluded to, it cannot fairly be brought forward as a *proof* text. Eusebius says, " As to the writings of Peter, one of his Epistles called the first, is acknowledged as genuine. But that which is called the second, we have not,

* See the First Chapter.

indeed, understood to be embodied with the sacred books, (εν διαθηκον) yet as it appeared useful to many, it was studiously read with the other Scriptures." "Peter's Epistles, of which I have understood only one to be genuine, and admitted by the ancient fathers." *

If, however, this Epistle still be considered genuine, the teaching of St. Peter would seem yet to be very difficult to render clearly intelligible in any sense that we should find it easy to admit. To do so, we must adopt principles of interpretation, which, though followed by many of the more superstitious Jews, are hardly considered sound by intelligent Christians. What is meant by no prophecy being of any private, i. e. *individual* interpretation? Perhaps the sense given by Bishop Horsley is the best, i. e. that prophecies are not detatched predictions of separate independent events, but are united in system, all terminating in one great object, the Messiah's kingdom.

This would render the twenty-first verse clear and intelligible, "for the prophecy came not of old time by the will of men, but holy men of God spake as they were moved by the Holy Ghost." The meaning must be that the predictions did not originate in their own minds, but in the impulse of the Spirit, who made the organs of these holy men his own instruments for revealing the future. It is no part of our object here,

* Eusebius, Lib. III, Chap. 3.

to discuss the nature of prophetic inspiration, or to call in question that there may have been particular instances of such inspiration, both under the Old Testament and the New. But when from such a passage, Gaussen goes on to secure the same degree of infallibility to the *whole* of the Old Testament, by asserting that *all* the Scriptures of the Old Testament and of the New are prophetic,* it seems time that some boundary should be set to the enormous extravagance, which, under the pleas and exigencies of supporting a system of supposed orthodoxy, would destroy the true character of a thousand holy laws, and proverbs, passages of history and songs of praise, and grind up *all* the finest utterances of holy men into mystic prophecies. Indeed, if we wanted proof of the pernicious views of Inspiration we are opposing, it is just such results as these which render the pretext of establishing the infallibility of the Old Testament, would convert the whole into a mass of mystical prophetic fable. "Joshua was *as fully* a prophet of the Lord as Isaiah;"—*all* of them wrote the words of which St. Peter tells us "that none of them spake by the will of man. Surely, this is what Coleridge so justly complains of, "the ever widening spiral ergo from the narrow aperture of a single text."

We have thus seen that while in the New Testa-

* Chap. 6: Sec. 4 and 5.

ment, the Saviour refers to the Old Testament as generally inspired, and as of Divine authority for the purposes for which it was given, yet this is not done in such a way as to assert the infallibility of every part. The other view even if made out at all from the New Testament writings, can only be supported by taking for granted the absolute infallibility of these writers beyond what they would have claimed for themselves as living teachers.   And further, it can even thus only be proved by straining the meaning of two texts, II Tim. 3: 16; and II Peter 1: 20–21; the former by a misinterpretation of it, and the latter being of doubtful genuineness, and requiring to be most grossly perverted and enlarged, before it can avail for the purpose in question.

The results of this discussion, however, will be made more clear in the following chapter.

CHAPTER VII.

THE INSPIRATION OF THE NEW TESTAMENT NOT INFAL-
LIBLE OR VERBAL.

NO Christian on reading the New Testament, will fail to feel the internal evidences of a much higher degree of inspiration in it, than in the Old, each taken as a whole. If there is any exception to this, it is in regard to the Psalms, (which, strangely enough, were ranked among the Jews, with Hagiographa or least esteemed division of their Scriptures,) but which are commonly bound up together with the New Testament. Christianity stands on a higher level than Judaism.

But is it necessary to faith in Christ and Christianity, that we should esteem every part of the New Testament to have been so dictated by an unerring Spirit, as to be infallible itself? We do not here go into the question of the Canon, but only speak now in regard to those books unmistakably authentic, and felt by all Christians to be of Divine authority. We need not question that their inspiration formed a holy guidance, rendering these Scriptures a sufficient aid to the faith of the good, and an authority resting on the Church similar to that exercised by the Apostles in their lives and teachings. But they are not, therefore, to be esteemed absolutely exempt from human infirmity. This is the conclusion to which we must come.

Indeed, the only way in which any other result has been obtained, is from first assuming that the New Testament teaches the infallibility of the Old, and then arguing *a fortiori* that these later writings as being more important and useful, must be infallible also. The inconclusiveness of this whole process has been sufficiently shown.

Nearly all the assertions of the New Testament Scriptures in regard to Inspiration relate to the Old Testament and not to itself. In the Discourses of our Saviour preserved to us, full as they are of allusions to the Jewish writings, not a promise is given nor a word is said in regard to special Divine assistance to be extended to any authors of books as such, which were yet to be written. There is no prediction of any *writings* to be given by Divine direction. The assurances of the Holy Spirit are sufficiently clear, numerous and decisive, but relate to a general direction of the conduct and words of the disciples, giving them wisdom for each hour, and "bringing all things to their remembrance." But not a word is said of any especial guidance of the pen, as distinct from the oral teaching. No command is given beforehand, as to who should write, or what should or should not be written. No intimation is made that any records whatever were intended to be given to mankind. Jesus had promised his inspiring presence to the Church, but not a word is recorded of further or special inspiration for any documents such as now form our New Testament. If, therefore, we admit as much Divine authority for the writings of an Apostle, as we should for his words and teachings, it is certainly all that the Master requires or requests.

The strongest promise of Inspiration, — the passage most urgently quoted from the lips of our Saviour is perhaps John 14: 25–26. "These things have I spoken unto you, being yet present with you, but the Comforter which is the Holy Ghost whom the Father will send in my name, he shall teach you all things, and shall bring all things to your remembrance whatsoever I have said unto you." Let any man read over carefully the whole of that promise of the Paraclete from the sixteenth verse, and he will I think perceive that it is the assuring of an Inspiring

Presence with the members of his Universal Church, a promise which, while *inclusively* it would give a peculiar and restored vividness to all his personal teachings, was to be also "*another* Comforter that should abide with them *for ever*," and be a fountain of new and progressive instructions as they were able to bear them. Not a word is said specifically about guiding their writings. " When they shall deliver you up, take no thought how or what you shall speak, for it shall be given you in that same hour what ye shall speak, for it is not ye that speak, but the spirit of your Father which speaketh in you." Matt. 10 : 19, or as Luke expresses it, " the Holy Ghost shall teach you in the same hour what ye ought to say." Yet this strong language was never regarded as conferring absolutely *infallible* wisdom and knowledge and propriety upon the speech even of Apostles in every case where they were brought before rulers for Christ's sake. Would Paul himself have claimed it, when he said, " God shall smite thee, thou whited wall," and afterwards retracted and apologized, saying, " I wist not brethren that he was the High Priest, for it is written, thou shalt not speak evil of the ruler of the people." Why then should we pretend to claim, or rather to *wring* out of the general promise of the Paraclete (John 14 : 26,) an assurance of infallibility to each of the New Testament writers which even the more specific assurances of Matt. 10: 19, were never intended to convey? We may and ought freely to concede to the Sacred and Canonical writings of the Church, the same Divine Authority and guidance that inspired the personal teachings of their authors but no more. That inspiration and guidance is all sufficient in each case for the purposes intended, and it shall be until the end of time. But all claims beyond this can only throw suspicion on what are valid and true; —can only make infidels of many thinking men, and fanatics of the unthinking.

If now we turn from the words of Jesus to those of the New Testament writers themselves, it will not be difficult to ascertain whether they claim as a whole, any marked or distinctive pre-eminence for the inspiration of their writings over that of their own personal teachings. It is true, indeed, that St. Paul mentions some in his day as declaring of him "his letters are weighty and powerful, but his bodily presence is weak, and his speech contemptible." This might have been consistent enough with some modern theories of Inspiration. But St. Paul at least never dreamed of such a distinction, and repudiates it. "Let such an one think this," he adds, "that such as we are in word by letter when we are absent, (alluding to I Corinthians,) such will we be also in deed, when we are present." Of the Apostolic preaching he uses language as strong or even stronger than anything he ever says about writing. " I certify you brethren that the gospel which was preached by me was not after man, for I neither received it of man, neither was I taught it, but by the revelation of Jesus Christ." And yet he ever felt that both he and Peter had this treasure in earthen vessels neither were "already perfect." Of his writings, he speaks in very similar language. " If any man think himself to be a prophet or spiritual, let him acknowledge that these things which I write unto you are the commandments of the Lord." If ever there was a man truly and consciously inspired of God, it was Paul. And yet the lines between in-spired and human wisdom so ran into each other, that he could not always be certain in himself which was which. There are times when he can only say, " *I think* I have the mind of the Spirit." I Cor. 7: 40. At other times, he " *supposes* " what is good for the present distress, having " no commandment of the Lord," or speaks by "permission and not by com-mandment." There were in fact in his experience, very different degrees of certainty and fallibility at-tending his own Inspiration. It is true that in the First of Corinthians, he uses such strong language as this, "I command, *yet not I but the Lord*, let not the wife depart from her husband," &c. And then he adds, " But to the rest speak I, not the Lord,"—and further on, after giving his judgment, he says, "I think also that I have the Spirit of God." Some have, indeed, thought that δοκῶ here, so far from expressing a doubt, is emphatic, and implies the highest certainty. But this only shows the extent to which the best men will sometimes wring a sense out of the plainest language to support a pre-conceived theory. Bloomfield approves the rendering, "I *trust* that I have the Spirit of God;"—"denoting full persuasion though modestly expressed."

Nearly all the assertions of the New Testament writers as to Inspiration however, refer to the *Old* Testament, and not to the *New*. Of their own and of each others' writings, (except in II Peter, of which we have before remarked,) there is none of that self-assertion, or peculiar claim for these Scriptures as of more authority or infallibility than their living instructions, which we might have expected to find, if indeed, any such distinction existed in their minds.

To such an extent is this the case, that it is to tradition alone or circumstantial evidence, apart from their own claims, that we are indebted for our knowledge of who the writers of the four gospels were. Matthew begins his gospel without any intimation to us, of who is writing, or by what authority he writes. It is the internal character of his work, or the tradition of the Church, which assures us of its value and inspiration.

Nothing is claimed for it by the author or any other New Testament writer. Even the traditions are most perplexing, not informing us how or by whom it was translated into Greek, from the supposed original Aramaic, in which it is asserted to have been written. " The history of the present gospel of St. Matthew," says Westcott,* "is beset with peculiar difficulties, and the earliest writers are silent as to the circumstances which attended its composition. While using the Greek text, as unquestionably authentic, they recognize unanimously the existence of a Hebrew Archetype, of which they *seem* to regard the canonical book as an authoritative translation, or representative, but still without offering any explanation of the manner in which this substitution was made. Papias, possibly on the testimony of the elder John (though this is not clear,) states simply that " Matthew composed his history in the Hebrew language, but each interpreted it as he could." † " In the next generation, the Greek gospel was used most commonly by Justin, though he is silent as to the authorship." Afterwards it was recognized as the gospel of Matthew. Mark also begins without announcing himself, and is nowhere endorsed by any other New Testament author, and the same is true of the third gospel, though addressed to Theophilus and referred to in the Acts.

* Introduction, p. 194.   † Eusebius 3 : 39.

But this gospel of Luke affords the most decisive possible disproof of any belief by its author in modern views of Inspiration. For though carefully stating the ground on which it claims a peculiar regard on our part, yet by never alluding to any infallible guidance and dictation, it repudiates in the most complete manner, the consciousness or belief on the part of the writer, that he was guided in any such manner. Let any one carefully study Luke 1: 1–4, and while he will be convinced of the perfect sincerity, carefulness and trustworthiness of the author who tells with perfect simplicity, the grounds on which we may "*know the certainty*" of the things most surely believed by the first Christians, it seems impossible to suppose that he had at the same time, another conscious, demonstrable ground of security against all error, one capable of superceding all the rest, — i. e. the dictating guidance of an infallible Spirit, and yet failed to allude to it. If he felt this, why not assert it, instead of recapitulating his other and more human advantages, such as, that the things he writes were delivered to him by those who from the beginning were eye-witnesses of them, and officers of the Church; — that he had had perfect understanding of all things, and arranged the whole in an orderly narrative. Why urge all this, when he could have accomplished the end in view, i. e. securing credence of his facts, much more effectually and simply by asserting the infallible inspiration of the Holy Spirit? Why produce the inferior evidence, and omit the more demonstrative? It is incredible that he should do so, if he were conscious of possessing it. That single passage settles the whole matter.

There is a work called the Apostolic Constitutions, the first part of which was palmed off as the genuine production of the Apostles, some centuries before the latter part or eighth book was written. And though the last is clearly a fiction, and Luke's preface a simple and elegant statement of the fact, yet if the two are for a moment compared, the reader will see something of that self-assertion which would have been natural, had Luke desired to claim infallibility for his narrative

In Book VIII. chap. 3–4 of the Apostolic Constitution, we read, " Our discourse hasteneth us to the principal part of the portraiture of ecclesiastical affairs, that so, when ye have learned this constitution from us, ye who have been ordained Bishops by us, conformably to the will of Christ, may perform all things according to the commands delivered to us; knowing that he who heareth us, heareth Christ, and he who heareth Christ, heareth his God and Father, to whom be glory for ever, Amen. Wherefore, we the twelve Apostles of the Lord, who are now together, give you in charge these our Divine Constitutions, concerning every ecclesiastical form; there being present with us, Paul the chosen vessel, our fellow Apostle, and James the Bishop, and the rest of the Presbyters and the seven Deacons." This work closes with giving a list of the Canonical Books of the Old and New Testament adding to them, " the two epistles of Clement, and the Constitutions dictated to you, the Bishops, by me, Clement, in eight books, which it is not proper to publish before all," &c.

Luke never claims even the endorsement of a single Apostle, for his infallibility, much less the dictation of an infallible spirit. He had faith that words of truth and simplicity wing their way to every heart that loves the truth, and that Preface proves his confidence well founded. But the ill judged and erroneous claims of his later followers are thus clearly refuted by his own words.

Rev. 22: 19, in regard to "adding to or taking from the words of the prophecy of this book," has, indeed, been sometimes quoted as if the Apostle John at least was commanded to assure us of the infallible dictation of the whole of the New Testament. But on the Continent of Europe, from the time of Luther downwards, several of the best critics assert that not John the Apostle, but John the Presbyter was the author of the Apocalypse. Not to
10

dwell on this, however, the words used are expressly confined to the Revelations, apart from the other books of the New Testament, which were not collected into the same volume for about a hundred years afterwards. Indeed, the book of Revelation was not generally received into the Canon till two hundred years later.

To sum up now what has thus been advanced as to the claims which the books of the New Testament make on their own behalf, there are passages which speak of some of these writings as inspired, and as such each Christian must accept them. We will not discuss how far he is bound to receive every one of the minor epistles, (that is a question which belongs to the New Testament Canon,) but these books are inspired, as the Apostles themselves were inspired in their conduct while living,—no more and no less. There are certainly many passages, which taken alone might seem to speak as if the books then received as Scripture, were all infallibly dictated. But the expressions are quite as numerous, and even far stronger in favor of this dictation of all the unwritten words and even works of the Apostles, when they debated, disputed and contradicted each other,* almost as much as modern Christians do, but when yet an inspiring spirit brooded over the whole and

* Acts 15: 2; Gal. 2: 16-18.

conducted the Church to the loftiest truths and most glorious results. Although when brought before priests, kings and rulers, the human element still remained in the Apostles, so that they made hasty and un-Christ-like replies, yet still what Jesus had promised was gloriously verified in their lives and words as a whole. " It is not ye that speak, but the spirit of your Father that speaketh in you." There were times when the inspiration rose within them, and became verbal and prophetic; there were others when the human element became more conspicuous. The promise was never meant to assert that every extemporaneous word a disciple of Christ uttered should be absolutely infallible. The promise, whatever it means, belongs to the saints of all time, and the Church at the Reformation rejected the interpretation that declared itself infallible. But it was a promise richly fulfilled of a guidance sufficient for all real purposes. The occasion was to give practical wisdom, and bring out of the depths of their pious hearts, its own inspiration, better adapted to each combination of circumstances, than any studied rhetoric or elaborated reasonings. There are occasions when the very imperfections of an honest, holy soul become the greatest perfection. And when we have sought truth with our best powers, the highest wisdom and inspiration which is in us at the hour of action, ought ever to be the same in its practical effects upon us, as if it were absolute and unerring certainty.

Now all this is plain and clear enough in regard to the lives and unwritten teachings of Evangelists and Apostles, and even of the saints of all ages in proportion to the exigencies of the case, nor does it make any Christian of experience in these things, doubt the living reality of Christianity. Indeed, he regards all other claims and views of Divine guidance now as fanatical. Why then is it, that when we come to the *writings* of the same men two thousand years ago, we should want to use the *very word inspiration* in a different sense, and question the reality of the gift, if it render not the individual document absolutely and verbally faultless? For the practical guidance of the Church, rightly received, the New Testament is the same thing as infallible, and yet speculatively, there must ever be allowed owing to the human element, room for vast exceptions.

In the Old Testament, (the inspired Preface to the New,) we have seen that Genesis is not scientifically infallible, when it says, the heavens and the earth and all their host were created in six days. All this is but the Preface to the Divine law which Moses gave the Jews, the wisest and best for the age and for the people. Moses was inspired to utter great truths in his day. It is of no importance whether he or Samuel began to commit these books to writing, and whether

Hilkiah or Ezra finished correcting the Pentateuch. Whoever wrote it, did so to teach the Jews that Divine wisdom and power founded all Nature, and gave to it, and to man, their present laws. The Cosmogony of the day in all those nations from the Oxus to Egypt and Phœnicia, taught the people as a part of the great unwritten creed, that the creation took place in six days, just about as it is recorded in Genesis, and the inspired writer would no more have thought of stopping to correct the belief of that age on that subject, had he known better, than he would have stopped to teach the Copernican system, and set right all their notions about the rising and the setting sun. His inspiration led him to teach the Jews this great truth, that God did it. Whether creation was effected by laws extending through vast ages, or by specific interferences, was not even the point, but *God did it.* That is the inspired truth which has given its vitality to Genesis.

And now when we open the New Testament, we may not, because we must not be afraid to admit that there are errors and discrepancies in it, just such as honest, earnest, pious men would be almost sure to fall into, because they were men, — some of them unlearned and ignorant men, but none the less truly inspired, enlightened and elevated by the spirit of God on that account.

Thus in the genealogies;—we need not follow all

the attempts to reconcile the plain discrepancies of Matthew and Luke, but just take by way of illustration the *number* of ancestors of our Lord as given in Matthew 1: 17. "So all the generations from Abraham to David are fourteen generations, and from David unto the carrying away into Babylon are fourteen generations, and from the carrying away into Babylon unto Christ, are fourteen generations." Now it is clear that fourteen were *not* all the generations from David to the carrying away into Babylon. Dr. Robinson in the Notes to his Harmony, clearly admits this, — "between Joram and Ozias in verse eight, three names of Jewish kings are omitted viz., Ahaziah, Joash and Amaziah.* Further between Josiah and Jeconiah in verse eleven, the name of Jehoiakim is also omitted. If these four names are to be reckoned, then the second division, instead of *fourteen* generations, will contain *eighteen*."

To account for this, Bishop Newcombe and others, have denied the genuineness of verse seventeen. But if it is not genuine, no part of the first two chapters are. "*All* external testimony of manuscript and versions is in favor of it," as Dr. Robinson admits. Such omissions sometimes do occur in these tables, often the Rabbis tell us, because the men were "wicked and impious." But this could hardly have been the case with Joash. At any rate, many worse kings' names

* See II Kings 12: 21; and 14: 1; and II Chron. 24: 27.

are inserted, and similar omissions occur in other genealogies, without any such reason being possible.* A
more specious reason is that these tables must have
been so arranged, and omissions made for the greater
convenience and ease of remembering the rest. But
in order to make out the fourteen generations in this
second case, the name of David has to be counted
twice, once at the last of the first series, and once at
the beginning of the second. If the writer of this
might have felt at liberty to strike out the names of
three generations for the sake of uniformity, he would
at least have left the fourth in for the sake of making
this number come right without counting the name of
David twice. No; it has been *a mistake*. Some careless scribe from whom Matthew copied the genealogi-
cal table had omitted these four names. This supposition is certainly more creditable to the integrity of the
writer of the seventeenth verse than to suppose he
knew at the moment he was writing "fourteen generations," that there were in reality seventeen. The
author of that verse, I think, believed just what he
wrote, although Strauss, of course, thinks he did not.
But Matthew was not infallible. So there will be
found an anachronism in Luke's statement in regard
to the enrolment.

But a more important matter for consideration here,

* See Ezra 7: 1-5, compared with I Chron. 6: 3-15.

than these slight discrepancies, is the very striking and *verbatim agreement* of large portions of Matthew, Mark and Luke, the three Synoptical Evangelists, as they are termed. To those who are familiar with the discussions on this subject, the following explanation will perhaps seem unnecessary, but for many readers they will be useful.

If any one will take Robinson's Greek Harmony of the Gospels, or even his English Harmony, and begin at section fourteen, he will be struck with the close similarity and even identical language in which each of the three Evangelists give their accounts of the Ministry of John the. Baptist. Or if any one will read together Mark 1: 2–8; Matthew 3: 1–12; and Luke 3: 3–18; he will be perfectly sure, either that these writers copied one from another, or else that all copied from some common pre-existing source of information. They, each of them for instance, quote Isaiah 40: 3, in just the same manner. The three accounts of the Baptism of Jesus, are almost equally similar. So in sections twenty-nine and thirty-one of Robinson, — the miraculous draughts of fishes, and the healing of Peter's wife's mother, and in many other places, it is not merely that the words attributed to our Lord and to other speakers are so similar, but that the narratives are in parts so word for word alike, as to assure the reader that they had before them some common source of information, unless as I have said, the the last copied from the first. It used to be supposed that this was the proper method of accounting for these and similar passages. A more close examination has, however, convinced many that there must have been, before either Matthew's, Mark's or Luke's gospel was written, a synopsis of the Life of Christ in common use among the Christians. This, the synoptical Evangelists embodied in those parts in which they thus closely resemble each other. In writing, every author added such further facts as he knew and wished to convey, and with such particular comments and explanations of the whole, as were necessary to make the gospel intelligible to those to whom he wrote.

The writer has before him a Life of Christ formed simply on the basis of inserting only those passages of the three first Evangelists, which are related by any two or more of them, and which, it is clear, must have formed parts therefore of the original synopsis. It makes a very complete history of Jesus, from the point where Mark begins, i. e. the Baptism of John. In fact, it puts us in a position to say that we know what that common mother gospel was,—the Synopsis which formed the basis of the first three.

Whether this Synopsis was even reduced to writing before the first of our gospels was composed, is an open and much disputed question. Westcott and others seem rather to take it for granted, than stop to prove that this gospel was oral and not written.   In Chap. III, on the origin of the Gospels, Mr. W. seems to think that "the spiritual position of the Apostles was incompatible with the design of forming a permanent Christian literature, while yet favorable to its formation."   He says, "they seem to have placed little value upon the written witness to words and acts, which still, as it were, lived among them.   The 'coming age' to which they looked forward, was not one of arduous conflict, but of complete triumph.   But while everything shows that the Apostles made no conscious provision for the requirements of after times, in which the life of the Lord would be the subject of remote tradition, they were enabled to satisfy a want which they did not anticipate.   That which was in its origin, most casual, became in effect most permanent by the presence of a divine energy."   The national character of the Palestinian Jews, was, he thinks, generally alien from literature.   "The rules of Scriptural interpretation, the varied extension of the law, and the sayings of the Elders, were preserved either by oral tradition, or perhaps in some degree by secret rolls, till the final dispersion of the Jewish nation led to the compilation of the Mishna.   'Commit nothing to writing,' was the characteristic principle of the earlier Rabbins, and even those who like Gamaliel, were familiar with Greek learning, faithfully observed it."

The Apostles, he says, commenced with preaching not writing, and this was the foundation of the Apostolic Gospel, yet it caused no drawback from its final completeness. " The Gospel was a growth, not an instantaneous creation. The synoptical Gospels were the *results*, not the foundation of the Apostolic *preaching*. The primary Gospel was proved, so to speak, in life, before it was fixed in writing. * * * The oral collection thus formed, became in every sense, coincident with the " Gospel," and our Gospels are the permanent compendium of its contents." " Till the end of the first century, and probably till the time of Justin Martyr, the " Gospel" uniformly signifies the substance and not the records of the life of Christ."

Perhaps this subject may best be illustrated by the so called Apostle's Creed, which was clearly the summary of the catechetical teaching, in which all the candidates for baptism were instructed orally before being propounded for admission, and which they were taught with an increasing uniformity, to repeat memoriter before the Church, on being received for baptism. " I believe in God the Father, Almighty, Maker of heaven and earth," &c. The first copy of this committed to writing, that we have, is that by Irenæus, but it had been in use orally a long time, and was a gradual growth, one or two of the clauses, such as that of the 'communion of saints,' the holy Catholic Church, and the descent into hell, being later additions. But it was the oral confession, long before it became the written creed of the Church. And it is supposed that gradually the substance of the united Apostolic testimony, as to the life of Christ, condensed itself into that mother Gospel which the three have made the basis of their written accounts of the Saviour.

That large portions, if not the whole of it, were, however, committed to writing before our Evangelists took the pen, seems to me almost demonstrable from the use of words so precisely the same in particular parts, while the freedom from exactness with which they use language at other times would seem to indicate that they did not generally stop to make extracts, but trusted to a memory which was quite familiar with the whole story. Luke 1 : 1, seems to allude to written accounts as verse second does to traditionary accounts at that time, whenever it was, pre-existing. It was not, then, that the Evangelists copied purposely one from the other, as some have tried to establish. There are no breaks, or marks, or changes of style, such as that would lead us to expect, but there is an easy flow, like that of men writing out what they had long been accustomed to talk over in the same language for the most part, and only in a very rough kind

of order. But it was yet often with that verbal identity of phrase which must have arisen from the precise
words having been previously written out somewhere.

In the Gospel of John, on the other hand, there is
no allusion to this synopsis, which can only be accounted for by supposing either that it was written
very early, even before the synopsis had come into use,
or at a period after the substance of it had been incorporated by the other three, and all that was esteemed
desirable was supplementary matter. Some have,
therefore, assigned to the fourth gospel the earliest
date of any of the four, while others more correctly
consider it (as the earliest traditions assert) to have
been written considerably after the other three. The
more numerous quotations from the other Evangelists, and the allusions to Gnostic heresies by John,
must settle this. Tischendorf has pretty well shown
that this Gospel must have been written and used in
the Church as early as the first quarter of the second
century or earlier, yet clearly not until the other
three had obtained currency.*

There is, indeed, nothing in all this that *need* interfere with the common views of plenary inspiration.
Yet a close study of the four Evangelists, comparing
them in this light, will show the human element of
Inspiration in a striking point of view. Perhaps the

* See Christian Examiner, July, 1866.

most important apparent discrepancy which is found between the Synoptical Gospels and John, is this, that from the former it is quite certain that Jesus and his disciples partook of the feast of the Passover on the night on which he was betrayed, while from the latter, (John) it would appear as if the Passover was not celebrated by the rest of the Jews until after sentence against him by Pilate. Robinson has very ably attempted to reconcile the difficulty by supposing that John is speaking of the Passover *festival* of unleavened bread, after the supper had been eaten.* He supposes, therefore, that the Saviour partook of the Paschal Supper on the same night as the rest of the Jewish nation, and that they had already partaken of it when he was betrayed. Perhaps it cannot be said that this view is absolutely irreconcilable with the language of John, as many have thought, and yet there are so many passages which seem to imply that *no part* of the festival had commenced when Judas went out of the supper room,† and the Passover was part of it, that the appearance certainly is that of an anachronism on the part of John.

Nor should it here in fairness be forgotten that there is a similar appearance of mistake in John 18: 3, where Judas with a band of men and officers, is

---

* See Robinson's Harmony, Greek Sections 133–158, Notes.

† John 13: 1, 29; 18: 28.

represented as approaching Jesus in the garden, with *lanterns and torches*, as well as weapons. We cannot say certainly whether the night was clear or cloudy, but this we know, that since it was on the night of the Paschal supper, it was the fourteenth day from the new moon, when it, therefore, was at the full. In the early part of the evening, the rays of the moon might have been kept somewhat from the garden of Gethsemane, by the shadow of the Mount of Olives behind which it would rise, i. e. in the east, but as at this period of the month, the moon rising when the sun sets, it must have been now far advanced on into the noon of night. If it were clear, the moon would now be shining down in full brightness on the marble splendors of that temple, under the walls of which Jesus must have passed before crossing the brook Kedron, to enter the garden of Gethsemane, under the shadow of its olive trees. And yet, whether shining or cloudy (and it clearly was not raining,) it seems difficult to conceive the necessity or usefulness of torches and lanterns at the full of the moon. Perhaps it was the mention of the torches and lanterns that suggested to Dr. Watts, these lines: " Twas on that *dark* and doleful night," &c., but a little reflection would have shown him that outside at least, it must have been just the opposite, nor is it easy to see how either clouds or mountains, shadows or trees could have made artificial lights useful as some have suggested. It appears more like the imperfection of the memory of an aged man so sure of his substantial accuracy that he did not stop to report and perfect his recollections.

I have thus expressed some of the difficulties that appear to stand in the way of the usual theory on the subject of Inspiration, both in regard to the Old Testament, and the New. But on the other hand I find the proofs of an overpowering Inspiration running through these books, and nowhere more evidently than in that very Gospel of John, the author of which appears, however, to have been betrayed by an imperfect memory into some inaccuracies, unimportant to his subject.

CHAPTER VIII.

AUTHORITY IN RELIGION.

THERE is a growing tendency towards a universal scepticism as to the old forms of expression in which the most vital parts of Christian faith have been enwrapped for centuries; and to the superficial, it may perhaps seem that the concessions we have made, might encourage this disposition to a dangerous degree. But there is also among the deep thinking and philosophical, a tendency earnestly promoted by men like Coleridge, to come around to the most fundamental principles of Christian truth as the only possible basis of all real knowledge and true philosophy.

A hundred years ago, Hume sneered at what he mockingly called 'our most holy religion,' because, he said, it is founded upon faith rather than upon reason. But one of the most profound philosophers of our day, Sir William Hamilton, shows that reason itself must rest upon an ultimate groundwork of faith, not only in Religion, but in all real science, and quotes from the writings of the good old Christian Father, Augustine, as containing the best declaration he can find of the relations of faith and reason in Philosophy. Nor will it be any real digression from the work before us, if, before going further, we here pause awhile, to show the proper province of Authority as distinct from Reason in Religion, the relations of the πιστις to the γνωσις.

There are some even in the Protestant Church, who assign so very narrow a scope for Reason in Religion, as to leave it doubtful if there is in their view, any such thing as *a Science* of Theology at all, and whether our knowledge of Religion and of God ought not to be a simple acquiescence and unreasoning reception of certain words of Scripture, without even any due consideration of all that they may possibly mean.

Others have denied the validity of all processes of reasoning as to the bases of Natural Theology, but referred as Dr. Mansel does, our knowledge of the very existence and attributes of a Supreme Being, to a mere direct and unreasoning feeling, a sort of instinct of our natures. This is pietism and not piety. John Stuart Mill in the seventh chapter of his Examination of Sir William Hamilton's Philosophy, has, it seems to me, incontrovertibly answered all the reasoning of Dr. Man-

sel, and reduced it fairly to the most absurd conclusions.

Practically it is most important that we should be
assured that Theology not only is a science, orderly
and clear, but one that is the simplest in its elements,
the most demonstrative in its reasonings, and the most
sublime in its conclusions; the most growing and
comprehensive of sciences, because, in fact, it embraces
and harmonizes them all. For as every scientific truth,
when discovered, enlarges our knowledge of the works
and character of God, thus enriching our Theology, so
all true reasonings lead but to fresh revelations of the
character and will of God. He, therefore, who de-
preciates Reason in Religion, despises the sources
of all our most advanced knowledge of Religion itself.

But yet, he who attempts to discover Divine truth
by any processes of Reasoning *alone*, and apart from
that just submission of the soul to true authority,
which reason requires as a previous condition, is also
the man who is certain to end in not having any religion at all. In this, Theology is not different from
every other science, but follows the analogies of them
all. "The undevout Philosopher is mad," anywhere
and everywhere.

To illustrate this, let it be considered in the first
place that the largest number and the most important
of all our beliefs, as well as actions, are as a matter of

fact, based, not on Reason, but on Authority. Let any man, Christian or Infidel, examine his life for a day, and see which ultimately moves or guides him in the most important concerns, pure reason or authority. If he is a *little* unwell, he may treat sickness by his own reason, but if the case become serious, the same man puts himself under the authoritative direction of his physician. Suppose the doctor were to come to his bedside, and say, " my friend, physicians are fallible, trust not to their directions, but reason out your own case; here is a work that refers all pathological symp-toms to their proper diseases, and here is the Pharma-copia. Put no faith in the authority of doctors, they are fallible, study for yourself. Determine from this book your disease, and see there your remedy." The patient would reply, " I have more faith in your authority on a question of health, than in my own reasoning on these books." And thus ever the more serious the case, the more does the mind seek authority rather than rea-son for its actual and practical guidance.

In family-life, suppose a parent to teach his chil-dren to receive nothing on his authority, or that of law, or custom, or the Sabbath School, or the Scrip-tures, but on their own *reason* alone, and their own sense of the right, the true and the beautiful! All will admit that the child must *begin* by copying holy examples, by obeying the instructions of parents and teachers, by yielding to authority, and this not from fear but *faith*, in order to form the best conceptions of life and virtue. Reason may come in afterwards to discriminate between the better and the worse, but there could be nothing to reason about, until a conception of first principles had been received by faith, upon the authority of some instructor.

Nor is this true only in practical *life and action*. It is equally so in matters of speculation. Take a case of the *purest* reason; where all shall depend on the correctness of some calculation. How does the astronomer gain the greatest final certainty of the correctness of the whole? Is it not when he and his friends have independently gone over the figures *many times*, or all come to the same conclusions by various processes. He thus becomes assured of the correctness of his own reasoning, from the *authority* of numerous tests. Certainty in the results of his reasoning, is based finally on *faith*. This final certainty is obtained by ninety-nine out of a hundred, not from any reasoning at all, but from faith in the word of others. Further still, the profoundest philosopher, where he receives one truth on his own reasoning, receives a thousand others upon the conclusions of proper authority. So little are the greatest and wisest guided by mere reasoning.

And this prepares the way for another remark, that

not only *practically* do we rest more of our conclusions on faith in authority, than on the deductions of reason, but that theoretically and philosophically reasoning itself on all ordinary subjects, even of a scientific character, rests upon a basis of *Authority.* Sir William Hamilton on this point, quotes the words of St. Augustine as strictly accurate. "We *know* what rests on *reason,* we *believe* what rests on *authority.*" But, Sir William adds, "reason itself must rest at last upon authority; for the original data of reason do not rest upon reason itself, but are necessarily accepted by it, on the *authority* of what is beyond itself. These data are, therefore, in rigid propriety, *beliefs* or *trusts.* Thus it is that in the last resorts, we must perforce philosophically admit that belief is the primary condition of reason, and not reason the ultimate ground of belief. We are compelled to surrender the proud "*Intillige ut credas*" of Abelard, to content ourselves with the humble "*Crede ut intelligas*" of Anselm.

Of course, in all this we must bear in mind that the term Reason is used in different senses by different writers. Thus far we have used it for the reasoning power simply, as distinct from those first principles, and direct, intuitive beliefs, which constitute that basis of authority on which all processes of reasoning are conducted. But there are some who, on the other hand, in drawing a distinction between the understanding and the reason, make it *comprehend* all those first principles which cannot be proved, and which (as Aristotle says) we must receive from some *authority.* Those who wish to exalt reason, then, make it include these subjective, intuitive and authoritative beliefs of the mind itself. This is a mere question of definitions. In this view of reason, authority is not only a part, but the most *vital* and fundamental part of all reason, instead of something separate and distinct if not opposed. Authority is thus a something without which reason could not for a moment exist, any more than a house could stand without a foundation ; and thus we see, as Sir William Hamilton asserts, that all *reasoning* must rest at last on *faith* in authority, and that faith does not rest upon reason, but the reverse.

All reasoning, therefore, is the comparison of seeming authorities, and thus discriminating more accurately the mere specious and seeming from the true and eternal. It is the art of weighing authorities, when they are only probable, and not absolute; of exploding the false, and separating the truth from the error it contains.

We see, then, that all which we call knowledge, even scientific knowledge, is the result of a union of the two, — reasoning and authority, — and is brought home to us as certain, not through the understanding alone, but through the united operation of the *under-standing* and *faith* in certain first principles which cannot be proved, but are received from some authority. Reasoning in science, without authorities, could never conduct us to the certainty of anything.

To apply all this now, first to Natural Religion, and then to Revealed, I desire to show that reason without authority in Religion tends to Atheism, while a blind reverence for authority without reason tends to superstition. There is, indeed, often more superstition in science than in religion.

1. Natural Religion at least must be considered, not only as a science, but a *pure science*; it belongs to the real as distinct from the formal sciences, (which latter are, in fact, simply forms, which the mind necessarily adopts in the presence of reasoning.) It stands at the very head of all real, pure science, embracing Natural Theology, and lying at the foundation of morals, of law, and of all true politics. But while the various theories on all these subjects, show how much erroneous reasoning may lead astray, yet it is not so much this that produces mistakes as the want of a clear recognition of the authority of certain *first principles*, upon which all true reasoning must be founded.

Dr. Mansel's Limitations of Religious thought appears to me to fall into just this very error, or at least it is liable to lead others into it. The eloquent

Author of Reason in Religion even while exhibiting as his own belief a most refreshing and eminently living, devout and worthy faith in God, in
Providence and in prayer, yet will not begin the
the attempt to *prove* the existence of a Supreme
Being. He seems freely to admit the futility of all
attempts to demonstrate God to the understanding, to
establish the fact of God-head by induction. He
concedes to the atheist, to the positivist the inadequacy
of such demonstration, the inconsequence of most of
the reasoning employed for this end. This may spring
from a certain reverence for Scriptural and Church
authority in Dr. Mansel, or [from the authority of the
Pure Reason in Dr. Hedge, but it might lead thousands
to Atheism; for a God who gave no proof of his
existence to my understanding, would be a Being,
whose existence I should have no right to recognize
reasonably. That is, it is through the Understanding
as the medial faculty that Reason enables us to know
the existence of a God.

It can and must, therefore, be maintained that Theology, — Natural Theology is a pure and perfect *science*, that the knowledge of God thus taught is an
ever growing science, the most perfect of all *demonstrations*, and the most excellent, comprehensive and
delightful of them all. Its language and that of
Scripture coincide. "Thus saith the Lord, Let not
11

the wise man glory in his wisdom, neither let the mighty man glory in his might, let not the rich man glory in his riches, but let him that glorieth, glory in this: that he *understandeth and knoweth me*, that I am the Lord, which exerciseth loving kindness and judgment and righteousness in the earth, for in these things I delight, saith the Lord."

It is becoming the fashion of the day to decry Paley and to show what most have long perceived, that all his arguments from design, so suggestive, so lucid and capable of being indefinitely extended, prove nothing to the man who chooses to disbelieve all his intuitions. But there is no proving a single truth of *any* real science to the man who pursues such a course, because, as we have seen, all reasoning rests ultimately upon the authority of intuitions. But to one who admits that where we perceive marks of design, we are so constituted that we cannot doubt the existence of a designer, — then all of Paley's arguments that there are marks of design; i. e. not of adaptedness but of adaptation in the physical universe, forms a complete proof through the understanding of a personal God though resting upon a basis of the purest reasoning.

And yet we are asked to concede to the Positive Philosopher, the futility of attempts to demonstrate God to the understanding. Again let us say, that while the understanding alone, and apart from the authority of intuitions, cannot demonstrate the exististence of a God, yet it is only because it cannot demonstrate *any thing else in science.* It is the want of a reverend and intuitive belief in *causation,* that is the sole cause of Comte's Atheism, the very essence of the Positive Philosophy, and Stuart Mill has well shown that this defect of his Philosophy, this confusion of all antecedents, those which are causes, and those which are only conditions, renders it absolutely impossible scientifically to prove or to know *any thing,* and only enables us to *arrange* what is already known.

But if we only start with the intuitive belief in causation, that whatever has had a beginning, must have had a cause, and if the world as it now exists, all complicated, ever had a beginning, it must have had a cause, then through a chain of antecedents reason will conduct all back and back inevitably to a first cause. And then Natural Theology, the knowledge of a first cause, his personal existence and attributes are demonstrable by science, and can only fail of being proved as such to the man who denies that *any thing* can be proved by induction, or denies some other of those intuitions, necessary to the scientific knowledge of any real truth. Is any one prepared to concede all this? Comte's Philosophy is science turned upside down. With the most lucid and beautiful method for arranging, *teaching* and explaining science, after it is once known, it would destroy the possibility of proving, that is of *knowing* anything. The secret of his error was a want of reverence for the Divine authority of intuitions. What had he to put in place of this? Mills well replies, " I am ashamed to say *Phrenology.*" This lack of a humble submission of the soul to the proper authority of these, and the seeking of their fuller, clearer revelation to the soul, is the chief danger in regard to Natural Religion. With the cultivation of this, a boundless field opens, and everlasting sources of new knowledge of God and duty are progressively attainable through and of the understanding.

Let any one study the history of Moral and Metaphysical Philosophy among those nations not favored with the light of revelation, as exhibited by Professor Maurice in the Encyclopedia Metropolitana, and he will see how this sort of scientific knowledge of a personal God was gradually educed through long ages, and much speculation of reason progressively, until first Anaxagoras, then Socrates, and then Platonism with its lofty Theism, gradually merging itself into richer streams of Christian truth, destroyed all other philosophy, and receiving baptism, entered into the Church, where it has since flowed on in the united tide of Reason and Revelation; and the Christian Monotheism is flowing onward at this moment to all the nations of the earth, the real basis of all other science.

And now to apply all this to Christianity; what becomes of Mr. Hume's objection that it is founded upon faith, and not upon Reasoning? We may admit the fact, and humbly accept and love Christianity just because it comes to us first of all as an *authoritative* revelation. Jesus "taught as one having authority," and not as the scribes. He did not attempt to demonstrate anything by argumentation, but claimed for his words the authority of the most simple enunciations of eternal truth, and first principles, which no reasoning can make plainer. His words are self-evidencing, and the pure in heart feel their authority by a direct appreciation, just as they thus "see God."

M. Renan, however, tells us that Jesus was a wonderful rustic of glorious intuitions, and who, if he had only had a good philosophical education, might have expressed his very profound views in a way more consistent with reason; that it is a sad pity he should have talked of God as a *personal* Father, and of Universal Providence, when in him first the highest Deity yet developed woke to consciousness. But what says Jesus of his own teachings? " Heaven and earth shall pass away, but my words shall *not* pass away." They are eternal. They are Divine. They speak with the authority of God directly to the soul. They are to be henceforth the axiom truths of all future possible religion.

Conceive Euclid, after he had finished his thirteen books, standing in the court of Ptolemy, and saying, "Kings and Emperors may rise and fall, Greece may forget her glorious history and literature, and the empire of the Ptolemies shall crumble, till Egypt is the basest of the kingdoms. Yea, it and Greece and Rome shall all pass away, but my words shall not pass away, but exercise a dominion over all coming time. They are revelations of Formal Science; and all coming ages shall build on what I have here wrought. And so Christianity comes to us, not indeed as a series of demonstrations of a formal science, but as the expression of absolute and eternal truths and the essence of all *real* science; truths that can never die, because they are final, and come home to all our hearts with the authority of intuitions, the authority of God. This is what Jesus meant when he said, "Heaven and earth shall pass away, but my words shall not pass away."

But Christianity is all simple faith, and nothing more, say some. It allows no room for progress, no scope for progress by reasoning. That view, however, is all pietism but not piety. One might as well say that the axioms of Euclid afforded no scope or basis for progressive reasoning or for any future progress in Mathematics.   Why, they are the foundations of it all.   And so we may say of Christianity, it is the fountain and foundation of the world's progress practically in the knowledge of God, and the morality of the human race, and its growth in all real science.   Look at the history of *doctrines* in the Church.   Christian truth is a growing thing in the earth, and the reasonings of the Church through ages, have led to a more clear and discriminating knowledge of all its truths and its morals, and made that knowledge progressively possible to each age.   Our own civil war has been, in fact, a great ethical struggle between an antiquated and a progressive school of Christian thought.   It all arose out of the Churches, and has succeeded in adding another victory to growing Christianity in the Abolition of human slavery.   And thus it shall be till time shall end, reason will find its scope in comparing the authoritative teachings of all revelations, and thus purifying Christianity from the misconceptions of even Christian men, and carrying it to further practical results, while reason in Natural Religion is bringing to light new illustrations of the wisdom and power of God from every science and fact in nature.

Indeed, I am convinced that we shall all increasingly see and feel that Natural and Revealed Religion are not two antagonistic systems, one resting on reason alone, to the exclusion of. Revelation, and the other on

Revelation to the exclusion of reason. Rather is it that all the intuitional truths of Natural Religion are authoritative *revelations* which God has given to be developed and made clear by reason, and that all the revelations of Christianity, whether in the Scriptures or through the Paraclete, or through history, or through the power of living Christianity in the Church, or through Providence working in national struggles like ours, are authoritative declarations of his will, and mode of governing the world. All are comings of the Son of Man, and of his kingdom in the clouds with power and with great glory;—all are means of developing the thought, the *reason*, and the progress of mankind to work on through the boundless future.

Indeed, the distinction between the Natural and the Supernatural, though so apparent and important so far as our weak powers of comprehension are concerned, must fade into obscurity and dimness until the lines become obliterated, when we view the revelations of God, in reference to his own exertions of power, rather than our knowledge of that power. For what work of God is there in Nature, which, when looked at intently by itself alone, does not become Divine and *super*-natural to the eye of man,—the frost upon a window-pane, or the growth of a tree, or the life in man. On the other hand, those wonders which we call supernatural and most miraculous, are all natural to

Him, all exertions of powers easy and regular to Omnipotence, in harmony with the highest and most Universal laws, and made wonderful to us only by the weakness of our own minds. The water changed to wine at the word of the Master, we call supernatural, but the dew and the rain are each season changing quite as wonderfully to the holy and contemplative soul, through absorbtion into the juices of the vine, and formed after thorough fermentation into wine. Thus a higher and more constant and observing faith in God, sees miracles *every where*, in every answer to prayer, in the life and death of every child, in every step of Providence, and in every drop of dew and flash of sunshine, while reason also afterward sees in the same events, order, harmony, law; and *both* see truly and not contradictorily. Thus by the true and proper relations of authority and reason, restored through Christianity to the soul of man, all religion, natural and revealed, becomes one harmonious science, by which we see and feel the Divine power and efficiency every where at work throughout the Universe, and learn each our own places, and duties and destiny.

It cannot be said that views like these necessarily cut at the root of all proper submission of the soul to authority in Religion. They seem rather to establish it upon a true, solid basis. For the sources of our knowledge of religious truth correspond to those of all other truths, and may thus be briefly expressed: God is our Creator, and has given us all our powers.   We can only see what He has given us the power to see. He has enabled us to learn many of his thoughts and purposes and laws, as exhibited in the physical world, in one of the three following ways:

1. By a direct, certain knowledge, which we call sometimes instinct or intuition, as that by which a bird knows how to fly, or a fish to swim, or man believes in the uniformity of nature.

2. In part they are received upon the authority of others, such as parental or traditionary teaching.   Thus it is that we learn the truths of history.

3. In part by reasoning or the observation of sequences.

In like manner, moral and religious truths are made known to us.

1. In part through our religious and moral intuitions.

2. In part through Authority, such as (a.) Scripture, (b.) the law of the land, (c.) Parental teachings, (d.) the voice of the Christian Church.

3. In part by Reasoning, or the observation of moral sequences, both immediate and historical.

Now the real basis, or measure of authority for believing anything, is the probability of its truth, i. e. that we perceive it as God intended we should, our perception of it corresponding to his thought. The authority of no one source of instruction is absolute or infallible, but rather progressive. There are all sorts of different degrees and shades of authority, in proportion as confirmed by experience. Even Mathematical truths have their degrees of uncertainty, because, however absolutely true in themselves, our minds are fallible, and may err in working them out, so that we never feel perfectly sure from a single calculation that the result is correct. Can we then say that any instruction we may draw from the Bible possesses absolute and infallible authority? This will not be asserted of the *English* Bible, which is only a translation; and very few would declare their *own* translation of the Hebrew and Greek infallible. Much less so, can be the opinions of any commentator, learned or unlearned, as to its meaning. So that to each man in this life, the authority of what he derives from Scripture, can only be probable, not absolute or infallible in any case. In questioning the absolute infallibility of Scripture then, we do not thereby destroy its practical authority, when if its letter were ever so perfect, our minds and understandings of it must necessarily remain imperfect. Everything *to us*, must have its own *degree* of authority, nor can anything be practically infallible, we being fallible.

But if we once admit any deviation from infallibility, it is asked, where shall we stop? what is certain? There is no infallibility in the natural sciences; repeated and careful experiment is there the only basis of any fair degree of certainty. No man dreams of infallibility in any experimental knowledge, yet sufficient is obtained to enable us practically to rely and act just as if our knowledge were absolute. There are laws of the expansion of steam and of air, of winds and storms, so imperfectly known at present, that the most skilful mariner can only act on the best light in each case, and leave results with Providence. But there are other laws of winds and storms and the expansion of steam so well known, that he relies on them as infallible, and pledges the lives of hundreds daily, and all most dear to himself, on that practical knowledge. It is just so with Christian truths. Some of these we may not be sure that we rightly understand; some of the records of the past we may suppose to a certain degree imperfect and fragmentary. But on all the great vital matters of Christian faith, each step is so confirmed by experience as to leave the whole practically infallible for our daily guidance, and there is just that measure of evidence which is adequate for the present stage of our development, constantly growing upon us. This is sufficient in matters of science, and sufficient for practical life in everything else beside religion, — why not in it? It is all the certainty that

the nature of the human mind practically admits, and
it is infinitely better for us than any fancied infallibility, which might make us rest in the letter of Scripture,
instead of walking by a perpetual faith in the guidance
of the Holy Spirit.

Prior to the Reformation it was popularly supposed
that the Roman Catholic Church was an inspired, and
therefore infallible body. That very belief, most of all,
corrupted it. The Protestants destroyed the last part
of that claim by setting against it the Inspired Scriptures, which, on the same grounds, were popularly considered infallible also. But there were men, even then,
who perceived that the Bible, though inspired, was not
therefore literally infallible, and the great truth which
must finally re-unite the living Church of all ages in
one, is the knowledge that both the Church and the
Scriptures are truly inspired of God, — temples in
which he dwells and walks, — yet are they not thereby
infallible, but ever living and growing bodies in the
power of illumination they possess for the ages and
nations on which they operate.

CHAPTER IX.

THE CHRISTIAN IDEA OF THE INSPIRING SPIRIT.

WHEN Jesus was about to leave the world, he promised to his followers an Inspiring Spirit to be with them to the end of time. It was to be their monitor, advocate and comforter in all their perplexities, and the suggesting "spirit of truth," which was to show them more of the counsels of the Father than he himself had unfolded; while it brought back his own teachings also to their remembrance, and thus inspired their writings as themselves with a perpetual and accompanying Divine presence.

In the Christian writings, this Divine Spirit is spoken of sometimes simply as a *Force or Power*, with the mysterious workings of which we are but little acquainted. "The wind bloweth where it listeth, and thou hearest the sound thereof, but canst not tell whence it cometh, and whither it goeth; so is every one that is born of the Spirit.*" Sometimes it is spoken of as *a law*,— that is, a power operating regularly, and with certain courses of uniform sequence. Paul speaks thus of "the *law* of the spirit of life in Christ Jesus, making him free from the law of sin and death, assurring us that there are certain courses that quench and grieve it, while most fully it is the the Paraclete, the gift of the Heavenly Father to his children through Christ Jesus.

The most powerful agents in nature are the most silent and incomprehensible ;— light, air, electricity. Indeed, we seem only just becoming acquainted with those most potent forces of nature, by which we are yet momentarily surrounded.

As in the physical world, so is it in that of spirit. How little do we know of the nature of the soul that animates our bodies, the spirit that worketh within us. Even individually, our philosophers from Plato to Abercrombie philosophize at utmost on the dispositions of the individual, but how little has been thought of those more *collective*, spiritual forces by which minds operate on each other. The power of sympathy, the force of public opinion, and of social excitements are some of these. We are then surrounded by spiritual forces operating on us, and we in turn on them, and are moved above all as Christianity and experience teach,

* John 3: 8.

by one great Animating Spirit, whose influence upon us is exhibited by several most remarkable figures or symbols.

But the gospel of John preserves to us the record of a promise that can hardly be called a figure, the promise of the Comforter; the Paraclete, a term used by him alone, either in regard to the Saviour or to the Holy Spirit. For when Jesus is recorded as saying, "I will pray the Father, and he will send you *another* Paraclete," it implies that he is one, the first, and typical representative of the idea. In the First Epistle of John, this is distinctly declared. "If any man sin, we have an Advocate [literally a Paraclete,] with the Father, Jesus Christ the righteous." A passage like this will perhaps best show the difficulty of rightly expressing in any one English form of expression, what is said of that 'other Paraclete,' usually called by us the Comforter.

The promise of the Holy Spirit is, as we have seen, common to all the Evangelists and the Epistles, but that this Spirit is the Paraclete and is that other Paraclete capable of even more than supplying the personal ministry of Jesus Christ on earth, is the assertion exclusively of St. John.

To find any one other term that shall fairly and fully express the meaning of the Greek παρακλητος, has been the unsuccessful effort of eighteen hundred years.

In the Vulgate, Jerome seems to have given up the task in despair, and used the transferred word Paracletus, substantially retained to this day in the Douay. But Jerome only complied with the usage of still older versions, and the Latin Fathers, from Tertullian at least, do the same. Even the first of all versions the Peshito Syriac has not ventured to translate, but only to transfer the original term. Indeed, the Rabbins have done the same thing. No other tongue has any single word that can fully express all that is conveyed in this term, as the note below will show.*

* Etymologically the word παρακλητος from the verb παρακαλέω, would mean *one called to stand beside and therefore to aid* another. The Paraclete would be in this view, simply an *aid* or *assistant*, one perhaps waiting to be called upon for his aid, before it is granted. In classic usuage, from the time of Demosthenes, at least, this term and the verb from which it was taken, seem to have been often used in a special sense, for the summoning of a man's friends to attend his trial. Hence a *paraclete* was a "helper," an "encourager" of the tried and persecuted, and at last technically, an official advocate or counsellor in a court of justice. Something like this has been the view taken by the early Latin Church generally, as Archdeacon Hare has well remarked, so that it is by them commonly translated "Advocatus." I will send you another Advocate. But the inadequacy of this, as a full English translation, has been well exposed by Campbell. The advocate pleads only in presence of *the Judge*, and defends his client's cause often in his absence. No doubt this is very much the meaning of the term, as applied in that only other New Testament passage in which it is used. "If any man sin, we have an *Advocate* with the Father, Jesus Christ." And so Le Clerc, and so Knapp in modern times, have most erroneously

And perhaps some are almost ready to turn back to the method adopted by the Rabbins and the Latin

rendered it in John's Gospel. Grotius goes still further, — "I will send you another *orator*."

Another rendering therefore, has been suggested, which however, is no nearer comprehending all that the original suggests. Theodore of Mopsuesta, was perhaps the first who suggested that "*Teacher*" was the true sense, and even the judicious Campbell translates it "monitor," "prompter," because the assistance of the Spirit is *within* a man's own soul, and not externally on his behalf. And if indeed the aid of the Spirit were only negative, like that of the demon of Socrates, and not positive, — or only instructing the intellect, but not persuading the will, or quickening the affections, then "monitor" or "teacher" might do. But these terms are evidently inadequate.

Far nearer to the true sense would be that of *Counsellor*, such as Knapp has well shown, that the Advocates anciently were. Not so much pleading in court *for* the man under trial, but standing beside him to counsel and prompt and show him how best to win his own cause. Yet it may be doubted if even this gives us the full view of that wonderful promise. "I will send you another Paraclete."

To gather the complete sense, we must look, not so much at the Classical, as the Hellenistic and Ecclesiastical usuage and developments of this term. The Hellenistic writers give a *warmer* sense, especially to the verb. With them, it signifies "to console," "to soothe," "to encourage," and even the Rabbins seem to have transferred this term in much this sense, as Tholuck has shown. In Job 16 : 2, the Septuagint has παρακλητορ, and the version of Aquilla, made about A. D. 200, has the very term of our text "miserable *comforters* are ye all."

Accordingly, nearly all the Eastern Church, as Dr. Hare shows from Origen downwards, give *consolator, comforter*, for the sense of the term as here used. And hence at the Reformation, when the Spirit was poured out anew, Luther, Tyndale, and our English translators so ren-

Fathers, and *transfer* the words of the promise, confessing that in its fullness, it is untranslatable. But this only confesses the difficulty, without even attempting to remove it. Nor is such a practice without injury, as Archdeacon Hare remarks, "as it not only obscures our perception of the word thus imported, but by severing it from its etymological associations, deprives it of a portion of its power." Or if to Anglicise a Greek term, may make it more truly comprehended by a Greek scholar, it must make it harder to be understood by the people generally. I do not believe that we thoroughly understand anything, until we can intelligibly express it.

The difficulty of translating the word arises from its *comprehensiveness*. Instead, therefore, of restricting ourselves to any one word, let us define it in as many words as may be necessary to the idea intended to be expressed. The Paraclete is "one called in to administer spiritual aid." In I John 2: 1, this aid is advocacy with a third party, as we have seen. "If any man sin, we have an advocate, a Paraclete, with

dered it in the fourteenth and sixteenth of John. Yet against this term it has been justly remarked by Campbell, that "the part of a Comforter, is in its nature merely *occasional* for a time of affliction, whereas that of monitor, instructor, guide, is to imperfect creatures like us, *always* needful and important. "He will teach you all things, and remind you of all I have told you."

the Father." But in the promise of Christ to his disiples on parting with them, it is a spiritual and internal aid more directly to the soul itself; and hence it has been so variously rendered Teacher, Monitor, Consoler, Comforter.

The work of the Paraclete is not to plead for the disciple against outside parties, but internally to assist his own soul, by supplying all that can strengthen it in itself. This is what Jesus had done while with his followers, and what that other Paraclete was now to do.

The term "comfort" in its modern sense is not by any means comprehensive enough for this broad promise. But the fact is that our English word comfort itself has changed its meaning since Wycliffe and Tyndale first introduced this rendering into the English tongue.

Our verb "to comfort" is taken from the Latin of the Vulgate, *confortare*. It used sometimes to be written in English as in French *confort*, and was then applied according to its strictest etymology, from *con* and *fortis*, to make strong by communion, as Hare shows.

The Comforter, in this view, is one who binds the soul of man together, so as to make it inwardly strong. The Paraclete is this Comforter, not so much in the sense of making us *happy in feeling*, as possessed of that soul strength which prompts to duty, and through self conquest, makes the victory over outside difficulties easy and delightful. Dr. Johnson utters in the Rambler, a thought most pertinent here, that consolation and comfort are words which signify "rather an augmentation of the *power of bearing* trial, than a diminution of the burden."

But our modern English word comfort, gives to the ordinary reader, but a very inadequate idea of this strengthening energy, which quickens and thus inwardly aids, included in that promise of another Paraclete, to administer spiritual and universal *strength*, in whatsoever way it is needed.

The term Paraclete to be rightly understood, must embrace nearly all these more specific uses of it, that we have discussed. It is the "comforter," not merely as making happy but strong, and full of holy conscious *power*, and therefore rid of all uneasiness, self-possessed and hence happy. It is the "teacher," or "monitor," but not a merely intellectual teacher, a *guiding* and *guardian* Spirit, as Calvin well shows, making wise in mind through the proper poise of the affections. It is the "*counsellor*," the friend whose aid may be called in upon every trial, or any emergency, with the certainty of success.

It is, indeed, the "*Inspirer*" of the Church. Tholuck well says, "many resolve the promise of Christ in regard to the Paraclete into that of *religious inspiration*. The Spirit of God never comes without a religious inspiration and elevation, but he enters into the heart of the believer in such "inspiration," yet even because *He* is in it, this religious inspiration is different from all others."

The Paraclete is then most completely an Inspiring Spirit dwelling in the believer in Jesus, and supplying his personal presence and work on earth, uniting the whole Church into one living energetic and Divinely guided body to the end of time. Such is the Paraclete. When Socrates stood before his judges, in the most solemn moment of his life, tried and condemed for introducing a new Divinity, he answered his accusers, that a guardian spirit was ever accustomed to admonish him when he was about to do anything improper, that it was his daily monitor, and that as that morning, when about to leave home, it had not warned him, he felt sure he was acting rightly, and they wrongly. The fact is, account for it as we may, the best and wisest men of all ages, have ever believed, because they have felt within them, the guiding presence of the Divine Spirit, felt and owned its power as another spirit, another self, working within their spirits, not a mere influence, but a guiding presence.

Shall we then say that this promised Paraclete has been the possession of the good men of all ages?

That the Spirit of God guided the Old Testament saints, David declares. But not in that new living character and power, here declared as the peculiar guide of the believers in Jesus; not as the Paraclete, the Holy Spirit that inspires, quickens, consoles, and gives life, energy and guidance to the renewed and redeemed, walking in the steps of the Master.

The Monitor of Socrates, which he professed to hear from childhood, of which he was accustomed to speak familiarly, and to obey implicitly, always operated, he says, in the way of restraint, never of instigation. And even David, when he prays God not to take his Holy Spirit from him, expresses no such positive conconceptions of the Spirit as Jesus promises to his followers, who after faith in Him are sealed with that Holy Spirit of promise, the Comforter, which is the earnest here below of our inheritance above. This Paraclete is to abide with the Church forever, and guide all its members individually, and still more to guide the onward movements of that Church collectively.

Sometimes the power of this Spirit is compared, as we have seen, to *the wind*, in respect to the mystery of its origin, and the power of its workings and effects. What so viewless, so noiseless, so seemingly causeless and mysterious, as the gentle first rising pulses of air? Yet what so powerful and exhaustless as the wind, that raises the swelling and resistless billows or bears whole navies across the ocean, age after age, unwearied of its toil? The subject of an equally mysterious and powerful influence is every one that is born of the Spirit. Socially, again, it is compared to a baptism of fire, or a tongue of flame, in its animating, warming influence on Christian character, purifying all that is true, and also consuming the dross.

Yet the gentle, brooding, affectionate dove of Palestine, with its delicate hues, but easily repelled presence, is its favorite symbol. That is given as the messenger bird of the Spirit. As the *anointing oil* of the sons of Aaron spread an invisible and unique fragrance around the consecrated High Priest, enveloping his presence in a peculiar atmosphere, so does the Spirit throw an unseen but heavenly influence around the true Christian. " Ye have an unction from the Holy One, and know all things," says St. John.

As *a seal* affixes an image and ratifies and confirms all promises, so the spiritual are represented as " sealed with that Holy Spirit of promise which is the earnest of their inheritance." It puts the stamp of God upon the brow of the Christian, impressing the intellect, heart and life with its divine character and image; the intellect in the convictions it inspires, the heart in the conversion it induces, and the life in the conformity that follows. And as an *earnest*, or a small portion of wages given in advance, so is this spirit a foretaste of heaven, — heaven itself begun below.

Mosheim says, in his history of the Mennonites, that they make but little account of human creeds, because they base everything on the spiritual enlightenment of the Holy Spirit. No doubt many of all ages, and all sects, have mistaken the working of their own spirits, for the teachings of the Heavenly Comforter and guide, and doing so, have become fanatics. But after all, the most pernicious evil that could happen to a church, or a Christian, is the losing faith in that ever living presence. And in this age of controversy and perplexity, the words of this last promise of Jesus, the promise of a Paraclete, should be our comfort and our stay. It will give a heavenly instinct, a fineness and discrimination of spirit, that will lead us through the most complicated mazes of error, however specious. It will form a perpetual Providence. In all the trials and temptations, and struggles towards the light of truth, let not ambition guide the Christian, nor love of ease, nor of fame, nor pride nor indignation against wrong and ingratitude. But if he seek and expect the guidance of the Paraclete, the counsellor as well as the comforter of the Church, he will find it. He has a right to seek for and expect its holy and perpetual *Inspiration*. The Church is and was ever intended to be an *inspired* body, and in the earliest and purest
12

periods of Church history, this was the full faith, one that modern Christians have strangely lost. And ever present Divine aid must be, as Christians, our faith and hope and expectation. Not that we are to suppose and to act with the conceit of any personal or official infallibility, such as the ministers of Romanism have ignorantly and haughtily assumed. St. Paul declares even of himself, " We have this treasure in *earthen* vessels, that the excellency of the power may be of God, and not of us." Inspiration and infallibility are two distinct ideas. The inspiration of the Paraclete is indeed infallible in its own abstract nature, its Divine element. But it will prove such to us, on each occasion only in proportion as it is sought for or called to our aid, as its name essentially signifies. Yet notwithstanding all our infirmities, it shall in its operation, be sufficient for all practical utility. That which supplies the highest and best wisdom we can possibly obtain at the proper hour of action, is, and ought to be for all practical purposes of guidance, the same as infallible in its effects on our conduct. We may rely upon it, therefore, thus, and this will be our comfort, in going forth as sheep among wolves, that in every exigency, we shall receive words and wisdom, and a guidance for the hour, a practical and holy inspiration ; not such as shall supercede the hardest mental labor and thought, or more especially prayer and study, but *through* them *all*, shall guide us to the wisdom of the most proper course and word for each occasion.

The promise of Inspiration is no more and no less *now*, than when extended to the canonical writings of the Church of the living God, the Holy Scriptures. Their Inspiration was the divine and strengthening power, giving energy to those who wrote those words of comfort and strength for all ages yet to come, through the spiritual strength and comfort that was in the writers. They wrote truths eternal, even when relating the history of things temporal, for their minds were fixed only on the eternal principles, which guided the temporary forms of outward events, and wrought them out of the eternal substance of inherent realities. It is an Inspiration exciting and requiring a corresponding inspiration in the heart of the reader to interpret it rightly and fully.

The venerable Wilberforce used to say that as there were probably "stars of which the light, though always travelling on its course, had not yet reached us." And he thought it might be somewhat like this with the light of the blessed gospel. He acted on that faith in commencing his attacks on the slave trade, and developed truths of Christianity that are now changing the whole world, and becoming the advancing light of this age of the church. Church history is a living, progressive development and application of the teachings of Christ through the Paraclete.

CHAPTER X.

THE NEW TESTAMENT DOCUMENTS.

THE most prominent writer of the New Testament is the Apostle Paul. His writings are the key and clue to all the rest. Nothing in regard to ancient literature is easier or more certain than the process by which we can trace back some of his Epistles to his own hand or dictation, and through such means, identify his style and individuality. Historically we can go back and back, until we find the Church at Rome through Clement, Paul's fellow laborer, somewhere in the reign of Domitian, which extended from A. D. 81 to 96, writing an Epistle to the Corinthians,* and saying, " Take the Epistle of the blessed Paul the Apostle into your hands. What was it that he wrote to you at his first preaching the Gospel among you?

* For one of the best reviews of the whole literary question as to Clement's First Epistle to the Corinthians, see Donaldson's Critical History of Literature and Doctrine, Vol. I, Chap. 2.

Verily he did by the Spirit, admonish 'you concerning himself and Cephas and Apollos, because that even then, ye had begun to fall into parties and factions among yourselves." Here at least we have one who had known the Apostle, identifying I Cor. 1: 12, as part of a first Epistle written by St. Paul to the very men to whom he was writing. These two Epistles to the Corinthians, that to the Romans, and that to the Galatians, even Bauer, one of the most extreme of the doubting school, cannot and does not call in question. And with these once admitted as genuine, it inevitably follows, that before A. D. 60, that is to say, within one generation of the death of Jesus, all the important facts and doctrines of Christianity, much as we now have them in the four Evangelists and the Epistles, were not only taught by St. Paul, but believed by all the Christian Churches scattered through Palestine and Asia Minor. They were catechized into them, and baptized into them ;— Rom. 6: 1–5; I Cor. 15: 1–11. There is not a New Testament doctrine, nor any fact of the slightest importance, but what can be shown to have been held by the great body of Christians then in substance as they are taught us by the rest of the New Testament now. There were some who doubted or denied Paul's Apostleship, some who were opposed to relaxing from the letter of Judaism also, some with strong Ebionitish or humanitarian tendencies, but none before whom these facts and doctrines had not been spread by Paul and his companions, as the authentic teachings of the Christian Church, so far as his influence and authority would carry them.

There is another book that must have been written substantially, if not precisely as we have it now, somewhere between the years A. D. 63 and 68, (that is still within about a generation of the crucifixion,) i. e. the Acts of the Apostles. It is written clearly to show historically the spread of St. Paul's doctrine of the entrance of the Gentiles into the Christian Church, as equals with the Hebrews in the kingdom of God, and without going through the initiatory rite of circumcision, or undertaking to keep the ceremonial law. It may not, as De Wette suggested, have been edited out in precisely its present form until later. But if so, it was edited from pre-existing and most authentic manuscripts and journals, so far at least as the accounts of Paul's journeys are concerned, edited with so little alteration from the contemporary documents, that even the first personal pronoun is left standing just where it was, as in Acts 16: 10, 11, 13, 15; 20: 13; 21: 15–18; 27: 1–37; 28: 1, to the end. This book is for all our purposes, therefore, a contemporary document, and shows that the chief facts of the gospel were taught and believed by St. Paul, and by the early Christian churches, especially of the Gentiles, very much as we have them now, in the four gospels at that early date. We thus know substantially, apart from the four gospels, that the facts in which they all agree, were believed and attested most solemnly by the primitive churches, planted by the Apostles and the evangelists. Whenever they were put to paper, (we speak now particularly of the first three,) they are chiefly but the writing out of an oral or mother gospel, already formed and preached and believed everywhere in Palestine, in Asia Minor, and even in Rome. Tacitus, born in Rome, and from ten to fifteen years of age at the time of Paul's residence there, was clearly familiar with the substantial facts of them, and probably had seen some written document, when he wrote his Annals.

How far we may rely on the Acts, as written by Luke, just in its present form, is one of the most interesting questions of Biblical Criticism. It would almost seem impossible that the author should have known of the death of St. Paul and not brought his biography to a regular close. This history which begins with so carefully a composed exordium, yet leaves Paul bound and in prison. " The ground of this silence lay (De Wette says,) in the work from which the Editor drew." He finds possible allusions to it in Ignatius, Polycarp, Justin's dialogue with Trypho, and

Tatian, but no direct quotation before Irenæus.* But in Clement's Epistle, A. D. 96, there are two passages, which, especially when put together, leave, I think, no doubt that Clement had seen the latter part of the Acts, either in its edited or unedited state. Near the beginning of the Epistle, he says, " Ye were all of you humble minded, not boasting of anything, desiring rather to be subject than to govern, *to give than to receive*." If this passage had stood alone, it might have been considered as one of those doubtful allusions, of which but little could be made, although there seems to be here a sort of partial reference to Acts 20: 35. " Remembering the words of the Lord Jesus, how he said, 'it is more blessed to give than to receive.'" This is the only well authenticated saying of Jesus Christ handed down to us through any other channel than the four gospels. It would seem, therefore, from the way in which it is brought forward, to have been so currently repeated in the ears of the early Christians, that it would have been dangerous on the authority alone of such an allusion, to have pronounced certainly, that Clement had seen the book of the Acts, from which it appears to have been taken. But in the latter part of this same epistle of Clement, we have in connection with another saying of Christ's from the gospels, this passage, "*Remem-*

* Introduction to New Test. 114-117, Sec.

bering the words of our Lord Jesus, how he said,
Woe to that man by whom the offense cometh." ֽHere
we have, I think, a clear case of the insertion of the
two halves of Acts 20: 35, in such different connections, as best shows a familiarity with not only the
sentence of Jesus, but with this quotation of it by the
writer of the Acts, which can only be fairly accounted
for, by supposing the book in current and familiar use,
just as we have it now. Either that, or the document
thought to be its source, must have been in Clement's
hands, not as a mere private journal, but as a classic or
canonical book. It is alluded to in these passages,
with just that familiarity, without excessive freedom,
that sort of love and reverence for its authority, which
so often marks the best of the Fathers in their use of
the writings of the New Testament.

But if this is so, then have we either the Acts of the
Apostles or a document that formed the foundation of
it, in established circulation at Rome, *before the close
of the first century,* containing a life of St. Paul brought
to just that point which shows it to have been completed between A. D. 63 and A. D. 68.

And the book of Acts alludes to the third gospel
(Luke's) as "*a former* Epistle," and therefore might
seem to show as early a date for that gospel in its
present form as any have ever thought possible to
claim for it, i. e. pretty certainly before the death of

St. Paul, — say A. D. 68, — and therefore at least two years before the destruction of Jerusalem.*

There are internal marks, such as the more close and bare adherence to the Synoptical basis, which have made Schenkel. seek to place Mark as the first writer of all the gospels. But, without being first penned, Mark's gospel may have confined itself most closely to the Synopsis. A much more conclusive test would seem to be the proportion of the quotations and allusions in the earliest of the Fathers. Any one who examines this test, will, I think, be convinced that Matthew's gospel was very decidedly the first to come into general use and acceptance among the Churches, that is, it is far more frequently and freely alluded to and quoted by the earliest Fathers. Mark, I think, would seem to stand second, and Luke third. This agrees best also with all the traditions. It is to this

* The above used to appear to me absolutely decisive, that Luke's gospel was written before the destruction of Jerusalem, and that the Acts, *as we now have it*, was also written before St. Paul's death. I confess however, now that Luke 11: 51; and Matthew 23: 35, would seem to show that both Luke and Matthew embraced the use of a synoptical gospel not fully formed until some time after A. D. 69, when if Josephus is to be relied on, Zacharias the son of Baruck was slain. (See Wars of the Jews, IV: 5, 4.) If so the Preface to the Acts and Luke are the work of a later Editor than the most of the text of Acts. The way of evading the force of this by reference to either of the other men bearing that name in the Old Testament, seems to me now too improbable to be fair.

view we should readily assent in regard to any other documents at the same distance of time.

The very great difference in point of current early acceptance between Matthew and Luke, thus indicated, would show even quite a considerable priority of date for the Greek version of the former to that of the latter. But there was before that a Hebrew or Aramæan Gospel of Matthew, " which each one translated for himself as he was able," until the inconvenience of this led to our present Greek version of it, which was considered of equal authority with the Hebrew gospel. Separate apparently from this was the prior synoptical gospel, either in a written or perhaps simply oral form.* On the whole, therefore, it seems clear that at as early a period as could possibly be expected, the history of the life of Christ, so far as now presented to us by the united testimony of any two of the synoptical gospels, must have been published orally at least to the whole of the Gentile Churches, and indeed to each member of them, before the writing of 'Paul's Epistles, i. e. before A. D. 70, and indeed before A. D. 60, if not 50.

The author of the third gospel claims, as I understand from Luke 1 : 1–4, and as even Renan concedes, to have been a man of the second Apostolic generation, (that is to have been the companion of the men about

* See ante, p. 66.

thirty years younger than Jesus, but who were eye witnesses of the later facts of our Lord's life.) This would place his gospel between about A. D. 60–80. One chief difficulty which renders so many critics unwilling to admit that Luke's gospel could have been written before A. D. 70, is that the prediction of the destruction of Jerusalem is so accurate, that it could not, they think, have been written before the event had taken place.

Without here discussing that question, I believe it will be found on turning to the passages referred to by De Wette, Renan, and others on this point, (Luke 21: 9, 20, 24, 28, 32, compare 32 and 36,) that they contain chiefly such general predictions of the destruction of Jerusalem, as his wonderously instinctive knowledge of what was in man, might even naturally have led him to predict. Coleridge used to say that a profounder insight into causes, was the foundation of the true prophetic foresight of events. There have been predictions in regard to the fate of slavery, and the beginning and the results of our own civil war, which to those who meditated less upon such subjects, might have seemed quite supernatural. It would for any such theory, seem unfair to post date the gospel of Luke in order that it might not contain predictions which came true. That Jesus foretold the destruction of Jerusalem, I believe, although some of the sentences recorded in Luke, were, I think, written *after* Jerusalem was destroyed, especially Luke 11: 51.

The rest of the New Testament Epistles of Paul, have almost all of them, that parenthetic style, and readiness to take fire and enlarge at the name of Christ, with several other peculiarities sufficient to assure us of their genuineness. The early forgers of spurious Christian writings have no imitations of style, or even thought carried to this extent, and whatever may be said of some of the minor Catholic epistles, there are no good reasons for doubting the three principal of them, — I Peter, I John and James, — are genuine, in spite of the denial of the last even by Luther. Whether the book of Revelations was written by John the Apostle, or John the Presbyter, written in 68 or 98, or at any time in between, there can, I think, be little doubt of its being a production of the first century, certainly before the end of the first quarter of the second, and perhaps among the earliest portions of the New Testament.

But with so many of the Christian Scriptures that are clear, and beyond all reasonable question, there is no need, but only infinite danger in preaching to the people such a doctrine of verbal infallibility, as shall make them give up the whole of the New Testament, if perchance an opponent can prove a probable mistake about some unimportant matter of fact, or a logician finds an illogical mode of stating an argument even in St. Paul's writings.

The true proofs of the Inspiration of these writings are to be found in the effects they have in all ages produced on the world, and do now produce upon the hearts of those who study and follow them. Just so the early Churches felt the proofs of St. Paul's Apostleship, the divine authority of his teachings. But suppose the disciples had urged, as some appear to have done, with regard to St. Paul, that none of these apostles were absolutely infallible, and had therefore said that we never could demonstrate that this or that particular instruction was binding? Would it not be fair to reply that even infallible instructions to men of fallible understandings, must after all ever be to a certain extent fallible, and that when we have obtained the best instruction the case admits of, that ought to be sufficient, and the same in its effects on us, as if it were absolutely unerring? Why then should we demand or expect or assert a quality in the New Testament writings, never esteemed necessary or possible in regard to the personal teachings of the writers while they lived?

CHAPTER XI.

OBJECTIONS AGAINST WHAT HAS BEEN ADVANCED.

IT often, indeed almost always happens, that in rising from low and partial opinions to higher and more comprehensive views in regard to any subject, there is an unpleasant feeling of change and privation, as if we were about to be robbed of every truth, even the most vital, to which we have thus far been accustomed. The Alpine traveller, who quits for the first time his native village, and climbs the mountain ranges, finds the house where he was born, and the streets in which he had walked, and the garden where he had played, all so curiously changed and dwarfed, and the relations of the entire valley so altered by the wider connections of it with the surrounding hills, that he feels as if he had lost his native place. And he cannot believe, until he descends, that it has been all there, only much more added to it. It is a strangely desolate feeling to perceive that "the truth and the Gospel that we have known are but a small home farm in the great universe." Even Martin Luther could not bear to give up the Ptolemaic system, which made his earth the centre of everything, for the Copernican, allowing that the earth's movement, and not the sun's, produced day and night. He feared in it irreverance to Scripture and to God. To be really irreverent to either would be a sin against Christianity that we would not attempt to compute. And many will esteem the views that have been expressed as tending to dangerous consequences. But while holding most firmly to these writings as the production of men who "spake as they were moved by the Holy Ghost," and therefore worthy of our highest reverence, being guides of Divine authority as a whole, and authentic expositions of Christianity, we shall best show our reverence for them by a love of the *exact truth* in regard to their composition, in preference to. such an idolatry of the letter of Scripture as must destroy the veneration the good man will ever feel for its essence and spirit.

The demands made upon us by the present century, to give up several of our old beliefs in facts supposed to be ultimate in Science, have been many. Seventy years ago, it was a matter of primary instruction in every school, that there were four, and but four, elementary substances,— air, earth, fire and water; now there are above sixty that we can at present resolve no further. Fire, light and lightning were considered substances, rather than vibratory motions or conditions of substances only thus partially made known to us. But it may be safely said, that in all these cases, where real and true science overthrows an old belief, it is by substituting some more general and comprehensive view in its place, which embraces all the long familiar truths of the old view, and gives us a larger amount of positive knowledge in addition.

We can perhaps conceive of some conceited youth who should say, " You have proved that air and water are but mixtures of gases, that a flame of fire is but the vibration caused by the combining of oxygen and carbon, and that many earths are but the combinations of oxygen with metallic bases, so that all that used to be considered the four elementary *substances* are not such, but only accidental conditions; therefore I will believe in none of them, i. e. in nothing. All is a dream. There is no such thing as matter." In spite of such dreams and doubters, we are quite sure that thinking people generally have acquired a much more positive and distinct idea of what earth, air, fire and water really are, as the result of the discussion; their old views being in fact superseded by broader, more general conceptions of each. And they have a firmer and more comprehensive belief in the existence and qualities of all.

In like manner, a true Christian is constantly finding his former crude religious conceptions superseded by more general ones; yet this need not lessen his faith in experimental Christianity, but should increase it, making his religion broader at the base, and therefore firmer.

I wish, so far as may be, to illustrate this truth in its application to the subject of Inspiration. There are now many Christians who feel that all the facts of the case require that we should give up the old and popular view of Infallibility. But then, they say that by relinquishing this, we give up the *certainty* of every thing, and are cut adrift from all the old authorities in religion; what have you to give us instead? On the contrary, it will be found that the old verities, so far as they are exact expressions of truth, all come back to us with new and higher certainty, and in more comprehensive, and therefore surer forms.

But to proceed in detail. It certainly cannot be supposed that *everything* in religion will be thereby cut loose and set adrift. All the great truths of Natural, that is, of Universal Religion, belonging to man as man, must remain just as certain as ever. The existence and attributes of the Supreme Being, the distinction of spirit and matter, of right and wrong, can not be thus shaken. There is a religion that belongs to man as man, a sense of moral obligation, arising out of the relations he sustains to God, to his own nature, and to his fellow-creatures. As these relations are more exactly perceived and defined in each age by the intellectual developments of mankind, so the moral and religious obligations of men are discriminated with greater clearness, accuracy and certainty, upon universal and eternal principles. There is, therefore, a science of Universal Religion, the most comprehensive and profound of all sciences, capable of leading to noblest results, and of affording the greatest support, indeed the only sure basis on which to build up the evidences of the Christian Religion as a true Revelation from God. No difficulties as to the infallible nature of Inspiration can possibly shake any portion of that. Experimental religion, with all the complicated and wonderful confirmations which it brings to the heart of the living Christian of the truth of what he believes, fairly, so far as it is really experience, belongs to Universal Religion. And *it*, in like manner, cannot be shaken by any of these difficulties. The chief difference is, that what he had supposed a special revelation established by miracle is now found and felt to be eternal truth and a part of Universal Religion.

Indeed, the whole of these present trials of our faith, are really necessary to bring the certainty of the great natural and eternal bases of all religion, and of real Christianity, vividly before the mind, and within the acknowledged range of our vital experiences. As it is in the dark night, that we see those stars most clearly, which are worlds of light, though hidden by the blaze of day, so there is a sort of eclipse of faith in regard to the Christian Records, that may render more clear to the pious heart, the fundamental principles of universal Religion, and thus end in giving a nobler view of these ultimate and strongest evidences of Christianity itself.

The objection we are considering, can only be supposed to have any bearing upon the evidences of the *Christian* religion, not on all religion as such. But really it cannot for a moment be believed to affect more than a very small portion of what are commonly included under these evidences. In Divinity Lectures on this subject, the discussion of Inspiration is naturally and properly left till all other points are fully established. If there is any exception to this, it is most illogical. The genuineness of the documents, the authenticity, credibility, and Divine Authority of Christianity, are all established *before* the subject of Inspiration is touched upon at all. Of course then these things are all supposed to be capable of being proved independently of it, although it may be dependent upon them. These most important points of

Christian faith, would be as capable of proof therefore, apart from any particular views of Inspiration as with them, and must and will be discussed quite independently.

It is true that sometimes Theological teachers have, as I learn for supposed convenience, inverted the order of lecturing, and begun with Inspiration first of all, for the sake of making their work more easy, when all were prepared to admit at the outset, the conclusion attempted to be reached. No doubt it makes the work more easy for the lecturer, where his students are docile, and already fancy that their ground is perfectly secure. But it is not fair, and must by so much, destroy the possibility of making his work solid. He who begins by lecturing on Inspiration, must in doing so, take for granted the existence and attributes of the Supreme Being, in fine, all the truths of Natural Religion, and all other portions of the evidences of Revealed Religion. How, for instance, does he obtain his knowledge of what books shall, and what shall not be included in the Canon of those Scriptures he attempts to prove all infallibly inspired? An objection brought against II Peter, might seemed to vitiate the whole, or arguments proving the Inspiration of St. Paul, or I Peter, or I John, might be believed sufficient to cover the book of Jude, or Solomon's Song. Perhaps nothing will better illustrate the loose and illogical manner in which this whole question has been discussed, than that such a course of treatment, such a *petitio principii,* should in different Protestant Institutions, have been pursued for twenty or thirty years together. Nothing but an undefined sense of the weakness of the arguments to prove the conclusion desired, could have led to the adoption of this course in a single case.

A more important objection to our view of the subject, is that it tends to Rationalism, and to destroy the due submission of the soul to Authority in Religion. Rationalism has become a technical Theological term, and is understood to imply a system of opinions deduced from Reason alone, as distinct from any acknowledged basis of Authority, especially any Scriptural authority whatever. To one who believes that holy men of old spake as they were moved by the Holy Ghost, although still believing them to be *men* who spake, and therefore fallible, the tendency of all the views I have advanced, is to exhibit in as strong a light as possible, consistent with truth, the Authority of Holy Scripture, as containing a Divine as well as a human element, a revelation of eternal and glorious truths. This I have already shown in the chapter on Authority in Religion. So far our object is just the opposite of Rationalism. And yet, of course, it must be the desire of every wise and good man to purge increasingly from his religion, all that is contrary to sound reason; in fact, to have nothing but a perfectly reasonable and self-consistent faith.

Mr. Lecky's History of the Rise and Influence of Rationalism in Europe is in fact a misnomer. In it we see a number of lively, vigorous, and original sketches, not of Rationalism strictly speaking, but of the struggle between Reason and Authority on several errors, which having been received in ages before the birth of Christianity, have been really expelled from the Church by the conjoined operation of Christianity and Reason, just as it was Luther's faith in the Authority of Scripture, not Rationalism, that over-threw that of the Pope.

In the number of the *Westminster* for October, 1865, there is a Review of Mr. Lecky's work on the History of Rationalism in Europe, containing an attack on Christianity. But the first paragraph of it expresses, in fewer and clearer words than we have almost ever before seen it conceded by such a writer, what were the characteristics of that living spirit in Christianity as distinct from all the highest and best philosophy of the age in which it appeared, that, eighteen hundred years ago, gave it the power to overturn all other systems opposed to its progress. It was "a principle which substitutes a spirit of *unselfish tenderness* for the hard, cold ideas of Greek and Roman polity." It taught that "the self-dependent magnanimity of Aristotelian ethics is a mere dream, and that its realization would fill the earth with tyrants. It obliterated generally the cruel distinction which Athenian philosophy drew between natural freemen and natural slaves. By its beneficent influence, slavery has given place to serfdom and serfdom· has merged into liberty. It has taught men that their mutual relations have no meaning and no force, except as based on an eternal and inalienable relation of all mankind to *a Father* whose justice cannot be wearied with iniquity and whose love is not to be conquered by ingratitude. In the slowly-working leaven of Christianity we discern *a living spirit*, for which we look in vain in the dreamy Theoria of Aristotle, or the ideal philosophy of Plato. We see in the vehement conviction of Saul of Tarsus, that the final issue of the great conflict will be the victory of truth and love, a victory by which the last enemy of man shall be destroyed, and God shall be all in all."

If this was the *living power* of that system which conquered all the philosophy and religion and established physical powers of the world eighteen hundred years ago, we may rest quite assured that the world will not *move backwards* from them in all the ages to come. The Church, including all churches, may have made great mistakes in carrying them out, — may have abused its authority, and claimed powers over the rea-

13

son that did not belong to it, and these abuses may and will all be swept away, but the world can never go backward again to consider Plato and Aristotle finality. The progress and philosophy of all the future must embrace the wisdom of all the past. And these principles, which Rationalism concedes to lie at the base of Christianity, have plenty of work to do in the world yet. And Mr. Lecky's work has done, and will do great good on all sides, so far as it causes such concessions as these to be freely made, such tributes to be paid to the eternal and living principles of that religion whose Author said, eighteen hundred years ago, "Heaven and earth shall pass away, but my words shall not pass away."

Able and valuable as the work is, it is not a *history* of any thing, but the illustration of certain points in the history of the decline of belief in magic, miracles, religious persecution, and other topics. The Critical History of Free Thought, by A. S. Farrar, ought to be a work substantially on the same subject, according to the titles. Yet, if the Bampton Lectures are history, Mr. Lecky's work is not. Nor is it fairly a vigorous sketch of certain triumphs of *Rationalism*, but rather of the struggle between *Reason* and *Authority* on several errors which had been believed in ages before the birth of Christianity, but which Reason, in conjunction with Christianity, has gradually been expelling from the Church. Rationalism is a system of opinions deduced from reason, as *distinct from* Inspiration, or opposed to it. But most of what Mr. Lecky calls Rationalism was really reasoning from what was thought to be inspired premises. He himself admits that " the success of *any* opinion depends *much less upon the force of its arguments,* or upon the ability of its advocates, than upon the *predisposition* of society to receive it." That is, it depends less upon Rationalism than the *authority* of certain previous states of mind in the community. Nor is it even true that the predisposition results solely "from *the intellectual type of the age,*" but far more from its moral and religious type.

For instance, Mr. Lecky undertakes to give the History of the Decline of *Religious Persecution.* Yet he never alludes to Roger Williams, the first legislator who incorporated perfect religious liberty in the statute books of any nation in the globe,—nor to Lord Baltimore, nor to William Penn, all Englishmen by birth and education. Yet where did Roger Williams, in 1639, nine or ten years before the power of Cromwell, get his principles? From his study of law? or from rationalism? His study of law no doubt made him long to incorporate his great principle in constitutional form. But it was his reverence for the *authority,* of what he considered a Bible truth, that made him seek and demand liberty of conscience, and feel that it was the *right of all.* So in England the rationalism of Hobbes, *made* him " the most unflinching of all the supporters of persecution," declaring that "the civil power had the absolute right to determine the religion of the nation," even when wielded by the profligate Charles II., and thus encouraging him to keep John Bunyan for twelve years in jail. It was not rationalism, — not even reason, but reverence for the authority of conscience, that in England was the source of both religious and civil liberty in the days of Cromwell, and of the commonwealth, and again in 1688. And where would freedom of conscience have been now, throughout the world, but for the English and American struggles? But it was the rationalism of Hobbes that made him so indifferent to the rights of conscience, as to put every man's religion under the thumb-screws of the politicians, however ignorant, profligate and vile.

The views of Inspiration which have been stated by me, tend ultimately, not to destroy, but to increase the spirit of reverent veneration for the Divine and therefore Authoritative in Scripture as in Providence, in History, and above all in the presence and teachings of the Paraclete in every true Christian experience. A proper view of this subject will lead to higher reverence for the Authority of Scripture, as the record of that ever living body, the kingdom of God and the Church of the Redeemed in which He lives and reigns, who walketh in the midst of the seven golden candle-sticks.

Perhaps then it might seem especially from some developments which have actually taken place, that the chief danger of these views may be found rather in a certain tendency to mysticism (such as we see in High Church Episcopacy, or in transcendentalism,) than to Rationalism. And here again, all turns upon the meaning we attach to terms. For there must ever be as the basis of every human belief, something that transcends the mere reasoning process, something that goes beyond and back of it, some basis of Authority on which all reasoning is grounded.

CHAPTER XII.

SUMMARY VIEW.

WE will now briefly review the whole ground, and especially the difficulties of those spurious views which fail to take into the account the Human Element in the Inspiration of the Scriptures.

I. One of the difficulties of the Popular and current views of Inspiration, is that it crosses Antiquity, and is in its present form a modern growth. At the Reformation, the Lutheran Church in its Confessions of Faith, said nothing specially about the Inspiration of the Scriptures. In 1582, however, in the Preface to the Formula of Concord, the Lutherans, as a matter of course, rather than of controversy, say, " We believe those sacred writings alone to be the sole and infallible rule to which all opinions ought to conform."

The thirty-nine Articles of the Church of England assert that the " Holy Scriptures containeth all things necessary to salvation, so that whatsoever is not read

therein, nor may be proved thereby, is not to be required of any man, that it should be believed as an
article of the faith, or be thought requisite or necessary
to salvation." Bunsen thinks it can be proved that
this was so worded because many of those preparing
it could subscribe to no more, and did not believe in
the infallibility of inspiration.

The Westminster divines, however, were in no
mood for so undecided an article on the Bible and its
claims, and from their utterances the Savoy Confession, and then the New England Confession of Faith
of 1680, took their rise. About nine years later, one
hundred Baptist ministers met in London and adopted
a Confession, almost in the very words of the Savoy,
except as to Baptism. Of all of these documents, it
must be allowed that the absolute Infallibility of the
Inspiration of the Old and New Testaments is one of
the most decided features, and put forth with that sort
of increasing decision and prominence which makes
us wonder why it was that the saints of all previous
ages were so defective in expressing these views, provided they as clearly and fully believed them. In fact,
it can hardly be supposed that the most learned and
careful of them did this. If any one will look over the
Confessions of Faith, historically, from the Apostles'
Creed down to those now commonly in use among
most of the modern evangelical denominations, nothing

will so much surprise him as the way in which faith in the plenary and infallible inspiration of every part of the Bible has only by degrees developed itself, with an increasing decision and exclusive force, as the source of all Authoritative religious teachings, to the exclusion of the Church on the one hand, and even of all the great principles of Universal Religion on the other. In the Apostles' Creed, a belief in the books of the Old or New Testament is not once alluded to, but only of some of the principal facts taught in the Church and in the Bible. But in one of the last of these documents, the *first* article is, that "the Holy Bible was written by men Divinely inspired, that it has God for its author, salvation for its end, and *truth, without any mixture of error*, for its matter." The existence even of a Supreme being, and of every thing like a Church, is deduced from this source alone. About a year ago, in a sort of convention of the Congregational Churches, at Plymouth, to re-affirm over the graves of their Fathers their adherence to the great principles of religious faith brought over by the Pilgrims, care seems to have been wisely taken to avoid in future pledging that denomination to any such extreme and untenable views. In fact, it is from a sense of the necessity of an abandonment of such extreme expressions by all Christian denominations, that we here point out some of the objections, theoretical and practical, to their further maintenance.

II. There is no such uniformity as we should expect to find, were the Scriptures written on the plan supposed by this theory. We do not dwell upon the obvious diversities of style, by the various writers, but of those varieties of thought that amount at times to irreconcilable discrepancies. Differences of this kind may and often do confirm the credibility of an ordinary witness, by showing that there was no collusion, but the distinct testimony of independent, though fallible persons. But the moment they are *both* claimed to be truths "without any mixture of error," proceeding from one infallible spirit; either all such discrepancies must be reconciled, or the infallibility be abandoned. The learning, the wearisome toil, and the subtleties of rhetoric, by which attempts have been made to reconcile all conflicting passages, will be looked upon by future ages as something astonishing, just as we now regard the ingenious controversies of the school-men in the dark ages.

The Genealogies of Jesus in the first seventeen verses of Matthew, all admit to be difficult to reconcile in any way with Luke. The forcing method of supposing that one relates to Joseph, the reputed father of the Saviour, and the other to Mary his real mother, is the most common. That is difficult enough,

but the assertion that there are just " fourteen generations," when in fact, there are eighteen, is an obvious mistake;—one of no practical moment to us
now, perhaps, except as destroying the claim to infallibility often made *for*, but never *by* the Evangelists.
In the Genealogy given by Luke, as we have before
shown, the name of Cainan (chap. 3: 36,) omitted in
the Hebrew,* is inserted agreeing with the Septuagint.
Thus the entire chronology of the world is extended
one hundred and thirty years, and an authority is
here given to the Greek translation of the Old Testament against the Hebrew, wholly at variance with
the infallibility of either, or the idea of unerring accuracy having been esteemed by the sacred writer,
of the same importance, as our Confessions regard
it now. The advocates of verbal inspiration, do not
now extend their views so far as to concede that
deviations as great as those between the Septuagint
and the Hebrew, altering the world's Chronology by
more than a thousand years, can be admitted without affecting the question of Inspiration. And yet
it seems impossible to deny that our Saviour and
his Apostles did practically teach this view, by quoting more freely from the Greek version, which was
avowedly inaccurate, than from the Hebrew, which
has been supposed infallible. There are altogether

* See Gen. 11: 12.

one hundred and eighty-one quotations in the New Testament from the Old. Of these, sixty-two coincide exactly with the Hebrew, and seventy-two with the Greek. There are *six* cases of quotations differing from the Hebrew, but agreeing with the Septuagint, and eleven differing from the Septuagint, and agreeing with the Hebrew. There are sixty-two cases of quotations agreeing nearly with the Hebrew, and forty-seven taken from the Septuagint, but with some variation; twenty-four cases of quotations agreeing with the Hebrew in sense but not in words, and thirty-two of quotations agreeing with the Septuagint in sense but not in words. These classifications may be found in Horne. Dr. Davidson and others have examined this subject more closely, but these are sufficient to show that the Septuagint was regarded about as nearly infallible, by the New Testament writers as the Hebrew. Even in Matthew's gospel, this is the case. Westcott, in his Introduction to the New Testament, divides the quotations made by Matthew into two classes, those passages which are quoted by Matthew *himself*, as fulfilled in the life of Christ, and second such as are interwoven in the discourses of different characters, (including Jesus himself,) and form a part of the narrative which may be supposed to have been the basis of the synoptical gospels. "Exactly in accordance with this supposition, it is found that the first class is made up of original renderings of the Hebrew text, while the second is in the main in accordance with the Septuagint, even where it deviates from the Hebrew." This makes it quite clear that Matthew, Hebrew though he was in the whole scope of his mind and purpose, had still no such idea of verbal inspiration, as made him feel it necessary to re-translate a mis-rendered passage from the Hebrew. It also shows, as do the whole of these quotations, made prevailingly from the Septuagint even where it differs from the Hebrew, that this version was considered sufficiently accurate. The Apostle Paul appears to have quoted both from memory freely, sometimes using one, sometimes the other with equal freedom, and varying at times from both. There are five or six such passages in the Epistle to the Romans alone. But where he makes a *long* quotation so as to turn to the passage, he generally uses the Septuagint. If there is any exception to this in other writers besides Matthew already discussed, it is in Peter.

In the book of Psalms, we have the same Psalm substantially inserted twice over. Ps. 14 and 53 with slight variations, showing that it had been accidentally bound up in two collections afterwards merged into one. Facts like these, and they could be multiplied to any extent, show that no such idea of verbal inspiration was held when the books of Scripture were being written. The honest truth-lovingness visible in the whole writings and conduct of the Apostles, is by far the most valuable evidence of the Inspiration of the New Testament.

III. The theory of Infallibility could have no consistency unless each translation were supposed to be equally inspired, or there were a universal religious language, with which each Christian was bound and able to become acquainted. Our modern versions, any of them are now much more faithful translations of the Bible than the Septuagint is of the Hebrew. Nor need we doubt that William Carey in Calcutta, Morrison in China, Henry Martin in Persia, and Judson in Burmah, were raised, aye, inspired truly of God to make their several translations, though far enough as they ever felt, from infallible, both they and their works. The Roman Catholic Church has often been blamed for holding that Jerome was inspired to prepare the Vulgate. But it is rather for allowing the people to attach an exaggerated idea to the term Inspiration, they are to blame. Either, then, these writings were not meant to be translated, or else not intended to be considered infallible. It is said that sea-weed and shell fish, two feet thick, were lately found to have grown on to the bottom of the Great Eastern, and scraped off. So these superstitious views of Inspiration, have gradually fastened themselves on the sacred text of the Old Testament, and of the New, like barnacles on the bottom of a ship, and while they do not destroy it, yet impede its native powers. True, a similar superstition has in all former ages generally come to adhere to the earlier religious writings of nearly every national religion separating them from later productions, and while preserving them from alterations, often impeding or destroying their original usefulness, fossilizing them in fact, and petrifying all their utility.

IV. Such a theory of Inspiration as that to which we object, would seem for any practical usefulness or consistency, to require not only an equally inspired, but infallible state of mind, in all persons *receiving* the sacred words. If the eye that perceives, is distorted or jaundiced, it may have the same effect practically, as if the object were mis-shapen or discolored, or as Whately puts it in his Rhetoric, " a change effected in one of two objects having a certain relation to each other, may have the same practical results, as if it had taken place in the other." Though a book may be ever so infallible, yet perused by a fallible mind, the impressions received cannot be relied on as otherwise than fallible. It is on this account that the Roman Catholic Church, when she superstitiously undertook to establish an infallible Revelation of Religion, was even more careful to claim for the Church an infallible power of interpretation, than for the sacred writings perfection of composition. And Protestants, when they overthrew the authority of the Church, put in its place the work of the Holy Spirit in the heart of each enlightened individual.

But it is only by slow degrees, that the uselessness of the whole idea of absolute perfection in the Revelation, while the man for whom it is made is imperfect, is perceived by the minds of many. Knowledge of truth must be and is a holy and slow growth of the soul itself. We may approximate in knowledge certainly nearer to perfection, but the Finite can only approximate, never reach the Infinite and the Perfect.

V. Indeed, this theory seems absolutely *disproved* by the whole course of the actions and assertions of the Inspired writers. In the first paragraph of Luke's gospel, where he enumerates all the grounds on which we are to know "the certainty of the things" recorded, this claim is omitted. But it would surely have been brought forward as most decisive of all, if Luke had considered it valid. The Apostolic Constitutions as we have seen, forged after a belief in Apostolic Infallibility had become popular in the Church, have just that self-assertion which would have been natural had Luke claimed infallibility. St. Paul also, "withstood Peter to the face, because he was to be blamed," and "walked not uprightly," but "dissembled," while the New Testament writers quote mis-translations from a well known but inaccurate version like the Septuagint with more frequency than from the Hebrew. But the practical objections to this view are really far more serious than any we have yet named.

VI. The error against which we are contending, has led to a loose, fanciful and spiritualizing method of interpreting Scripture, which has for ages been the bane of the Church. By this means, each religious leader easily makes the Scriptures themselves seem to the flock, to teach any conceit or error of his own, and to clothe it with all the authority of infallibility. When it was once taught that all the directions of the Pentateuch were not merely religious instructions for the Jews, but in every word an infallible revelation for all ages and nations; all typical and prophetic of Christian truth, every bell and pomegranite on a priest's garment, became mystical, and the very snuffers of the candles seemed more divinely significant, to the Christian Church, than they were literally and originally for the Jews. Any passages of Scripture hard to reconcile with each other, or with well understood facts, were by a new spiritual interpretation, stripped of their contrariety. Alexandrine Jews like Philo, led the way, perhaps from still older philosophical commentators upon Homer of a kindred spirit, and in an elevating cloud of mysticism doubted or denied the literal obligatoriness or truth of many commands or histories of

the Old Testament, while yet quite sure of the infallibility of those spiritual lessons drawn from them by
this species of interpretation. Origen in the third
century of the Christian era, carried this allegorical
method of interpretation still further, at times denying
that portions of the Old Testament had any true literal
meaning, and systematizing in the Church a vicious
system of interpretation, never thoroughly got rid of
since, but especially revived in the Protestant Church
under Cocceius. This was all the natural result of an
exaggerated theory of inspiration, and it led at the
beginning of the eighteenth century to a re-action of
the most terrible kind against all love and reverence for
Scripture.

VII. This idea of Infallibility, further, evidently
stultifies Intellectual and Moral culture, where most
implicitly carried out, and to a fearful extent. Nothing
is indeed so elevating and morally enlightening as the
study of the Bible, conducted in a natural and devout
manner, without any sceptical desire to find flaws on
the one hand, or superstitious dread of meeting the
proofs of a human and fallible element on the other.
But quite opposite is often the effect of Biblical study
on the mechanical principles of infalliblity. Galileo
was preached against by a Dominican from the text.
" Ye men of Galilee, why stand ye looking up into
heaven," and was brought before the Inquisition for

saying that the earth moves, and thus contradicting the Church and the Scriptures. We smile at all this now, and equally at the zeal with which Protestant Priests defended Hellenistic idioms as not Hebraisms, but necessarily the purest Greek, because the chosen vehicle of the inspired writers of the New Testament. Yet even Beza considered them as "gems with which the Apostles had adorned their writings." And within about thirty years at Andover, so intelligent and progressive a theologian as Professor Moses Stuart, sneered at the objections of geologists, and "the theory of gradual formation which makes some thousands of years necessary in each of the six days," and thinks "they will deserve more consideration when any two respectable geologists are agreed," and when the earth shall have been penetrated more than "an eight thousandth part of its diameter. He reminds us that it is not necessary to suppose that acorns were created first instead of oaks. Dr. Pye Smith was still more recently considered quite a dangerous heretic for doubting the universality of the Deluge, and where is the writer whose orthodoxy is esteemed safe, who has openly doubted the Chronology of both Usher and Hales, and ventured to believe in the much higher antiquity of the race of man on the earth? A few scientific Professors may have ventured to hint in ambiguous phrase of the "pre-historic races."

One or two Reviews like the Edinburg have at last broken the shell, and allowed that the Bible was not written to teach us scientific matters like these, but only to be accused of laxity and infidelity. None I think can question, that at least until this time, the obstructing force exerted against the freedom and progress of science, in order to keep up respect for these views of verbal inspiration, has been very great. Every scientific association knows something of it. Nearly every child is taught in his school books, as unquestionable fact and inspired truth, things which, so long as believed in, must condemn him to utter ignorance of the most important scientific questions of the day. If the early records of the Old Testament were studied freely and by all, as ancient fragments, and as such compared and put side by side with other ancient fragments, fairly though reverently, how much might be done to render Bible classes a thousand times more interesting and instructive, and to secure a progressive knowledge of the earliest historic periods of the human race. Now, on the other hand, many intelligent parents are keeping their children from these classes lest their minds should be prejudiced in the name of reverence for the Bible, against all scientific study of these matters. In fact these wrong views of Inspiration are so used as to pour contempt on Natural Religion. All God's other revelations of himself, whether in the course of nature, in Providence, or in History are ignored and slighted. The Bible is treated as infallible, they as fallible, and our interpretations of *it* are clothed with an authority which is in all cases denied to our interpretations of *their* instructions!

In this respect, there has been a singular and retrograde movement among many of what are called Evangelical Christians within the last hundred years, very marked and very fearful; one that must tend to an increased deadness to all religion, especially among those who find proofs of the fallibility of certain portions of the sacred records. There were many incautious expressions in several of the earlier Protestant Confessions, in which, intending merely to oppose the authority of Romish traditions, it was asserted that God had been pleased to commit the revelation of himself, "*wholly* to writing,— the other ways of God's revealing his will unto his people (as by dreams and visions) being now ceased." Yet it always used to be allowed that the light of nature, and the works of creation and providence do manifest the goodness, wisdom and power of God. In the life of Neal, the author of the History of the Puritans, he himself gives in 1739, in his old age, a beautiful testimony of the grounds of his own faith, thus: "My greatest concern is to have rational and solid expectations of a future happiness. I rely very much on the rational notions we have of the moral perfections of God, not only as a just, but a benevolent and merciful Being. *   *   * In aid of the imperfection of our rational notions, I am very thankful for the glorious truths of Gospel revelation, which are *an additional superstructure on the other.* For though we can receive nothing contrary to our reason, we have a great many excellent and comfortable discoveries built upon and superadded to it. Upon this *double* foundation, would I build my expectations with an humble and awful reverence of the Judge of all the earth, and a fiducial reliance on the mercy of the Lord Jesus Christ to eternal life."* But in place of this double foundation, all the other revelations of Universal Religion are by many ostentatiously discarded. The written Scriptures are declared to be "*the only*" rule of faith and practice. And a quotation, (not from Chillingworth, but probably from a printer or proof reader of his, falsely attributed to him,) expresses the whole matter with an unfortunate exactness, the Bible and "the Bible alone *is* the religion of Protestants." While it is in part true, as Butler declares, (Part II, Chap. 1,) that the Bible contains a re-publication of the Religion of Nature, a more exact view would surely be, that it is a supplement to it, and not intended to be construed independently from, but in

* History Puritans, Memoir, p. 35.

accordance with what it supplements. Modern Bibliolatry puts the two in antagonism, the one to the other. The true religion of the present must embrace all that has gone before. The whole Church of the future groweth into an holy temple, only by incorporating materials from every dispensation and Revelation of the Past.

No doubt, it is *easier* for the unlettered Christian not to trouble himself with the dim speculations of Natural Religion; and he who cannot find time, or mental and moral capacity for both, will indeed find the written word a lamp unto his feet, and a light unto his path, wondrously illumining the path of life. But there are few Christians who will not be spiritually improved by the faith in and study of Natural Religion, for it is the true key to open all difficult texts of the Bible. And for those who can do this, (and who cannot?) any other course will be that path of idleness that always ends in spiritual feebleness. A stronger faith in the great principles of Universal Religion is the chief want of our day, if only to correct that weak and effeminate pietism which so many mistake for true piety.

VIII. These views of the absolute infallibility of the written word detract from the proper view and reverence for the Church, as a practically inspired body. That there is a mystical body of Christ, in which he dwells and walks, and which justly claims great authority, the Scriptures plainly declare. In former ages, the Roman Catholic Church, with plausibility, assumed to be alone that body, possessed of the keys, and as such, to be infallible. The Protestants detected and exposed this error, but have many of them fallen into a worse, which is that the Church of Christ is not an *inspired* body, but a sort of voluntary society, or aggregate of such societies,—only that, and nothing more. The Church of Christ includes all who love and follow Him. And though the membership of it may be invisible to mortal eye, it acts with a visible and inspired power and authority upon each age, nation and community, leading it forward with a heavenly instinct and superior wisdom. There is the home of the Paraclete on Earth. Thus all become in measure inspired with the presence of the Saviour, the life of God. Each individual Christian has the Spirit in degree, even alone, but he will also recognize a voice speaking to him through the Christian community with which he associates. Our modern visible churches are perhaps all very much like different classes in a large school. One may be a little in advance of, or another behind the rest. Some particular branches of study may be prosecuted most advantageously in one class, and some in another; but wherever the Christian studies, he should do it with a loving faith in the value of the instructions of the whole school. Notwithstanding the bickerings of sects and parties, the true Christian will love the Church of Christ as the Jerusalem which is from above and the mother of us all, free with her children from subjection to any undue authority, but guided by the animating spirit of Him who founded it. Rightly regarded, it utters not a mere verdict of the majority, but the voice of God in the earth, asserting the foremost truths of each age to mankind, and inspiring men with the loving and holy thoughts of Christ's own nature. But a right practical view of the Church cannot and does not co-exist with a wrong and superstitious view of Scripture.

IX. But the greatest practical evil, which renders these mechanical views of Inspiration most dangerous and mischievous, is, that if a single mistake can be exhibited, it leads men to suppose that the Divine authority of the whole is disproved and at an end. One plausible objection practically shakes faith in the *whole* as Divine. No doubt, if we want a guide merely to the study of Geology, the writings of Sir Charles Lyell will give us a more correct notion of the processes by which this earth has become what it is, than the first chapter of Genesis. But as an instructive declaration that in the beginning God planned out the whole, Genesis teaches a class of truths beyond the province of the mere geologist, whose examination

stops with the latest positive results, and extends back
·only to the physical and intellectual, but does not
necessarily extend to personal or final causes. All true
theology does just this, and reads in creation just what
Moses read there,—the dispositions of Him which are
revealed in all these works, and which open up to us
the very heart of God himself. M. Comte, who denies
a personal God, may be as sincere a believer in Geology as Sir Charles Lyell, or Dr. Buckland; but the
Divine Inspirations, which lie back of the merely intellectual science, and ·reveal to the intuitional nature of
man the most important of all truths connected with
the study of Geology, may be lost to him who rejects
the treasures of Divine truth and love contained in
Genesis, because of the cracks and flaws of the earthen
vessel in which it is placed. On the contrary, these
ought to enable us to discriminate and feel that there
·is an excellency of power behind the whole. Here,
then, is the great and final misfortune of the error we
have been considering,—it tends by reaction to produce the most terrible and Atheistic form of Infidelity.

14

CHAPTER XIII.

THE TRUE VIEW OF THE INSPIRATION OF THE BIBLE.

THERE is an interesting little work put forth by the late Dr. Alexander, of Princeton, on the Evidences of Scripture, and published by the Presbyterian Board of Publication. In determining what books have right to a place in the New Testament Canon, the author says three methods of settling this have been attempted: 1. The Authority of the Church, i. e. the Romish Church (which Dr. Alexander considers arguing in a circle): 2. Internal Evidence (adopted by the Reformed French Church): and, 3. Historical Testimony, which he considers the true view. The question to be decided, is, he thinks, a matter of fact, whether the books of the New Testament are indeed the production of Apostles. Mark and Luke, he attempts to prove, though not themselves Apostles, wrote under Apostolic direction.

Now if we should grant all that is thus claimed, it would appear that exactly as much infallibility belongs to the Inspiration of the New Testament as arises from its being written by Apostles, *and no more.* Our own position is, that the official Apostolical books of the New Testament have in that fact the assurance of Apostolical Inspiration. But as the Divine Authority given to these men to establish Christian Churches did not render their spoken words infallible individually, and nothing of that sort was ever promised them, nor thus understood by themselves, or by others around them, so the sacred writings, while containing in the aggregate a system of the highest Divine authority and inspiration, are not to be considered as individually and perfectly faultless. To be more specific :

I. This Inspiration does not prevent a peculiar and human style from adhering to each author, and a general National or Hellenistic style from belonging to the whole of the Greek sacred writings. Although the teachings, so far as of the Divine Spirit, must be in themselves infallible and absolute truth, yet the human element which comes into play, first in *receiving* the Divine communication, and then in recording or *uttering* it, is clearly not absolutely immaculate, but of finite wisdom in both these operations. It therefore colors the communication by the medium through which it passes, as to the figures, the style, and to a certain extent with the thoughts of the writer. So far as he fails to perceive or to express perfectly the Divine idea, there is at least room to suppose possible imperfection. Without disputing that the Divine Spirit *could*, and in some particular cases may have perfectly guarded a particular communication from all tinge of human infirmity, it may be safely asserted, that so far as style at least is concerned, it has not seen fit to do so. There is no *evidence* or assertion of such an absoluteness of spiritual dictation usually, but there is every possible evidence of the contrary.

II. It will, we suppose, be by all admitted that the Inspiration of the Bible, does not cause infallibility to adhere to each part absolutely and separately from the whole. The declaration that "there is no God," is only true in its connection "the fool hath said in his heart." The cloak recorded as being left by St. Paul at Troas, though most useful as showing the general simplicity of the writing and perhaps helping to prove St. Paul's liberation from his first captivity in Rome, and so fix the date of the Epistle, is beyond this, useless to us religiously and not to be spiritualized. Some have seemed in former days to think that a religious truth must be found or forced into every statement of the Bible. All the secular narratives and varieties of style, idiom and statement, become most useful as showing the simplicity, honesty and humanity of the writers. The differences of the Evangelists are important in this respect, establishing the characters of the distinct writers, each with his separate purpose, and marking him off as an individual.

But this view needs carrying out much further than ordinarily has been done by those harmonists, who to make the writers appear infallible, have strained and stretched each narrative on a Procrustean bed, or denied its identity with the same facts differently recorded on account of some slight inaccuracy in one of the relations. There needs a more loving, confiding view of Inspiration, than the mere servile and verbal one. The letter killeth,—the spirit giveth life. We certainly want a more wise appreciation of the Scripture as a whole, and of the character of its Inspiration allowing us to rectify individual mistakes by the tenor of the whole.

III. Nor again, is even the whole of Scripture so inspired as to lead us into all needful truth independently of the Holy Spirit guiding our hearts, or Providence our lives. We must be inwardly enlightened to read aright the book of God.

IV. In fact, the Bible is not inspired in any such way as to render us independent of all of God's other revelations of Himself and his Will in nature or in science, in Providence or in grace. The teachings of all history, past and present, contain as surely as the Bible, lessons from God to be diligently studied, and the whole form the Scriptures of the true Christian. " We are not to look for truth only in one book, or set of books written centuries ago. But all truth is God's truth, all created things are his book, and all light is from the Father of lights."

V. The Bible is not so inspired as to prevent or restrict the freest discussions as to matters of chronology or science generally. We certainly have no right to be more certain that our interpretations of Scripture are correct, than that our interpretations of these elder Scripture are. We may and do mistake in our renderings of both. The Bible was not given to teach us science, it was given to awaken our religious life, and each book of God can best inform us on those subjects for which it was specially intended.

VI. A distinction should therefore be made, in reading the books of the Bible, between those truths the particular writer seems to have been inspired with, and specially designed to teach, and those other opinions, religious as well as secular, which the writer expresses incidentally, or arising from his age, country, or condition. The writers in the Old and in the New Testaments express views on many subjects besides those it was their object to communicate,—opinions received from early education, national prepossessions or prejudices, and the intellectual and moral atmosphere of the age in which they lived. These may be true or mistaken; but unless it could be shown that their inspiration not only taught them the new and higher knowledge, but restrained them also from accepting or expressing any of the imperfect views of their age, which they had imbibed as men, we must allow that their forms of expression and of thought may have been colored by these circumstances. Are we to receive all these views, sometimes asserted, but more frequently only *implied*, as infallible? These opinions are on various subjects, philosophical, historical, political, or religious. No one supposes the belief of the sacred writers was correct, according to our standard, in regard to the motion of the heavenly bodies, the firmament, the rising and setting of the sun and moon, &c. So also, when Matthew informs us that fourteen was the number of the generations between David and the carrying away into Babylon, was he not mistaken in a matter of history?

And now in regard to their religious views. The Apostle Paul was, we know, brought up at the feet of Gamaliel, one of the few great and popular Rabbis of his time, who had at least, less prejudice than most of his brethren against Greek literature, and had more acquaintance with it; — a sort of Erasmus of his day beside St. Paul a kind of ancient Luther. Is it not probable then that some of the Alexandrine theology may have been incorporated' into Gamaliel's words to the young man Saul, and worked themselves out in his doctrine of faith? He himself, though so tolerant of the Apostles, even when the zealous Saul was imbruing his hands in their blood, is said by the Talmudists to have turned afterwards and written or approved a formal anathema upon the Christians. Perchance then after leading on Paul to a certain point he as many timid reformers have done before him, he turned back as they do, while his bolder young disciple went forward. But that some of Paul's incidental theological views have an Alexandrine cast, cannot be questioned, and these may have been obtained from his liberal teacher of early life. At any rate, they are more ancient than himself, and are the repetition of the current views of the best informed and most advanced religious thinkers of his day. The doctrine of the vicarious and injurious consequences of Adam's fall, which in the fifth of Romans, was made an illustration by way of antitype of the vicariously redemptive work of the second Adam, was a pre-existing Jewish development found more fully expressed in their writings. Yet in certain sections and ages of the Christian Church, this illustration from the Rabbinical education of St. Paul's day has been the foundation of whole systems of Theology, tremendous and terrible enough. Surely without disparaging the Apostle's Inspiration, it might be allowable to question much that the Jewish doctors had taught him. Yet Dr. Gill has cited these opinions as certain proofs of truth, because St. Paul brought up a Pharisee, incorporates them as his own in a mere illustration.

The history of all religious opinions, in the Bible as well as out of it, is being studied with more care now than formerly. And as a farmer who should buy a field sown with wheat, would give more for the field for the sake of the crop, though not for the sake of the weeds which yet formed a part of it; so in dealing with systems of religion, there will be seeds spring up, not sown by the husbandman, but which have been re-producing themselves hereditarily, or lying latent, ready for development in the soil. They do not give value to the true wheat of Divine truth, but cannot well be separated from it, except by time, or the great final harvest, till when, both must and will grow together, inseparable often practically, even though not indistinguishable to the eye of the Theologian.

VII. But with regard now to those truths which we must suppose it to be *the great object* of the Inspired writer to communicate, we can, I apprehend, still distinguish between the truth which his own mind was specially excited to perceive and to express, and his expression of it, which latter, owing to the human element in him, will ever be more or less imperfect. The tooth of time has eaten into the stone work wrought out by the chisel of a Phidias, and many an Apollo and Hercules, by the hand of a rare old master, comes down to us rain spotted and worn from its exposure of ages. Yet in making our casts, and filling our sculpture galleries with copies of these, we prefer properly to retain them with their unsightly ravages, and not to attempt the restoration of them to what we think they ought to be. The outline of figure is not injured by these imperfections; not injured as it would be by any attempted patchwork, or by rubbing down into smoothness the whole surface of the original. Yet this is what is daily being done to the hopeless disfigurement of the proportion and beauty of the whole, by the forced Harmonists.

VIII. The human element in the Scriptures then, while not destroying their divine spirit or authority as a whole, any more than do the defects of the lives of the Apostles, clearly admits of certain imperfections. These will even be found very useful in their final purpose, exciting within us a conception of perfection, beyond what we ever find realized in that which is written, and enticing forward our minds to learn more of the idea of God than any mere words can reveal

They lead us to seek knowledge and inspiration from God's other manifestations of his will, and thus cause the whole, and not a mere part, to form the full revelation of God to man.

If then the statement were true that "the Bible, and the Bible *alone*, is the religion of Protestants," it ought to make us all as it has made the Puseyites, pity Protestants, not indeed for the glorious revelation they embrace, but for the other glorious revelations of the Divine will, which they ignore and reject. It might almost tend to make one a Papist, as it has done many and would do more, did we not find the Church alone, (and still more, any one sect of it,) inferior as a guide for faith, to even the written word alone. The Protestants, however, who have incorporated into the words of their confession, this sort of reliance upon the Bible "*alone*," are, in nearly all cases, much better than their creed. None have more personal faith in the teachings of Providence, of conscience and of the Spirit than they. It is only the Church that is excluded at the utmost by that word "alone."

IX. Perhaps, then, a truer view of the purpose of these holy writings, would be this: that when we have faithfully studied them, in connection with the whole of what we can obtain of God's other revelations of his will, we may arrive at truth in every point of doctrine, duty and knowledge, with a precision and certainty proportioned to our necessities. This we clearly cannot obtain from any part of God's whole revealed will, while turning away from or neglecting any means of knowing the Divine teachings completely. There are many religious truths progressively revealed by Natural Religion, by science and history, which yet cannot be learned from the most diligent study of the Scriptures alone. Though the New Testament is to the pious mind a sort of supplement, nay, more a key to the religious understanding of the entire body of them.

X. God's true revelation, as a whole, expands with each age. For a man with an historic Bible in his hand, which was avowedly growing for fifteen hundred years, to assert, without the least proof, that revelation has ceased growing ever since John died, and that all possible advance for ever more is impossible, is to declare, what is so contrary to all the analogy of God's other works and teachings, that it would require at least a special and miraculous revelation to render it credible.* The Jew looked backward for his Paradise, but the Christian looks forward for his. He who compares the books of the New Testament with the mass of the writings of the early Fathers, will find such a new life in them, and such a wide separation between

---

* See Isaac Taylor's Ancient Christianity "On the dependence of the Modern Church upon the Ancient," p. 50 Phil. 1810.

the two, that he will be in little danger of doubting the inspiration of the former, for they will inspire him, if a Christian man. But their lustre may prevent him from seeing the true value and inspiration of the early Church and its writings. It is not, however, the Past independently of the Future, that is finally to exhibit the fullest measures of God's inspiring Spirit and presence, for,

XI. The Church is an inspired, a living and a growing body. There has ever been an invisible kingdom of God growing up amongst men. This has been through time thus far, and it shall be till time shall end, growing not only in numbers, but in the knowledge of God and the practice of true religion, growing in grace and in higher, holier inspirations. But the New Testament, and indeed the whole of the Bible, is now thoughtlessly held by many Christians to be inspired as the Church is not, and as even the Apostles were not inspired, either in their lives or in their personal teachings. And this view has been pushed, to the exclusion of all the instructions of Natural Religion. In this respect, our theology has retrograded as Protestantism has become more intensely and antagonistic to Romanism.

The Church is not, it never was, and never will be, an infallible body; but it is a living, and therefore a growing body, exhibiting, in connection with its earliest and holiest writings, and a perpetual Providence and influence, God's hand in the world, his laws more and more exactly unfolded, his Paraclete and personal presence more closely drawing near and walking with man again in the garden in the cool of the day.

To all this we may anticipate one objection. Where, then, shall we find an infallible and complete Revelation ? And to this we reply frankly, No where on earth. The Roman Catholic asks the same question of the Protestant, and professes to find it in the teachings of his Church. But when pressed, that body of Christians is divided as to where the final solution of difficulties is to be sought, — whether in the Pope, for instance, or in a General Council, and whether the decisions of the Council of Trent are or are not binding on all true Catholics. Meanwhile, numerous mistakes and contradictions of all tribunals appealed to, have satisfied Protestants at least, that it is not to be found at all where thus claimed.

The Protestant has professed to find this guidance in the Bible "alone." But acknowledging himself but a fallible interpreter, he admits that it is only the spirit that renders the book such a guide to him, in proportion to the imperfect measure in which he possesses it. An infallible revelation is not necessary for man, and it is not possible, while man has an ever-changing and progressive nature. It is an ideal thing, which can always be obtained by the sincere Christian with suffi-cient accuracy for his own practical guidance, but not theoretically, or for all other ages and climes any where. It is as mistaken as the dream of the Papal Church, that in order to enjoy Catholic unity, it is necessary to have a universal ecclesiastical language.

No one considers infallibility necessary or possible, practically, in any other branch of knowledge, however vital; why, then, in this, the most profound in its researches, abstract in its essential principles, and com-plicated in its details of them all? Even in mathe-matics, we may form a conception of a circle, or a tri-angle, but who ever made or saw a *perfect* circle, or triangle, or straight line? And who would talk of a final and complete system of mathematics? A com-plete Revelation is possible only in the same sense, and to the same extent, as an infallible and perfect knowledge of any, or rather of every other science; religion being the most comprehensive and the most complicated of them all.

One may conceive of Euclid standing before his royal pupil Ptolemy, when he had finished his immortal work and saying, "your kingdom will pass away. Egypt will become a heap of ruins and of mummies. Rome itself will fall. New arms will change the tactics of war, and science will alter the arts of peace, but this book contains truths that will live as long as time lasts, and be eternally the same, while space itself remains, and their dominion over men, increasingly recognized as civilization progresses."

Jesus stood before the wise men and philosophers, and brought a system of absolute religious truth from heaven to earth, from God to man, and he says, " Heaven and earth shall pass away, but my words shall not pass away." But it was ever intended that both alike should grow in all their projections into the future.

However ignorant a man may be of external evidences, if he begins to live a Christian life, he will find himself at once brought into accord with the eternal laws of being and of his own nature as nothing else will bring him. When Jesus stood before that solid marble temple at Jerusalem, and declared that his words should never pass away though it should crumble, the Roman arms were doing for Judaism what civil war and science have been doing for our country and age, i. e. breaking up and unsettling old and cherished opinions. That was an age of lingering superstition among the people, and of wide spread scepticism among the priests, the rulers and all the men of thought and power. Two thousand years have since then rolled by, and the Roman nation has passed away, and all the then existing dynasties have passed away ; ages, fashions, customs, opinions, all have gone, but He who sat then King upon the Mount of Olives, and his words, and his throne have not passed away. His kingdom in religion, as Euclid's in mathematics, is more extended than ever.

There are some things, thank God, that never change. Some truths are so elementary and absolute, that they cannot be simplified, just as there are some substances in nature, so perfectly pure and uncompounded, that they never can be reduced to anything more elementary, and are therefore indestructible. So it is with pure religion, or what is the same thing, true and absolute Christianity. Our Saviour claims for his words, just this kind of abstract immutable quality. Heaven and earth are all complex, mutable and therefore destructible, but those words which reveal the ultimate laws of God and abstract truth, are eternal. When we obtain knowledge only by the instruction of others, we are never perfectly certain of its correctness, but when it is reduced to an inward perception, an intuition, we also know that it can never be shaken. The school-boy learns his multiplication table by memory, and so long as it is thus only learned, he knows not but what there may be some error in the printing and he may be learning it all wrong, or but that some new discovery may change it. But when he sees by an inward perception of immutable relations that twice two must make four and ten times ten are one hundred, he never again can fear that the progress of Mathematical science will push that aside as untrue or absurd; for so long as the relations of numbers continue, so long must that certainty remain whatever else changes. He has seen by an inward vision of his own, its correspondence with eternal truth and its relations.

And so, if some person should assert that bye and bye in the progress of things, lying and fraud would be proved to be virtues, and truth and honesty, crimes, it would only convince each wise and moral man, that he who made such an assertion, understood nothing of morals. And it is by just such a certain and clear inward perception, that the Christian's experience assures him at last, and beyond all words, of the immutability of pure Christianity.

Men usually begin by receiving the New Testament on its external evidences, just as the school-boy begins to learn his multiplication table mechanically out of his book. And the one continues to be about as dull as the other so long as only thus received. Nor does such a person thus obtain any certainty, but what some stronger evidence may arise upon the other side, and overthrow his faith; for there may be some flaw in a link of his historical chain of authorities, some hidden fault, and the strength of any chain is only that of its weakest—not its strongest link. Or new facts may come to light, or new discoveries of science or history, and upset the whole. So he must live in perpetual doubt, and conflict against science, history, providence.

But he who walks with God, and experiences the power of grace, and lives in the truths of Christianity, *knows* that the religion of Jesus is no dream or delusion. He may meet with a thousand specious objections that he cannot answer, but he has an evidence within himself that nothing can shake.

The lad who studies his Euclid aright, will very soon get intellectually to such a point, that if you should attempt to prove to him no such person as Euclid ever existed, or that half of these demonstrations were in use before, or that the whole book is but an invention of subsequent times to which an ancient name had been attached, though he might not know enough of history to refute you, he would reply, " one thing I know by an inward perception, that it is all immutably and indestructibly true. Thus also, is the Christian assured of the worth of the fourth gospel no less than the three synoptics, and of the book of Revelation as well as Paul's Epistles.

It is in this way, and in this sense, that Christian men feel and know by an inward experience, that Christ is the Rock of Ages against which all waves of time and change dash harmlessly, and the chief corner stone of that great and living temple, the Church, in which God dwells and walks with man again on earth. On it, the Apostles, laboring together, wrought as wise master builders, laying the foundations. On it, holy men, saints and reformers have labored ever since, building with various successes, some of hay, wood and stubble, and some of gold, silver and precious stones. And this building still "*groweth*" unto a holy temple, for an habitation of God, through the Spirit. Here we enjoy the presence of Jesus, and the enlightening and comfort of the Paraclete. All form parts of God's revelation of himself to man, reason and conscience begin the work of Natural Religion, all history, all Providence, all experience, no less truly than the written word, forming parts of the great Revelation in which even men first enlightened themselves, reflect in turn through the Church the light of eternal truth to others. Just as the moon and planets though naturally opaque substances, reflect back on other worlds the light they have received from the sun, so do the Redeemed of all ages contribute to our faith; and thus the Bible, the Spirit and the Church are not separated but made tributary to the onward progress of Revelation, Inspiration, Christianity in the earth.

CHAPTER XIV.

THE BEARING OF THE WHOLE ON EXISTING RELIGIOUS EFFORTS AND DENOMINATIONS.

IF the views before advanced are correct, the great fault of Roman Catholicism has been, not claiming that the true Church is a perpetually Inspired body; but that because Inspired, it is therefore *Infallible*, infallible especially in that exclusiveness which has led it to excommunicate some of the most intelligent and living portions of the true and Universal Church.

On the other hand, the great error of Protestantism has been in supposing that *the Bible* because inspired, was therefore necessarily infallible, and especially in believing this book "*alone*" a complete guide, to the exclusion of all other revelations and sources of spiritual improvement.

Infidelity has made the still worse mistake of regarding both the Christian Scriptures and the Christian Church, not only as fallible, but as *false* instead of, though containing errors, yet, living and therefore progressive developments of religious truths, and sincere and earnest efforts to adapt eternal verities to the nature, times and circumstances of particular ages and races. It is this shallow conceit of Infidelity that has made it throw its whole efforts into antagonism to the wisest and best men of each age, made it negative instead of positive, and always quarrelling with and fighting against the good, instead of working with it, and making it better.

The true view is that while there is a perpetual approach towards more absolute and exact views of theological and religious truth in each age, as in other sciences, yet but little of our knowledge can be called final, nor can it be considered in any respect complete in expression as regards the forces, causes, consequences, or Divine purposes connected with our religious life here.

Yet we are so created, that religion is necessarily not only a part of our nature, but the Supreme and ruling portion of it; the chief instinct and of increasing power in proportion as man rises to the pure and spiritual Being which the Heavenly Father intended him to become.

The teachings of *Universal* Religion are, therefore, the fundamental basis of all true politics, forming the principles of wise and just laws. While the separation of Church and State is well, and the most perfect freedom of religious opinions desirable, yet Religion as such, is the necessary and eternal basis of all true government. Christianity is essentially a remedial system and its kingdom is not of this world. But the eternal principles of religion and therefore of Christianity, so far as coincident with them, belong to man in all his relations. Christianity has nowhere directly forbidden either polygamy or slavery. It permitted each in practice merely teaching that "from the beginning it was not so," and was to be tolerated only in deference to the imperfections of then existing systems. And they have not been destroyed by any violent crusade from without, but by the working of certain antagonistic principles of universal religion within. These have caused them to disappear by degrees, as leading to results incongruous with the highest and best teachings of humanity and religion.

But the Church, though a voluntary society, is yet Divinely appointed for the cultivation of the Religious life on the basis of Christianity. There may, of course, be other societies for the culture of certain special virtues, such as temperance, or particular benevolences, or for the study of Universal Religion,— pure theism. These need not be antagonistic to Christian Churches, and ought not to be considered necessarily so in their ends or means, nor need union with any one preclude fellowship with others.

In the most ancient times, and again in the most modern, some have attempted rigidly to draw the line between the teachings of Jesus, and that of his Apostles. Dr. Priestly, indeed, considered not only that the reasonings of St. Paul were in parts inconsequential, but that Jesus was a mere man, "peccable and fallible." Yet many, perhaps most of the modern Unitarians would probably be disposed to make a distinction just there. Without considering the teachings of the Apostles absolutely final as to what is pure Christian doctrine, the instructions of Jesus, so far as they can be distinctly ascertained *are* so considered and believed to be of binding authority.

The great mass of the so-called Orthodox Congregationalists, Presbyterians and Baptists, are accustomed to regard the entire teachings of the New Testament as a finality; those of the Apostles as perfect and equal in authority to those of Jesus Christ, but deny similar weight to the teachings of the Church or writers of any period at all subsequent.

With most of the Episcopalians, however, the teachings of Christ and his Apostles in the New Testament together with the Fathers of the first four centuries, seem to constitute the authoritative declaration of what Christianity is.* The Greek Church includes even more than this;—the decision of the first seven Ecumenical Councils, concluding with that held by Photius in Constatinople in 879–80.

The Roman Catholic considers Christianity an equally living, growing authoritative system in all ages. Christ, the Apostles, and their successors are alike exponents of what Christianity is, and the Pope as the successor of St. Peter and the centre of Unity, is in their view the Vicar of Christ upon the earth.

Each of these various opinions sincerely upheld have been useful as presenting different and interesting aspects of Christianity with particular prominence.; each, however, imperfect and needing to be corrected by reason and by each other. But all such reasoning must be founded on the authority either of those intuitions which form the basis of Natural Religion, or those various Revelations which come to us through the Scriptures, the Paraclete, Divine Providence, or the teachings of the Church.

For the State, there are certain principles of Universal Religion, as of morality, (the last forming a part of it,) contrary to which, nothing can rightly be enacted, or stand, but to uphold and support which, by suitable means, is the true duty and policy of every government; while all things should of course

---

* See Cary's " Testimony of the Fathers," — Preface, p. 82.

15

be left as free as possible, so as to develop the spontaneity of the human affections in choosing the right, the true, the just, the beautiful and the holy.

There ought to be and there will be a large and increasing class of men of the highest moral and religious character, who will desire to cultivate religious knowledge in this most strictly and exclusively *scientific* aspect, as the true basis of legislation for this country, and the wisest for all mankind, and they ought to have liberty to do so fully and freely.

Daniel Webster in his argument on the Girard Will case, however, took a different view, and maintained that *Christianity* was a part of the law and public policy of Pennsylvania, it having been a part of those of England, and of all Christian nations, so that no public *Charity* can be supported as such by the common law of England, except it be a *Christian* Charity in its essential spirit. I have carefully studied his argument on this subject, but would observe *first*, that the decision of the Supreme Court sustains the Girard Will, to break which was the object of his speech; *second*, that the argument though abundantly proving that religion of some kind is the natural and necessary basis of the laws of every State, and thus reflects the governing ideas of the people on that subject, yet this does not prove that *Christianity* should be the basis of civil law, but rather that those universal principles of religion belonging to man as man in every age and climate, should be the fountain of all the legislation of states and nations; *third,* that this whole argument of Webster is built upon a special clause of the Constitution of Pennsylvania, in which it differs from that of nearly all the other States, and especially from that of the *United States*, which was amended on purpose to declare that "Congress shall make no law respecting an establishment of religion, or prohibiting that free exercise thereof, or abridging the freedom of speech or of the press." In expounding what this clause means, Judge Story says, "the right of a society or government to interfere in matters of religion, will hardly be contested by any persons who believe that piety, religion and morality are intimately connected with the well being of a State, and indispensable to the administration of civil justice. The promulgation of the great doctrines of religion, the being, the attributes, the providence of one Almighty God, the responsibility to him for all our actions, founded upon moral accountability, a future state of rewards and punishments, the cultivation of all the personal, social and benevolent virtues;—these can never be a matter of indifference in any well ordered community. Indeed, it is difficult to conceive how any civilized society can well exist without them. *   *   *   This is a matter wholly distinct from that of private judgment in matters of religion, and the freedom of public worship, according to the dictates of one's conscience. The real difficulty lies in ascertaining the limits to which government may rightfully go in fostering and encouraging religion. *   *   *   Probably at the time of the adoption of the Constitution, and of the amendment to it, now under consideration, the general if not the universal sentiment in America was, that Christianity ought to receive encouragement from the State, so far as such encouragement was not incompatible with the private rights of conscience, and the freedom of religious worship. An attempt to level all religions, and to make it a matter of State policy to hold all in utter indifference, would have created universal disapprobation, if not universal indignation."

Probably the clause respecting freedom as to religion, can be best illustrated by the next sentence as to the freedom of speech or of the press. The prohibition of abridging liberty of speech, or of the press, does not secure an absolute right to every individual to speak, or print, or write whatever he might please, without any responsibility, public or private. That would allow each citizen to destroy at pleasure, the peace, reputation, property and safety of every other, and corrupt society by obscene and immoral publications. But the meaning is, that every man shall have a right to speak, write and print his opinions on any subject, without prior restraint, so that he does not injure any other person in his rights, or disturb public peace, or attempt to subvert government or good morals.

So, therefore, in prohibiting the establishment of religion and all restraints on the free exercise thereof, it is the free exercise of *religion*, not *irreligion*, which may not be restrained, and this clearly supposes that there is an absolute and eternal religion belonging to man as man, and which, therefore, is not to be confounded with the immoral teachings of the Mormons, and such persons against whom the United States' laws of marriage rightly operate as a restraint. The Chinese has a right to build temples, and offer incense, and the Persian to worship the sun, and the Turk to spread his carpet and erect his Mosque in honor of Mohammedanism in the United States. But if the Turk attempt to practice polygamy, the United States' law may restrain him, and the basis of that law is, that it is contrary to natural religion, and therefore to public policy. The experience of these last few years has demonstrated to our people, that the same thing is true of slavery, and therefore its prohibition has been introduced into the Constitution itself.

Lactantius, in his Divine Institutions, (6 : 8,) has preserved to us some admirable teachings of Cicero on this subject. " Law, properly understood, is no other than right reason, agreeing with nature, spread abroad among all men, ever consistent with itself, eternal; whose office is to summon to duty by its commands, to deter from vice by its prohibitions, which however to the good never commands or forbids in vain, never influences the wicked either by commanding or forbidding. In contradiction to this law, nothing can be laid down, nor does it admit of partial or entire repeal. Nor can we be released from this law, either by vote of the senate or decree of the people. Nor does it require any commentator or interpreter beside itself. Nor will there be one law at Athens and another at Rome, — one now and another hereafter, — but one eternal, immutable law will both embrace all nations and all times. And there will be one common Master, as it were, and Ruler of all, namely God, the great Originator, Expositor, Enactor of this law, which law, whoever will not obey, will be flying from himself, and having treated with contempt his human nature, will in that very fact pay the greatest penalty, even if he shall have escaped other punishments, as they are commonly considered."

We say, then, that in this country, and in this age, and with our Constitution, while Christianity, as such, is not, and cannot be established as a national religion, yet that our Christianity, so far as it is the expression of the great truths of universal religion, and of the true remedy for offences against it, is of necessity the basis of all our laws. The great and immortal truths they contain give their perpetuity to the laws of Moses. And it ought to be the study of our wisest legislators, and philosophers, and divines, to show from experience, from the history of legislation, and of all various religions true and false, but especially Christianity, what are the eternal teachings or laws of universal religion on all subjects, and so to prove these teachings as to cause them to be reduced to the settled customs, institutions, education, and law of the land. Religion and law must, moreover, both of them, be *historically* developed. They are growths of man's moral and spiritual nature. Thus much for the relations of Christianity to *the State*.

But now the question remains, What must be the effects of the views of Inspiration we have seen alone tenable, upon the different religious denominations of our land, most of which have been more or less affected by what Coleridge calls Bibliolatry?

In some respects, it might at first appear as if they were about to tend towards Unitarian and in others, to Roman Catholic views. The Unitarians have been right in asserting that the written teachings of the Apostles were not necessarily or absolutely infallible, any more than their lives or verbal instructions, and their free yet devout examination of the Scriptures in the light of Natural Religion, is worthy of the greatest commendation. Dr. Pye Smith, in his work on the Person of the Messiah, while in the first edition he severely denounces Dr. Priestly for his sentiments on this subject, ends in later editions, as we have seen, in earnestly pleading against his own denomination for more liberal views on Inspiration.

But, on the other hand, Unitarianism, so far as it, in common with many, perhaps most other Protestant denominations, has set itself against *Church authority* and reverence for that growth of Christian doctrine and moral teachings which has arisen from ages of experience and traditionary practice, has cut itself off from one chief source alike of conservatism and of safe progress, i. e. experience, and exhausted much vital force in theorizing. In many respects, it is free from prejudices, and is broad and noble, enquiring and progressive. It has produced writings on morals, of a tone, beauty and thoroughness which are admirable. It has given a style and tone, and universality of culture to many of the writers of New England, that have brought together the best results of philosophy and Christianity, and made the world feel their harmony. But so far, its effects have been confined chiefly to writing. As a religious denomination, its congregations and churches have diminished, and been poorly attended, its members scattered, and it has not presented enough of old established and positive religion to feed the masses of the people. It has occupied itself too much with negations instead of positive truths. It has been anxious to limit its contemplations too much to the finite, while man never works so naturally or successfully as when grasping after the infinite and the eternal. The immensity of our late national struggle has done its adherents the greatest good, infusing a life and vigor into their movements, unknown before, making them more practical, instead of merely theoretic, and their religion the working Christianity of Him who went about doing good, while actuated by faith in right and justice and other eternal verities. The Sanitary Commission is one of its noblest products.

With regard to the particular questions at issue between the Unitarians and Orthodox Christians, the views of Inspiration which have been advanced will of course concede this, that instead of now insisting that each passage of Scripture must be interpreted in a manner perfectly consistent with every other, and taken in a sense that will make it harmonious with the whole, it is clear that we must weigh the language of each writer by itself, and may consider whether even the same writer is always quite consistent with himself. This Neander has felt at liberty to do on many points, and discriminates the Pauline from the Petrine view, and that of John in his " Planting and Training," with great suggestiveness. But then this system of interpretation, to be properly carried out, requires a much more accurate study of an author's words, and of the *history* of pre-existing views in the community to which they were addressed, than has been customary by any class; and it is here that new and higher ideas will lead, and are leading many Unitarians to a greater similarity of views with many Orthodox, as to the sense of Scripture. Yet others are going off more nearly to a simple Theism and the elimination of all that is super-humanitarian from their Christianity.

Of this, at least, there can be no doubt, that while the post-Nicene and ante-Nicene Fathers may both be examined as witnesses of the general belief of the Church, their controversial forms of expression, founded on all sorts of imperfect interpretations of Scripture, cannot be final or binding upon us. There must be a greater breadth and charity in all our creeds and all our churches. Most of the conservative portion of the Unitarians seem to feel increasingly, not only that Christianity is a Divinely inspired system, but its Author and Head is not to be regarded as merely human and fallible, but as a truly divine and final Authority as to Christianity itself. Some do this in the Sabellian sense, which also appears to be the essence of Dr. Bushnell's God in Christ. In fact, the modes of expression and views of the Orthodox and Unitarians often now approach so nearly to each other in their mutual dread of those who would do away all that is final and authoritative from Christianity, that it is impossible to draw a line of distinction that shall bar their intercourse and exchange of views, without great mischief to both parties equally.

On the other hand, the Roman Catholics, in coming to this country, have lost much of their Romanism, and are daily losing more. Their extreme veneration for the priesthood wears rapidly away, and Priests and people are becoming more truly Catholic, well educated and progressive. Indeed the Pope himself in proportion as he is losing his temporal power, has lately, it is said, become more enlarged and charitable in discipline. In order to win back the Greek Church, not under the Russian Patriarchite to Papal unity, it was said he had consented to allow the Priests of that branch to be married men, a reformation, it is to be hoped, that may be extended to other sections of that Communion also. The lines of distinction between the Roman Catholics and the more ritualistic and energetic portion of the Episcopal Church, are daily diminishing, so that to what extent the Romish Church may be eventually modified, it seems impossible to conjecture.

The views of Inspiration we have discussed, have certainly led to great desires for the introduction of the element of a positive Church authority, in proportion as the old literal faith in the verbal inspiration of the written word of Scripture has given way. This was unquestionably the process by which Dr. Pusey himself was led to his present position, and it has been at Oxford, the basis of the High Church movement. It is the chief reason why, among thinking persons of all classes, who wish for a practical religion in which to bring up their children, not contrary to reason, yet not resting on the individual reason alone, independently of Authority, so many have become Episcopalians.

There is, therefore, every reason to believe that this movement will increase in proportion as larger numbers of educated persons adopt modern views on the subject of Inspiration. As people are more educated, they see and feel the advantages of the division of labor, and are therefore more willing, when they get the best advice from those who have studied any subject most thoroughly, to accord to the adviser a degree of authority which more superficial persons accord to *their own* reasons alone. Hence there is a voluntary yielding of the judgment to Church authority, both natural, wise and increasing with intellectual and moral culture, which has thus far led many to join those who have pleaded for it most directly. The experience of many ages in an unbroken line, though not essential, is yet a great recommendation to any system of practical guidance. It is this that has led the powerful intellect of Brownson into the bosom even of the Roman Catholic Church, and thousands of others in England and in this country.

But after all, what is the Church properly considered, for whose authority so much may be claimed? The Church properly is the whole body, laity and clergy together, not the clergy alone, much less the clergy of any one sect. Our Christianity is the voice and testimony and experience of all Christians, modern even more than ancient, because the experience of the former is the result of all the wisdom and piety of the latter, and therefore more reliable. The opinions of the excommunicated and excommunicating sects are often alike to be weighed. Dr. Channing's view is more important than that of Pope Pius the Ninth, and those of the laity are as valuable on many points as those of the priesthood. Each one will be right in many things, where the others will be wrong. Every one will suggest much, and it is the province of reason to exercise a sound, critical faculty, and decide the claims to his obedience amid apparent conflicts of the authorities. But that the Church, that is the experience of the best informed Christians, on any subject is and ever must be one great authority, to each individual, there can be no doubt. It is here perhaps in the absence of respect for Church authority, that the Unitarians have seemed most defective, and the Roman Catholics and High Churchmen most superabounding. They stand in natural antagonism. The Unitarians have proved profound moral philosophers, and admirable guides to the State in all questions of natural right and wrong, and those points of statesmanship which are connected with universal Religion. But while their books are read, their houses of worship are not filled. Like the Theophilanthropists of the last century, their speculations are profound, and beautiful, their culture is wise, but their *worship*, and that which evinces reverence appears defective.

On the other hand, amid all the cumbrousness of antiquated forms, there is among the Episcopalians, a cultivation of living piety, a habit of worship, reverence for authority, such as every wise parent wishes to inculcate in his child, and every wise statesman upon all the members of the community. As a system of religious, practical education therefore, Episcopacy gains where Unitarianism loses. If the two could, as they will ultimately, so blend as that each shall respect and gain the good points of the other, and lose individual narrowness, there would arise a greater breadth of

Churchmanship, and a greater warmth and reverence among Unitarians. The life of Robertson or Arnold may illustrate the one, and perhaps works like Ecce Homo the other.

The strong hereditary hold which Presbyterianism in the South and Congregationalism in the North exercise upon very many of the most wise and moderate and truly respectable worshippers throughout this country, and through Protestant Europe, makes it natural to ask, What will be the effect of the coming wave of opinions as to Inspiration upon their prosperity? Both of these denominations were founded originally upon a most implicit faith in every line and letter of Scripture. "Every pin of the Tabernacle is precious, and must be made according to the pattern showed in the mount." Such were the Presbyterian arguments with Whitfield, when he sought to preach in Scotland; to which he found it best to reply, " True, but all are not called to make pins." There is, however, a period in the history of each denomination, in which it becomes naturally conservative and historical, and therefore certain to be the claimant of an authority within itself. It has been thus with both of these denominations, in measure, as well as with the Lutherans and German Reformed, and this as well in Europe as in this country. It will, therefore, not be natural, and perhaps not wise, for denominations thus situated, to take the lead in any progressive movements expediting a change, however certain. Their policy has been and will be no doubt conservative, and leaning rather to oppose than foster even those learned and really eminent leaders, who, like Dr. Hanna in Scotland, and Dr. Davidson in England, would have piloted them to a more secure anchorage ground. Yet, in good time, all opposition to the views of these teachers will quickly die out, and new pastors arise, who will silently accept the results of their learning, labors and conflicts, wisely combining with them the authority of religious teachers, (but without disturbing the older members,) while embracing the new generation in thought and spirit. It is thus that all bodies of men grow, both political and religious organizations. It is well for the masses that it should be so. Meantime each Christian man and minister must and ought to labor peacefully, and not antagonistically, where the head of the Church has placed him, and in his own appointed work. Sometimes I have felt sad to see the denominational leaders frowning upon a man like Dr. Bushnell, of honesty and earnestness, and trying by ridicule, sarcasm and bitter denunciations, to keep all things as they were, even at the expense of truths known or easily knowable by those who speak loudest in opposition to them. But this too shall pass away, and the men with it. Let discord only be avoided, and worship preserved, and practical religion diligently cultivated. In one or two generations, Christian men will be no more concerned at the loss of verbal inspiration than at that of the six literal days of Genesis, or of the belief in the Copernican theory.

There are, however, two denominations which have become the numerous bodies they are by most aggressive strides, rather than by the hereditary principle,— the Methodists and the Baptists; the former by the bold attacks of *reason* upon seeming doctrinal abuses, and the latter by a more exact compliance with the literal demands of Scripture *authority* in regard to the ordinance of Baptism. Both of these denominations, however, owe most of their real success, not to their different peculiarities, but to the point on which they both agree, i. e. in being earnestly and aggressively Evangelical, attacking sin everywhere, with high faith in the power of the Holy Spirit to make man a new creature, morally regenerated to God and goodness. Connected with this, the Methodist has used an able but avowedly human system of religious culture in the shape of classes and society meetings, while the Baptists have claimed the words of Scripture as their authority for the entire pattern of their Ecclesiastical regulations.

So far, then, it might seem as if Methodists could and would more easily adapt themselves to the broader views of Inspiration than Baptists. Perhaps they will find less external change to make in the form of their arguments or creed, which depend more on reason, and less directly on the Bible. But both will be found to rest ultimately upon certain great intuitions, and both have professedly been unqualified supporters of the most literal views of Bible Inspiration. Doctrinally, however, so far as creeds go, the Methodists, adopting substantially the thirty-nine articles of the Church of England, from which they sprang, have differed from that body only in giving them an exclusively anti-Calvinistic interpretation. Methodism is therefore as free as is the Church of England itself, to embrace by. those articles much wider views of Christianity and of the Scriptures than has thus far been common, but for which ample room can be found without the least disturbance, in proportion as the leading thinkers of that denomination adopt them. It would not for a day impair any of their zeal, but much extend their usefulness. _ Indeed, it would build up the work of personal religion in each man's heart and experience, as the foundation of all the best evidences of Christianity. All reasonable methods of cherishing and cultivating this are really parts of Christianity. Nor can any objector lay his finger on a word that need be altered in their fifth and sixth articles, which alone allude to this subject in their Confession.

With the Baptists this is somewhat different, though their disadvantage is less than might at first appear. They have ever denied the binding authority of creeds, and though several Confessions of Faith have been drawn up, many of their best churches have steadily refused to adopt any of them, and each association or church has altered, or composed, or declined to adopt any confession, pretty much as they have seen fit. One of the most venerable of these confessions, and one of the mildest and best, is that of the First Baptist Church in Boston, embraced about two hundred years ago. Most of those drawn up since have been modifications of· one adopted by one hundred Baptist ministers in London, in 1642, which is indeed, except on the subject of Baptism, almost identical with the Savoy Confession of the Congregationalists, and mostly copied therefore from the Westminster Confession of the Presbyterians, except in the matter of Church Government.

Other Baptists, wishing for something less antiquated in theological phraseology, especially on the subject of the Divine purposes, have very generally adopted a confession drawn up for the New Hampshire Baptists thirty or forty years ago. This has been again variously modified or dispensed with, so that, practically, no denomination is more unfettered by creeds, though perhaps none more generally agree among themselves in sentiment, than the Baptists.

So far this agreement, and all the expressions of it that I have seen, unless it be the first, have been very literal and plenary in their views of Inspiration. Perhaps their strict conformity to primitive customs, as to the subject and manner of administering baptism, is in some cases the natural consequence, in others possibly to a certain extent the *cause* of this.

Twelve years ago, when writing at length on the Progress of Baptist Principles, I did not then think this view amounted to what might fairly be called bibliolatry, either in them or in others, who from the same acknowledged premises, adopted different conclusions as to the particular ordinance of Baptism. But I now find myself inclined to suspect too exclusive an attachment to the letter of Scripture, among all those who hold as I once held to plenary Inspiration; and see with regret such men as the able Professor, Dr. Robinson* of Rochester, not ashamed to declare that he

---

* I allude to a note on p. 25, of a published Address of his delivered before the Rhetorical Society of Rochester Theological Seminary, delivered May 15, 1866, in which the author says, "For the benefit of those who have been so much concerned for his orthodoxy, that he believes implicitly and explicitly, 1. In the plenary Inspiration of the Holy Scriptures, 2. In the existence of God, in his decrees, &c." — I cannot but regret to see such a Confession of faith so endorsed, most especially placing a belief in the existence of a Supreme Being *after* that

holds now, and ever expects to hold on to this view. Even where many compensating statements of the living presence and inspirations of the Holy Spirit in the Church, are so upheld as to counteract much of the evil, it is impossible not to dread the formality and deadness that must arise, if the denomination does not outgrow the contracted expressions and narrow views on this point that are in danger of stifling its life and growth.

What then ought to be the bearing of the discussions recorded in former pages and agitating all Christendom on the Baptists as a denomination? I say at once and frankly, that before every thing else,

of what I must call the exploded dogma of plenary inspiration, in every sense of that phrase, that such an asseveration must have been intended to convey to his readers. On reading it I felt that some one ought to speak out on this subject, at least for the sake of the rising ministry of our Denomination. In a very different spirit Dr. Hovey of Newton has seemed to treat the matter in a sermon preached at Newport and other places, and condensed in a recent number of the Watchman and Reflector. But the widely prevailing ignorance of the difficulties of this whole question among ministerial students, otherwise intelligently and laboriously educated, but allowed to remain terribly in the dark on this Inspiration question, in most of the Evangelical denominations, is to my mind, one of the most fearful signs of the times and has alone induced me to write this work. Should I have succeeded in leading some of them to think on this subject for themselves, prayerfully and with a supreme love for the truth at any cost, my purpose will have been fulfilled.

young men preparing for the ministry, ought to be led to freely study, candidly, fearlessly and for themselves, this as one of the most important of all the theological points likely to come up for discussion in their future ministry. "The priest's lips should keep knowledge," yet few of them have much on this subject to keep. The plan of putting the complicated and difficult study of Inspiration *out* of its proper order, into the first lectures of a course, when the minds of students are fresh and green, with the critical faculties unsharpened attrition, and no basis laid on which to *prove* anything theologically, and before even the existence of a Supreme Being is discussed, is a fundamental error. They are thus, no doubt, most ready to believe everything, without proof or difficulty, and this makes it very easy work for the instructor, but must tend to make them sadly superficial, if not blind leaders of the blind, so far as all this is concerned.

There is a natural and an eternal order in theological study, as in that of every other science, i. e. from the most simple to the more complex; and as in all the Natural Sciences, the proper arrangement makes more than half the difference as to whether a student *ever* gets a correct conception of the whole, so is it equally essential in theology. Where this order is violated, young men leave the seminaries with minds shallow, and confident, but asleep; praised for a docile orthodoxy, but quite unable to meet the spiritual wants of intelligent hearers, or enquiring young members who go off in crowds to hear those who can command the respect of their minds and feed them as well as touch their feelings. Soon these ministers begin to read, grow cautious, misty, preaching a half starved theology without point or aim or conviction. It then generally takes them years, often a life, before they are worth anything as preachers, because they have no clear, strong, undoubting certainties on Inspiration or any other subject.

I know the fear of rendering young ministers sceptical, makes old professors careful. So they ought to be. But if pious and earnest young men, who give up their lives most sincerely to the study of religion, with the most disinterested motives, cannot be trusted with the truth, who can? Life is short. For twenty or thirty years there have been seminaries where progress in discussing these subjects has been almost imperceptible while theological literature has been full of it, and every year, new classes have issued. Nor have I known a single case in which a more thorough, simple and honest course has been pursued, without a firmer and more living faith in the great and Divine reality of Christianity resulting.

But what is the duty of those persons, ministers and

members of all Christian Churches, who become convinced, as many are daily becoming, that those verbal
views of the infallibility of Inspiration in which they
have been brought up, are both unnecessary and erroneous? Shall they stifle, or abandon such convictions
for fear of wounding weak brethren, or rather for fear
of being wounded by those stronger in a blatant
volubility of orthodoxy; or shall they conceal their
belief by unworthy professions or evasions?— God
forbid! The love of truth and of Christian honor
must ever be held supreme in the soul and life of
every Christian. Not to be afraid or ashamed of a
truth at any cost is one of the earliest and most
important lessons Christ taught the world by his life
and by his death, and Christianity has since taught
this by all its goodly company of martyrs. If it
should cost the severance of dearest Christian ties, still
to shrink from it would be irreligious.

But on the other hand, the lack of sufficient meekness, patience and forbearance is the besetting sin
attending increased knowledge, with a want of continued reverence, love and zeal for the old and common
truths of Christianity. Indeed, often doubts and
neglect of universal religion, are apt to be the besetting
dangers and sins of those whose characters formed on
one set of instructions, find suddenly that some of
what they held to be infallible, is only proximate.

Such persons should beware that they do not lightly or hastily throw aside any of those duties, or habits of the religious life or of usefulness to others to which they have become accustomed, without strong and adequate reason. When Jesus came as a reformer of the Jews, he urged upon his disciples that except their righteousness should exceed that of the Scribes and Pharisees, they should in no case enter the new dispensation. In proportion as our knowledge becomes larger, it will require and acquire a more earnest, vigorous and practical piety of life. Where this is not the case, it were better for a man to have gone on unawakened in the old routine. Larger views will either make a man better or worse, more exact in duty as well as in speculation, and more afraid of neglecting even a Christian usage, or a delicate feeling. Often it is otherwise. Men throw off too easily and too fast the restraints and duties to which they have been accustomed, though more necessary to their soul's health than ever. There should be even a higher and more spiritual self-consecration to the service of God, of Christianity and of humanity; of truth and of goodness, connected with those broader views of the Inspiration of the Scriptures, and of every Christian man. If Dr. Pusey and his friends have found and exemplified this in one way, shall not others find it in more natural, useful and practical directions?

16

No man should be in haste to alter his position in the Church of Christ from any advance in his own views, but rather by patience with the faults of others and a more holy, circumspect, and Christian life, lead others to see and feel at last, that he has a faith that comprehends more and therefore can endure more. To be candid without being censorious, or impertinent, or impatient at the oppositions of malicious, ignorant and bad men, who yet fancy that they are doing God service in vituperating and slandering him, is what the Master has taught his followers to endure — oh, how patiently! — for the good of others. All this we must learn to bear for the sake of each other. It is a part of that law of vicariousness, which the cross of Christ was intended to reveal to man, as the chosen method by which alone, the enslaved of ignorance and error are ever to be redeemed.

Jesus did not withdraw from the synagogues of his native land, nor was he ever formally expelled, but was still considered a poor Jewish Rabbi till falsely adjudged guilty of blasphemy, and declared by the High Priest to be worthy of death. Nor did his followers cease to worship and meet in the temple, long after the day of Pentecost, or to consider themselves as other than a Jewish sect in Palestine. Only gradually did the young Christian Church become separated from the Jewish synagogue, and then by no act of its own,

but slowly and unwillingly through that of the Jews.
Indeed, so slow and cautious was this process, that for
ages out of respect for them, Saturday was generally
held as sacred, especially in the East, as the first day
of the week. Both were and have ever been held as
festival days of the Church, and the fast of Friday
was so fixed to avoid them both.

With perfect candor then, but with perfect meekness and humility, let every Christian of every sect
avow all the new truths he may see, retaining fully his
love and charity for those who may not think with him,
and leaving those who have the least love, to
move in the work of schism and separation, if it must
be so. Certainly it becomes not those who are themselves only in a state of gradual development, to be in
haste to form new sects, and new antagonisms; they
should rather aim to be legitimate growths from the
ancient tree, inheriting all its vigor and sap, and
differing from it only in the new and higher fruitful-
ness of the young graft.

One or two things, however, are especially de-
manded of members of the Baptist denomination, by
the larger views of Inspiration that have been suggested in .this work. One is to rise above the mere
literalness of Scripture interpretation, (not indeed by
neglecting the laws of close criticism,) but by combining with them a more full and charitable adherence

to the Spirit. Several years ago, I wrote a little work on the Progress of Baptist Principles, in which I advocated the view that while we should take every means of exhibiting our Christian fellowship with all true Christians, yet that the ceremonial communion of ordinances had better be kept up by each denomination of Christians in conjunction with those with whom they agreed on the subject of ordinances, so as to avoid discussions. But I *now* feel, that with the far more important points of affinity, that every year is opening up of a most spiritual character, closer unities ought to and will increasingly prevail. All the Presbyterian Churches are thus attempting to unite. And if it should appear that Christian brethren of different denominations can increase their love and sympathy for each other by partaking *together* of the Eucharist, instead of in their respective Churches only, no ecclesiastical fetters should restrict them from doing so. I once believed that dissensions would be saved, by those only who agreed as to points of ceremony, being united in the same Church, all, however, fully recognizing each other's Christian character in appropriate ways. But the Associations of young men in Sanitary and Christian Commissions, on the battle field, in the tent, and in all our large cities, have given such an increasing importance to these new spiritual affinities, that every effort should surely be made, without destroying any existing institutions or denominations, to draw all who earnestly love Christianity, in such ways as they find expedient and most free from controversy, to exhibit their love to Christ and to each other freely, subject to all proper laws but without narrowness or jealously. Each denomination will prosper according to its love.

I have thus spoken practically of the bearing of these views in regard to Inspiration, upon different Christian denominations, as they exist in this country. But in the meantime, it is impossible to shut our eyes to the fact, that outside of the pale of the Church, that is, of all regular Christian Churches, even of the loosest organization, there have been quietly gathering large numbers of young men, some wild and thoughtless, and anxious to escape the restraints of Christianity, but others sincere, earnest, well educated and conscientious, who seldom ever attend church, but are sceptical as to all Christian doctrine, and still more ill-grounded as to many of the most vital teachings of Natural Religion, because none have taken the pains to advocate them on such grounds as they are prepared rightly to appreciate. The numbers of young men of this class are annually increasing, and their weight and influence in politics, in literature, in society are augmenting daily.

In fact, there is in New England at this moment a sort of moral and religious chaos, through which almost all thinking young persons have to wade,— a slough, not of despond, but of vague, dreamy and dangerous visions, through which many never come out safely to a recovered and firm foothold of clear, consistent faith in any thing religious. There are indeed many compromises made, such as subsiding into a quiet, professed respect for morality, even a love for Christian teachings which however are being rapidly undermined. Some move, like Brownson, to Roman Catholicism, for the sake of its authority, and some to open Infidelity and even Atheism, or the modern epicureanism of free love and the absence of any moral system. This is terrible but true.

Just what Boston is to-day in these respects, Alexandria in Egypt was sixteen or seventeen hundred years ago, when Ammonius Saccas and the New Platonics mixed up Platonism and Christianity in the schools of that city. There all sects of philosophy and Christianity met, were discussed, fused, blended and left as a residuum,— such a singular union of philosophy and Christianity, that, while it contained the foremost religious thinking of that day, it also embraced many gross errors. Platonism, the best system of philosophy, at last melted into Neo-Platonism, and gave way utterly before the earnest, practical piety of

Origen, who united the full appreciation and love for the good points of both, as others had partially done before. The Alexandrine Christian faith, which he thus developed, swept before it the results of all the philosophical thinking of the Oriental and Greek systems. Henceforth, by degrees, the Christian Church became the seat of all the philosophy of the world, combined with a higher, more fervent and heaven-born spirit, gathered from the lips of Him who spake as never man spake, and rendered practical by the earnest lives of all the members of the Christian Church. Every one strove for practical godliness, with a zeal that nothing could quench, and a breadth of experiment and speculation that left nothing in life untested. This was what gave the Alexandrine school a potency and influence which it never wholly lost, and the remains of which are distinctly traceable to this day. We have hardly yet fairly outgrown it in the West. In the East it ended, however, in countless bickerings and controversies, that could only be imperfectly quelled by the subjugating force of Mahomet and his simpler confession enforced by the sword, " There is one God, and Mahomet is his prophet."

That many of the sects and opinions of the present day are doomed ultimately to die out, or be crushed out, as were these sects of Platonism, Orientalism, and Christian Gnosticism, cannot be doubted. But in the meantime, a searching sceptical philosophy, seemingly antagonistic to Christianity, will gradually compel the old-fashioned literal views of verbal Inspiration to give way, and many may be disposed to think that all our Christianity will give way with them, and be carried down the stream of time like a wrecked mill on the side of a swelling stream, and just as Platonism was swept away before the rising tide of Christianity.

But it was Christianity that absorbed philosophy, and not philosophy that ever did or could absorb Christianity with its Theim. Now there are new schools of Infidel philosophy, antagonistic to Christianity, rising up, and confidently predicting its downfall before them. Yet the Atheism of Comte is little more than that of Aristodemus, whom Socrates refuted, and the Pantheism of the Germans is but the re-vamping of that of the Vedas, that *growth* is the only eternal principle, — a belief conquered by Platonism in Greece. Philosophy and Christianity wrought out, ages ago, in the hearts of all, the firm belief in a personal God, from the wreck of Atheism and Pantheism, as Prof. Maurice has shown in his admirable history of Moral and Metaphysical Science, in the Encyclopedia Metropolitana.

The world grows in knowledge, and does not go backward. It will never let any of the great truths once wrought out on its surface die ; and hence it may be safely predicted, that while our Christianity will be much improved, sifted and refined by all the present processes of modern thought and philosophy, it will absorb them, and not they it. This was the idea of Coleridge, when he used to say that henceforth Christianity was and would be the only possible philosophy, and this is, above all, what Jesus meant when he said, " Heaven and earth shall pass away, but my words shall not pass away."

CHAPTER XV.

TRUE EVIDENCES INDICATED.

THERE are some, perhaps, who have read this volume thus far, and are ready to lay it aside with
the feeling that they have not time or ability to settle
remote questions of the genuineness, authenticity and
credibility of documents near two thousand years old.
And they ask, How shall I assure myself of the right-
ful Divine Authority of Christianity over my heart and
life, beyond my own personal feelings and experience
as a Christian? The effects of Christianity, as a system, upon human life, upon marriage, and upon law,
are perhaps three of the best practical evidences, and
may help to indicate in what directions new confirmations are to be found. But it is only when the attempt
is made to substitute some other system for Christianity, that the value of this sort of proof can be fully
appreciated. It is hard for a busy man, who breathes

every second, to believe that the atmosphere is pressing on his body always to the extent of a ton on every square foot of surface on his body, or to conceive of the importance to his life of so clear, colorless a vapor, so imperceptible to all his ordinary senses, as this. But let him try what it is to do without it, by an air pump, and he is soon convinced practically. Or let him seek to substitute some other gas in place of it, and he will agree that it will never do to give up breathing air.

So it is with Christianity; and this is why, at the close of the first French Revolution, Napoleon, as a statesman, and Coleridge, as a philosopher, considered Christianity as the only possible philosophy for the future.

I. The horrid and wholesale destruction of the best lives occasioned by that attempt to do without this system, have convinced many. The value Christianity has given to human life, is best seen by looking at the *frequency of suicide* wherever men are not controlled by its principles. Look at Japan, the most civilized of the Eastern nations, where it is officially ordered and sanctioned by the wisest and most important citizens. Look through China, along the banks of the Ganges, and in France and Germany. Just in proportion as faith in Christianity is swept away, murder and suicide become common, and any little momentary trouble, that seems insurmountable to an excited imagination, ends in the destruction of what may have been a most highly educated and valuable life. It was just the same in ancient Greece and Rome, before Christianity, as a system, gave a sense of immortal value to every human existence.

Perhaps it will be said, that such is the innate love of life, that on a large scale this matter is not worth counting. But look at the bearing of this system on a wider scale, and see. That must be the truest and best system of morals that furnishes the best vital statistics. Indeed, that is the principle of " natural selection," by which worn-out races are swept off the earth, to make room for those who have most of the truths that protect existence, most of that growingness and tendency to improvement which are the result of vital stamina. The purest system of religion is the best protection of life and all its powers. On this continent, Christians and the old Indian tribes stood face to face. Why have the Indians died out, and the white race increased? The sense of the value of life has been one important means. American Christianity has been the chief cause of our rapid, healthy growth. Pitcairn's Island is, perhaps, one of the most perfect of statistical proofs of this effect of true religion.

The United States fosters an increasing population, and has a horror of all the Old World crimes of Greece and Rome, and the Atheistic philosophies which prevented the increase of nations. Christianity gives value to human life, and it is not mistaken. It connects the present life with immortality, and we all see immortal consequences attached to the conduct of every human action here. All the future of generations grows out of the past. Individual, family, social, national characteristics are handed down hereditarily.

No man acts well or badly in example, or thinks a new thought, or writes it in a tract, but it will produce effects a thousand years hence. Every action of each life produces a habit, every habit a character, every character an hereditary influence, working on endlessly, — so that all the future shall legitimately grow out of the past. "No man liveth unto himself." He who shapes every action of his life by the thought of eternity, alone has got the true clue to greatness, goodness, and the proper course for each here. "By patient continuance in well doing, seek for glory and honor and immortality." Such shall find eternal life. The system that teaches that, gives the only law of life for *this* world that is true and wise and good for nations. The world will never let it go, having once found it.

II. The connection of Christianity and Marriage, now demands our attention as one of its best evidences.

One of the great forces which, after three hundred years of conflict, and after every sort of examination and opposition, placed Christianity upon the throne of the Cæsars, was the last thing which seemed likely to do so — its teaching in regard to marriage, its opposition to divorce, polygamy and licentiousness of all kinds. The heathen temples, priests, priestesses, worship and mysteries were all connected with lusts and abominations so gross that respectable Roman matrons and maidens of high moral sense could not bear to go near them. The priests and philosophers tolerated and encouraged all this to get strong and rich men on their side, and the religion of the masses became worse and worse. Christianity opposed it all. This contest began about divorce at pleasure. The first divorce ever issued in the Roman Empire was about three hundred years before Christ, when one high in rank and influence publicly divorced his wife, just as Napoleon I, divorced Josephine, because she was childless. Hitherto the Romans had farmed, fought, and robbed, and murdered, but had been manly and pure in their domestic relations. But now followed, with increasing wealth, scandalous licentiousness, and the heathen temples encouraged it, and the Jewish doctors tolerated divorce about at pleasure on the part of the husband. At last, powerful wives sometimes divorced weaker husbands, to ally themselves to more ambitious and successful men. Herod the Great had ten wives, some murdered by him, some by the intrigues of the various children, and a few divorced. His sons and grand-children did worse. Herodias, a grand-daughter, divorced one uncle to marry another, *i. e.* the Herod who beheaded John and mocked Jesus. Drusilla, another grand-daughter, divorced two husbands and married Felix.

Now, a hundred years before the first divorce in Rome, Malachi, the last of the old prophets in Judea, had protested vehemently against divorce at pleasure, as contrary to natural justice, in leaving a wife without comfort in age, when youth and beauty were gone, and leaving the children without proper education — indeed as a crime against all right religious feeling, and the true companionship for age (chap. 2: 14–16.) John the Baptist, four hundred years later, commenced a practical denunciation against the Herods on this account, and lost his head. Jesus announced the true idea of marriage, and was crucified, but the Christian Church, as Paul's writings show, fixed here one of the greatest practical contests with the paganism and corruption of the age. Then, to avoid divorces, Christians became *more careful about their marriages.* This was one of the wonderful and good effects. The Church was informed of each intended marriage and consulted, and the Christian minister pronounced the nuptial benediction in the name of God, and registered the names of all married thus, in the church book. This was the origin of marriage, being considered not only a *civil* contract, but one religiously blessed.   With the heathens all was different; there were no registers, and such were the concubinage, the divorce and polygamy and loose connections, that no one knew what woman was married and who was not, or what children were legitimate.   No wife was safe and no mother, no husband and no father, except only among the Christians.   Their marriage was open, registered for life, and sanctioned by the religious community as above reproach.   And a father could feel sure when he gave away his loved daughter to a Christian that it was to a protector *for life*, when her beauty was faded and he was dead.   By degrees the best people wished their children to be *thus* united, and all other connections were looked upon, as the Church looked on them, as suspicious, disgraceful, and, where not real marriages, wrong.   This was Christianity.   It restored the original law of God.   This was the great battle it fought for family ties, and it banished paganism and conquered.

Now the question is, Will the world ever be willing to part from this?   One might as well ask the Southern slaves if they will ever wish to re-enact slavery. Revolutions do not move backward.   Christianity will be better understood and better lived up to in all future ages, but such a system will never be given up. It has always been just on this ground that the battle has had to be fought between Christianity and its foes practically. Many in youth, therefore, from ignorance or error, oppose this religion, but as men get settled and are fathers and men of weight and respectability they abandon their opposition, because they see how essentially and fundamentally Christianity is connected with all the truest and dearest ties of earth, — with all that makes it safe now to give away a daughter in marriage — all that can promise a sure and comfortable companionship for old age in the wife of youth. Take away the Christian ideas of marriage and its holy laws, rightly understood, and there can be no peace for the world.

Many persons bring forward the laws of Christianity to disprove and correct loose views of the relations of the sexes. But our point is, that Christianity is a true and divine power in the earth, proved by the great victory over man's lower nature, and upon which the whole progress of mankind, the education of youth, the preservation of age and the respect for woman all depend. If marriage is not divine, there is nothing divine, nothing solid on earth, nothing left that a good man, woman or family need wish preserved in all the institutions of mankind. And marriage and Christianity support each other as divine gifts, holy institutions from the Father of lights.

III. The effects of Polytheism upon ancient international law, and those ideas from which all law springs, have been admirably illustrated by Hon. R. H. Dana, Jr., in a very original and important manner in his introductory lecture on International law at the Cambridge Law School. The substance of his argument is as follows:

"Ancient civilization was essentially polytheistic and autochthonal. That is to say, each separate people and nation was supposed to be a distinct creation, having distinct gods. On this feeling Plato and Aristotle say that strangers — that is, barbarians — are natural slaves. Under this system there was not, and there could not be any such thing as philanthropy cherished; there was no brotherhood of nations recognized. The languages of foreigners were despised and hated as proofs of a distinct, perhaps hostile origin, and war or isolation were looked upon as the natural relations of nations to each other; and war itself became finally a real blessing to the world, as breaking up the still more unnatural isolation which was the desired and pictured condition of a blissful nation. Horace and Virgil both give this as the true picture of happiness, and Cicero speaks of the counting-house of the merchant as fit only for slaves of freedmen, not for honorable citizens. In fact, almost all commerce was piracy, and there is extant the copy of a treaty between Carthage and Rome, in which it . is agreed that the vessels of the latter shall be allowed to pass the Straits in the pursuits of war, commerce and piracy.

" War, too, was carried on not for the redress of grievances merely, but as a natural pursuit; the entrails were inspected, and all other auspices, and if these were favorable to success, it was considered a just war and a pious duty. The city attacked was considered accursed, doomed, and justly destroyed, the war not terminating with a white flag of surrender, but all being put to the sword or sold as slaves. Everything — the life, liberty and entire property of each inhabitant belonged to the conquerors as a right, and one that was expected to be exercised. The Jews who would have torn up the pavements to stone to death an adulteress, would have taken all the wives and virgins of the captured city to their harems, the children as slaves. So did the Assyrians and Babylonians make war, and so the Romans; sixty thousand slaves were sold on the capture of one city, eighty thousand after that of another, until the market was glutted, and the conqueror, whose nightly suppers cost ten thousand dollars, sold slaves at sixty-two and a half cents each. Ninety thousand slaves were sold after the conquest of Jerusalem.

The conquering chiefs abused the bodies of the slain as Archilles dragged about that of Hector or chained them, if living, to their chariot wheels to adorn their triumphal return; the betrayed rather than conqured Jugurtha was thus served, who, when unchained, was cast naked into a dungeon, and only after six days' starvation was there put to death.

" Indeed, slavery thus so multiplied that Gibbon, who seems to look back with peculiar complacency on the old institution, says there were about sixty millions in the Roman Empire. But this is too little; fully three fourths of the inhabitants were slaves. Every son, also, was the natural slave of his father, and never emancipated by being of age, and the wife and all the slaves of a man were subject to his will, so that no process of Roman law could cross a man's threshold to inquire why he put slave, or wife, or son to death! In fact, the ancient civilization, which, so far as *material* and outward matters went, far exceeded ours, was based on two great principles — hostile gods and different races. But there was in it all a total lack of *spiritual* life.

" Christianity, based on one God and the brotherhood of man, has introduced humanity, brotherhood and equal rights, into international law out of the idea of the common divine origin of man. When Jesus asked who was neighbor to him that fell among thieves, he erected a standard of humanity, towards which international law has been climbing up for eighteen hundred years. An eye for an eye, and a tooth for a tooth, to love a neighbor and hate an enemy had been the theory and practice before. But under the early Christian leaders an enthusiasm for humanity sprang up, and there was, in their view, neither Jew nor Greek, barbarian, Scythian, bond nor free. And this system advanced first to a share in power in the Roman empire, and then to dominion. Christianity, not searching timidly for truth, as Philosophy had done, but teaching it as an authority and an institution, changed the whole views of man.

" The councils of the Christian Church, with all their imperfections, are yet a just and noble monument of an intellectual kingdom arising, — one that broke down the old national barriers, mastered every language as if it had received a new gift of tongues, and even established a universal language to harmonize races more thoroughly. The sons of serfs became Princes of the Church, Archbishops of Canterbury, and Popes. The Crusades, though a sad error, yet united nations in new relations. Chivalry, though bad, was war itself humanized by Christianity. Under Charlemagne the idea of unity was pushed to the illegitimate length — one God, one race, and *therefore but one king*. But Christianity introduced resident Ambassadors whose persons are sacred, prisoners of war, with the idea of a *lawful* enemy expecting treatment according to the laws of war. Even *arbitration* has, by the late treaty of Paris, been introduced into modern treaties as a regular method of avoiding war.

"Here, then, lies the contrast of international relations. War then was considered the natural and normal condition of nations, as now peace. War then had no limits but in the destruction of the weaker. Now it stops when the just object is secured for which it was undertaken. Then, a city surrendered was doomed. Now, it is turned over to just government; the officers are paroled; and in our late war so also were many thousand privates. In 1863, Dr. Lieber, by request of government, drew up, for the treatment of our prisoners, regulations published in Europe, and in a fair way of being almost universally adopted. Private property is always respected now on land, and subject to confiscation at sea only in open court. Anciently, law did not at all extend to the sea. If now any one doubt what have been the results of the words of Him who on the hills and shores of Galilee scattered his words of truth as a sower his seed, we have only to turn him to the progress of international law for the illustration and proof of all." So argues one of our ablest authorities on the history of International law.

IV. But the most important of all the evidences of

Christianity is, and must ever be, the effect it exercises in strengthening the will of man to do right.

While the error of a few is that over-strength of mere will which we call obstinacy or self-will, the error of the vast multitude is *feebleness of will*. The bodies of most control their minds. How many eat where reason would say abstain, or drink that which steals away the senses! How many are too feeble of purpose to lay aside an interesting book or pursuit at the hour when it infringes on other duties! What hours persons waste in profitless reading or talk! Indeed, there is a fascination and tyranny about the *present*, whether company, passion or pleasure, that we are all ashamed of afterwards.

The ancient moralists felt this as much as we do. Seneca says, in language quite as strong as that of St. Paul, that he sees the right and admires it, and the wrong and hates, while yet he practices it. Many persons seem to think it enough to admit all this, without attempting to overcoming it. In fact, to be weak of will, amiable, and easily turned, they think a sort of Christian virtue. Yet it is one of the most radical of vices. For all character is determined by *the will*, which is therefore essential to all virtue. The glory of every human being is to have a strong will, (which need not be self-willed,) but bowed ever reverently to truth and justice and eternal law, and the Supreme Lawgiver. But there must be a vital strength of will, in order to choose the right.

How to obtain this, is a question to which many answers have been given by different persons. Our strength is not the same on all subjects nor in all circumstances and associations. Weakness or strength of bodily health has much to do with this. Exercise and repose affect it. An over-tasked nervous system will often be weak and irresolute, when half an hour's vigorous exercise or a sharp walk in the open air will renew it. The hour of the day will have much influence. On first rising, in the morning, the resolution is comprehensive and strong, while at night it is often feeble. Hence the most successful men generally plan out the day early, and make their mark while the will is vigorous and undistracted. Sleep often restores this faculty. Habit has still more to do with it. Every success makes a future one in the same matter more easy and natural, while every instance of being subdued by circumstances makes every similar temptation proportionably powerful. Association has much to do with it. In the company of those we respect we are easily led.

He, therefore, who would rule his own spirit, and be strong, must attend to these conditions. Habits that secure the most perfect health are hence most favorable to virtue. Sound sleep, vigorous exercise, proper food, fresh air, thus become Christian duties, to be secured at almost any cost.

But there is *one* habit, which, more than any other, before the business and confusion of the day be entered on, will strengthen the wisdom and the *will*, i. e. the practice of forecasting the whole difficulties, dangers and plan of the day devoutly in prayerful communion with the Heavenly Father. They that wait upon the Lord shall renew their strength. As the moulting bird recovers youth and renewed energy, so has man, in all ages, been found to do from real communion with the Father of Spirits. The power of vigorous *will* is thus most effectually increased and restored. Men rise new beings, both in the direction and force of their resolutions. Dean Trench has thrown this thought into a most beautiful little poem : —

> " Lord, what a change within us one short hour
>> Spent in thy presence can avail to make !
>> What heavy burdens from our bosoms take !
> What parched grounds refresh as with a shower !
> We kneel, and all around us seems to lower ;
>> We rise, and all the distant and the near
>> Stand forth in sunny outline, brave and clear ;
> We kneel, how weak ! we rise, how full of power !
>> Why, therefore, should we do ourselves this wrong,
>> Or others, that we are not always strong, —
> That we are ever, ever born with care, —
>> That we should ever weak or heartless be,
> Anxious or troubled, when with us in prayer,
>> And joy and strength and courage are with thee !

17

These are some of those evidences which he who tries practically will become thereby assured of the Truth and Divinity of Christianity. And without such evidences, all other will be but of little value.

THE END.